BLEEDING GREEN

A season on the run with Real Calcio FC

BLEEDING GREEN

A season on the run
with Real Calcio FC

Matt Gibson

Matador
9 Priory Business Park,
Wistow Road, Kibworth Beauchamp,
Leicestershire. LE8 0RX
Tel: (+44) 116 279 2299
Fax: (+44) 116 279 2277
Email: books@troubador.co.uk
Web: www.troubador.co.uk/matador

ISBN 9781780883694

British Library Cataloguing in Publication Data.
A catalogue record for this book is available from the British Library.

Typeset by Troubador Publishing Ltd, Leicester, UK
Printed and bound in the UK by TJ International, Padstow, Cornwall

Matador is an imprint of Troubador Publishing Ltd

*To the Sunday morning footballer, especially the late Tony Young,
a Real Calcio player and friend*

With every book sold a donation will be made to
Leukaemia Care and the Paragon Foundation
which supports sports-based charities

REAL CALCIO FC

Formed: 1998
Founder: Nick
Honours:
- Catford and Bellingham League Division Five South Champions 1999
- London West League Linesman of the Year 2003 – not sure this counts
- London West League Division Three Champions 2007
- Chopper Savage Cup Winners 2009

Team Colours:

Shirt: Light / faded green
Shorts: Black with no elastic
Socks: Green with holes
Sponsor: GJ's pub, who gave us £300 ten years ago; they got back their investment in about two weeks. It might be time to renegotiate our £30-a-year sponsorship.

Ground: Garrett Park, Earlsfield, London, SW18.

SQUAD MEMBERS

Phil

Position:	Goalkeeper
Age:	32
Favourite team:	Celtic or the Super Hoops as he calls them
Job:	Works in radio, has a face for it as well
Pre-match meal:	Two sausage rolls and a pint of full-fat milk

Although people often have their doubts about Scottish keepers, Big Phil (or Phaal, as he screams) has rarely let us down over the years. We have had some really dodgy keepers in our time. He is a breath of fresh, battered, Irn-Bru-fuelled air. Ironically he scored our first and solitary European goal in a tournament in The Hague a couple of seasons ago.

Hugh

Position:	Full-back
Age:	34
Favourite team:	Cork City, or is it Rovers?
Job:	Lawyer, the intelligent player in the team
Strange fact:	Never owned a mobile phone

A group of us used to play five-a-side most weeks and Hugh was always man of the match, yet come eleven-a-side he never seems quite the same player. He is still probably one of our better players and always gives one hundred percent when he isn't injured, which seems to be a rarity these days.

Pete

Position:	Full-back
Age:	43
Favourite team:	Celtic
Job:	Banking, sometimes pays for his £5 subs with £50 notes which is a real pain in the arse
Looks like:	Richard Fairbrass from Right Said Fred

Wrong side of forty now but still seems to have bundles of energy despite the fact that he became a father last season. He loves to forage upfield and thinks he is Ryan Giggs; as soon as he passes the halfway line he only has eyes for goal and there's no point even asking him to pass. Spends most warm-ups, when we have them, either playing with his kid or trying to recreate Celtic's goals from the previous weekend.

Tom

Position:	Centre-back or full-back
Age:	28
Favourite team:	Tottenham
Job:	Schoolteacher. I wouldn't want to be in his class
Plays like:	Martin Keown in the infamous 'Battle of Old Trafford'

Had an excellent season last year although does tend to moan before the match, during the match (mainly at me) and afterwards even if we have won. Got particularly upset last season when I subbed him so he then flagged me offside every time he had the chance to despite the fact that I was onside most of the time.

Chris

Position:	Full-back or goalkeeper
Age:	33
Favourite team:	Real Calcio – he actually told me last year he supported us
Job:	Graphic design, though he doesn't work too hard as his out-of-office is always on, saying he is on annual leave
Favourite car:	His clapped-out old Volvo he won off a mate at poker five years ago

He comes from that great football nation, New Zealand. However, a couple of years ago we had five Kiwis in our team and despite the fact that rugby union is their national sport, they were probably our best players. He dies for the cause; three years ago he played on in goal with a broken leg – albeit without realising it was broken, but he did say that it felt a bit sore second half. He has managed to crash his car into a bus twice on the way to games; looking for the hat-trick this season.

Del

Position:	Full-back
Age:	32
Favourite team:	Watford
Job:	Media, I think it just entails going out on the piss with clients the whole time
Looks like:	Someone in a boy band with his bleached blonde awful haircut

Thinks he is a centre-forward but is lucky if he gets a game at right-back. He is going out with my old boss but luckily I don't have to play him now as I have left the company. When I worked for her he played every week up front and never got substituted especially in games close to my work appraisals. He loves a big Saturday night out.

Jack

Position:	Centre-back
Age:	45? Looks a lot younger
Favourite team:	Arsenal
Job:	PE teacher; he is probably fitter than the kids he teaches but is probably the only PE teacher who smokes
Claim to fame:	He reckons he coached Jack Wilshere in his youth

He is probably the only lean member of our team despite being the oldest. Although he lives closest to our home ground he is often the last to arrive, with a fag in his mouth. Occasionally plays in goal and insists on wearing no gloves even if it is pissing down with rain.

Smithy

Position:	Centre-back
Age:	37
Favourite team:	Crystal Palace
Job:	Casinos, spends half the year 'working' in Las Vegas
Football hero:	Alan Pardew for scoring the winner in the FA Cup semi final twenty-odd years ago

'Smithy' is the shout we all hear when he goes for header after header. Has managed to lose what pace he had in the last year or so and sometimes likes to take on the opponents' centre-forward in our box which usually leads to us conceding a goal. He likes to inform the attackers after about eighty minutes that he had them in his pocket all game although last season there must have been lots of moths in there too.

Anton

Position:	Right midfield
Age:	26
Favourite team:	Liverpool
Job:	Not sure but they haven't taught him how to send emails as he never replies to my emails asking for his availability each weekend
Dream holiday destination:	Magaluf

Our fleet-footed winger and the only fast player in the side. He often moans at half-time that we never get the ball out wide to him and we always promise we will second half but, alas, rarely do. Very laid back, he managed to miss our flight back from Amsterdam last year and ended up taking the bus back instead, not that this seemed to bother him despite the fact it took him over eight hours.

Miles

Position:	Left or right midfield
Age:	34
Favourite team:	Ajax

Job: Trader. Does alright judging by the size of his house in Kensington

Claim to fame: Played at the Thailand national stadium

He was signed from a leading club in Amsterdam. Well, he came over two years ago and was looking for a decent team to join and when he couldn't find one he came to us. Never ducks out of a tackle, which has become quite expensive for him, as the fines for bookings have increased to seven pounds now. We still aren't sure if he is left- or right-footed.

Wilky

Position: Left or right midfield, much to his annoyance

Age: 30

Favourite team: Whoever is top of the Premier League

Job: Spends most of the year on a Contiki bus travelling round Europe

Favourite player: Ryan Nelsen. I think he's the only player he knows from New Zealand

Another Kiwi who plays for us when his girlfriend allows him to, which isn't much these days. Likes to think his best position is centre midfield but the rest of us beg to differ. He throws his toys out if things don't go his way; luckily we have a big pram.

Danny

Position: Centre midfield

Age: 36

Favourite team: Liverpool and don't we know it

Job: Sales director for a travel company, when asked he always replies with this. He can't just say he works for a travel company

Favourite
player: Himself

He doesn't like to leave his comfort zone of the centre circle. Needs to lose some weight though; a diet of burgers and chips could put pay to that. Only green food he has ever eaten in his life is green M&M's. However, he is probably the best passer in our team and isn't shy on informing everyone that he is. Member of the committee.

Nick

Position: Centre midfield

Age: 35

Favourite team: Rushden & Diamonds although they have now folded (a bit like his football career)

Job: Works for the council, spends a lot of time sacking people for no reason

Post-match ritual: Never showers

Had a shocking season last year but then again I'm pretty sure he had a shocker the season before that as well. He also mastered the act of missing chances that were harder to miss than score last season. Very injury-prone and if there is an injury you have had you can guarantee Nick has had it ten times worse. Has a disastrous love life but his dedication to the cause can't be faulted; he got dumped by the love of his life after three years at 9.00am one Sunday last season but was still at ground on time where he got no sympathy from any his team-mates. Member of the committee and founder of the club.

Bo

Position:	Centre midfield
Age:	27
Favourite team:	Peterborough United
Job:	Chemist. I'm hoping he can find a cure to our lack of goalscoring
Strange fact:	Decided to go a year without sex. More than making up for it now

Without a doubt our best player but this season he has found a decent Saturday team to play for and will only play when we are short. I told him to therefore expect a weekly phone call. Nick and Danny are happy he can't play this season, though, as it means one of them will not be shunted from centre midfield. Was on Peterborough's books as a youngster but their loss is our gain.

Jim

Position:	Left midfield or full-back. Should be centre midfield
Age:	27
Favourite team:	Watford
Job:	Gambling industry. He must owe the team thousands with his dud tips each week
Claim to fame:	Claims he has never missed a penalty, although not sure he has ever taken one either

Jim, who is my brother, has the Gibson trait of no pace although he had a great season last year and was Player of the Season. I like to think that he picked up his skills from watching me in his youth but he begs to differ.

Tworty

Position:	Left midfield or forward
Age:	36
Favourite team:	Arsenal
Job:	Banking. He must be the only banker that starts at nine and ends at five
Footballing hero:	Charlie Nicholas. He reckons he plays like him and was a hit with a ladies in his twenties as well

Another left midfield or a forward who, when clean through, has the habit of veering off to the left towards the corner flag. In one game last season he must have done this four or five times and I began to think that there must have been a couple of pretty dolly birds over there that had taken his fancy.

Damo

Position:	Forward
Age:	35
Favourite team:	Manchester United – he lives in Sussex… what do you expect?
Job:	Travel. He has recently written a report, which he hopes to sell, on how to rent out foreign property. This is quite ironic seeing as he hasn't managed to rent out his apartment in Egypt in the past two years
Strange fact:	Ran the London marathon a few years ago but didn't get under four hours which really annoyed him. Being a determined lad he decided to train harder and run it again the following year where

he ran an even slower time. We love reminding him of this

Only likes to play home games and will only play away games against weaker teams. He does live in Brighton so I suppose he has an excuse. He has never missed a penalty for us in ten or so years, which is all the more amazing as every spot-kick must bobble four or five times before trickling into the bottom left-hand corner. Member of the committee.

Paddy

Position:	Forward
Age:	30
Favourite team:	Man Utd – although he's never been to Old Trafford
Job:	Civil servant I think. He works nine to five, has a two-hour lunch break, 35 days holiday and works five minutes from home. He enjoys the perks of his job
Footballing hero:	Frank Stapleton, who scored the only goal he has seen Man Utd score live at some London ground many years ago

'Twing. There goes my hamstring, Paddy.' With Nick, he is the most injury-prone player at the club. However, all was forgiven when he scored the winner in our cup final two years ago and even more remarkable was that he scored it with his head, especially as he usually really good at avoiding headers despite being over six foot. Has dined out on scoring that goal ever since.

Paul

Position:	Forward
Age:	26
Favourite team:	Tottenham
Job:	Soldier. Serves God and Country and occasionally Real Calcio
Pre-match ritual:	Slagging off Arsenal and telling us how long it has taken him to drive from Cambridgeshire to wherever we are playing

He has just come back from serving in Iraq. With our renowned lack of ammunition from our midfield he will seem a million miles away from there. Tom's brother.

Carl

Position:	Forward
Age:	31
Favourite team:	Everton
Job:	Helicopter pilot/ art dealer/ diamond dealer/ dolphin trainer/ Prince William's bodyguard
Favourite country:	Denmark, Sweden and Norway. Anywhere where there are tasty blondes he can work his magic (bullshit) on

He is probably the only Kiwi in London who supports Everton. He is also probably the only centre-forward in London who failed to score last season. Still living off the hat-trick he scored a fair few years ago which won us the league. Probably has the most success with the ladies but also speaks the most bullshit to them. Was overheard telling a girl on one of our end-of-season tours that he was a cousin of Russell Crowe and was a helicopter pilot who lived in Chelsea when in fact he is a carpenter who lives in Streatham and shares a house with about half of Auckland.

Gibbo / Matt / me

Position:	Centre-back or forward
Age:	35
Favourite team:	Tottenham
Job:	Sports management, though I struggle to manage Real Calcio
Pre match ritual:	Spending half an hour on the phone listening to people saying they're five minutes away when they haven't even left their flat

Now in my mid-thirties and still don't have a set position. Played everywhere last season and am still no closer to knowing which position I play best. Some members of the team reckon it is probably linesman. Tom is hoping I'm not his centre-back partner this season. He reckons he shouts at me more in ninety minutes of Sunday football than he does all year to his little kid. Member of the committee.

"You haven't been on the winning team for the best part of two years"

Two days before the start of the season and Nick, Danny, Damo and I decide to meet up to discuss the coming campaign. The four of us form the 'committee' of Real Calcio and run the team, which has the main bonus of guaranteeing we all start in our favourite positions.

The plan, at the end of last season, was to meet in June to discuss new players, pre-season friendlies, finding a sponsor and training. As usual, the meeting is happening at the last minute, and with two days before the season kicks off there is no chance of any of the above happening.

We choose the usual boozer in Victoria. It's old and run-down but it has fruit machines, sells pork scratchings and pints that are less than four quid, shows the football on TV and has a nice busty blonde barmaid who pretends to like us so we will buy her drinks.

Nick, Danny and I arrive at more or less the same time before Damo bursts into the pub five minutes later.

"We're gonna win the league, we're gonna win the league and now you're gonna believe us, we're…"

Danny stops him mid-song. "Liquid lunch, Damo? We may have been relegated last season and in theory we should be playing teams weaker than us. But we got relegated the season before and look what happened."

"Nice to see you're full of confidence, Danny, two days before the season starts."

We're hoping that this season we can muster eleven players each game, get to the ground on time, start training and contend for the title rather than endure our annual relegation battle, which usually ends in relegation.

The four of us have played together since we formed the team back in 1998 and have watched each other get slower, develop wider waistlines and score fewer goals as each season has passed. What we lack in ability we make up in enthusiasm, although by November, when it's cold, wet and we're struggling for numbers, it dwindles and we wonder why we don't take up golf instead.

Danny is champing at the bit. "I can't wait for the season to start. I seem to have spent every Sunday this summer getting dragged by the missus to DIY shops, National Trust houses and garden centres."

"Hang on, Danny," says Damo. "I didn't think you even…"

"I know, Damo. I haven't even got a bloody garden. That's what makes it even worse. We're looking at stuff to put in a garden we haven't even got! I don't know how my missus's brain works sometimes. We haven't even put an offer on any house yet either. She also bought me membership to the National Trust as part of my birthday present. I'm thirty six, for fuck's sake, not fifty six. National Trust? I should be getting memberships for swanky clubs off Park Lane."

"Steady on, Danny. I can't quite picture you in a swanky club," says Damo. "Club with a stained carpet by the bar, serving watered down warm lager for two pound fifty with a dance floor so sticky your shoes stick to the floor, yes. But a members' bar off Park Lane? Do me a favour."

"Anyway, back to football. I can't believe the season is starting on Sunday and yet again we haven't even had a pre-season game. I haven't kicked a ball since our final game last season but reckon I can bang in a hat-trick come Sunday."

"Tell me about it," I say. "I've played the odd game of five-a-side, though. Nick and I played on Wednesday, didn't we, Nick?"

"Well, we turned up. Wouldn't call it playing, though, Gibbo," replies Nick, fearing an avalanche of abuse from Danny.

"Come on, lads, spill the beans. I sense you got a thrashing," says Danny with a huge grin on his face.

"You and your mouth, Gibbo," mumbles Nick.

"Well we were part of a twenty-three goal thriller in Clapham," I say gingerly.

"And in that south London thriller, how many goals did you boys get then, Gibbo?" says Danny.

"Three, Danny, but…"

"Three? You lost 20-3? Fuck me, this is fantastic. I can't wait to tell the rest of the boys this. They scored seventeen more goals than you. *Seventeen* more goals than you. Sorry, I needed to say that again as I never thought I would ever say that about a football match, and I'm so glad you and Nick were playing."

"I banged in two, though, Danny. Two crackers as well. One with my left foot and one where I beat… "

"I don't give a shit about you scoring, Gibbo. I bet you would prefer to lose, or should I say get absolutely thumped 20-3, and you score two goals, than win and you score none?"

"Tough one that, mate. I can't answer that. My mate Quinny played as well as we were short and after the game I asked him whether he had ever lost 20-3 before. He reckoned he had at rugby and they considered the scoreline a thrashing as well."

Even though I scored two goals in the five-a-side game, I was pretty dire. My first goal was an open goal and the second I scuffed in via my shin. The only thing that gave me an ounce of satisfaction was that Nick was just as bad. The team we were playing weren't great; we just made them look it.

When stretching before the game pretty much every bone in my body cracked. My hamstrings and calf muscles were really tight and when I tried sprinting I couldn't believe I had got even slower. During the game I was really off the pace, the ball wasn't sticking to me, I couldn't pass to a teammate for love or money and I lost one ball with a wayward shot that ended up in the car park.

"How did you play, Nick, in this thumping?" presses Damo, knowing the probable answer.

"Not too well, mate, funnily enough, although I probably just shaded Gibbo. Anyway it was only a pre-season five-a-side to blow off the cobwebs. I will be firing all cylinders come Sunday."

"Like you were last season?" snipes Damo.

"OK I wasn't the best last season, I agree. Anyway, on a brighter note we even have enough players for a sub on Sunday."

Having a substitute on Sunday has been quite an alien concept to Real Calcio over the years. We aim to get eleven players each week and if we get twelve it's a bonus. Thirteen is a once-a-season luxury and the only time we had fourteen players, bar the cup final, caused us more problems than it solved.

We didn't know whether to start the players who arrived late as substitutes, when to make the substitutions and whether to bring off the players who had performed badly even though they were the most loyal players over the season. You also feel that you have to get all three substitutes on at some stage in the game, and in the one game we had three substitutes someone got injured immediately after we put our last one on. We were left with ten men for the last twenty minutes in which we managed to turn our 2-1 lead into a 3-2 loss.

"Have any of the other lads been playing over the summer?" asks Damo. "I saw Anton and Tom a couple of weeks ago on the way back from the pub. They told me they had done nothing all summer, although they assured me they would be fighting fit come Sunday. They were both pissed, munching on a kebab and looked like they had enjoyed the pubs and fast-food outlets over the summer, so I'm not too sure."

This doesn't bode well, especially as Tom is an excellent player and is the one I rely upon to cover up my mistakes most weeks.

"I saw Paddy the other day," says Nick. "He's had a bit of a nightmare over the past week. Someone has been stealing his post and the poor lad has had his identity stolen. Football and getting fit has been the last thing on his mind, although in all honesty getting fit never has been on his mind. I'm also not sure who I feel sorrier for, Paddy or the poor bloke who has been left with his identity."

"Imagine that – you go to the trouble of stealing someone's identity and you end up being Paddy, a man who is thirty but looks forty and is skint," says Danny.

"Gibbo, what about your brother and Bo? Are they in good shape for Sunday?" wonders Nick. "Surely, being in their mid-twenties and full of energy, they've been keeping fit over the summer?"

"They've been playing a fair bit in some five-a-side league. I played for them once, thought I did OK but I've never been asked again."

"Don't call us, we'll call you then, Gibbo. A bit like most of the birds you meet."

"Whatever, Danny. Anyway the team we are playing Sunday just missed out on promotion last season so they could be a bit useful. It would be so nice to start with three points and really put down a marker for the season."

"I can't actually remember the last time we got three points," sighs Nick.

I spot my opportunity. "I can, mate. It was the first game in the New Year in Richmond. I banged in a hat-trick. One with my right, one with…"

Nick doesn't let me finish. "Shut up Gibbo. Shit, I can't believe I walked into that. We haven't won for eight months then and I was injured in that game anyway."

"Three games is all we won last season," says Damo. "Hang on, Nick, I'm pretty sure the two other games we won were in December when you were in New Zealand."

19

"Good point, Damo, he was," I say gleefully. "Fucking hell, Nick, you haven't been on a winning team for the best part of two years. Hope you are starting on the bench then come Sunday."

"Some run that, Nick. Anything else you want to set yourself up for?" says Danny, trying not to laugh.

"Whatever. Anyway, I'm feeling confident about Sunday. I can feel the Nick of old coming back this season."

"The 2003 version, I hope, as I'm pretty sure that was the last good season you had," I suggest.

"I was actually OK – I emphasise the OK – in 2008 as well, Gibbo."

Nick will be the first admit that he has really struggled for the form the last few years. We have all progressively got worse and worse but until about four years ago Nick was a goalscoring midfielder who used to instil fear into our opponents. He was the best out of the four of us, which isn't saying much, but the fact he hasn't been on a winning Real Calcio team for two years suggests his influence on our games has pretty much completely waned.

Damo turns serious. "We need to make sure everyone is down to Wandsworth Common early on Sunday so we can have a decent warm-up and do some stretching. I'm fairly sure with some people it will be the first bit of exercise they've done since last season. I sent an email to the team just before I came here."

"Look at you," I jump in, "trying to be organised for the first time in your life, Damo. And lo and behold you've told everyone to go to Wandsworth Common, when in fact we're playing in Wandsworth Park."

"Shit. I didn't realise that, Gibbo."

"Just when we are trying to come across as more professional to the rest of the team – well, a bit professional as I don't think we have ever had an ounce of professionalism in our fourteen or so years to date – and you've gone and told everyone, two days before the game, to turn up at the wrong place."

"OK OK," says Damo, embarrassed. "I'll call everyone tomorrow and tell them that the council have moved our game. The lads will never know it was my inability to read the fixtures and venues correctly."

"They will when we tell them," says Nick with a snigger.

"Thanks a bunch, mate," replies Damo, rising from his seat. "Anyway, I'd better go now. I need to get the train home."

"Make sure you get the right train, mate, and arrive at the correct destination," I say, laying on the sarcasm. "Don't go getting Brighton and Bournemouth confused when you see the departures board. Apparently the trains back there are on adjacent platforms which could prove problematic for someone like you who likes telling everyone to go to the wrong ground each week."

"Ha! That's rich coming from you, Gibbo," says Damo. "Last year, if I remember rightly, you were sat on a train at Waterloo and needed the toilet so you got off the train and went on the train on the opposite platform that had toilets. Then just as you were doing your stuff the train set off and you heard the words 'Welcome to the fast train to Bournemouth, first stop Farnborough' or something similar."

"That ended up being the most expensive slash I've ever had as the conductor charged me full fare and also fined me twenty quid for not having a ticket. He wouldn't believe my story, the miserable git. I mean, it could happen to anyone."

"Course it could," says Damo. "Anyway lads, got to dash. Make sure you have an early night Saturday as we need three points Sunday. I'm looking at you, Gibbo. Surely you can have one week away from Clapham's late-night watering holes?"

"That'll be tough, mate, but I'll give it my best shot."

Nick, Danny and I end up having a few more drinks discussing everything but Sunday football and the team formation we would play. I learn that Nick flew to Sweden when he thought he was flying to Denmark. Oh, and that Danny pulled some bird from *Hollyoaks* who couldn't get him out the house quick enough the following morning.

"If you don't perform like Bo did last night you're off"

I wake up and switch on the TV to watch *Match of Day* just as they are showing Goal of the Month which has some fantastic finishing. Great volleys, thirty-yard free kicks and players taking on four players before scoring. I can safely say Real Calcio won't be scoring goals like those today, or during the whole season, although I wouldn't put it past our opponents' forwards taking on our whole defence before scoring. We don't care if we score off our backsides, knees or shins; any goal these days is a bonus.

I clamber out of bed, get my gear together and realise that I haven't washed my boots from our final game of last season (not that they were washed much throughout last season) and that instead of buying football shinpads I had actually bought hockey shinpads. Oh well, if the season starts going pear-shaped at least I have an excuse to take up hockey.

I jump on my bike and set off to Wandsworth Park and sure enough the phone goes. Here we go, I think to myself – who is running late/lost/can't play because their dog ate their boots or some other crap excuse I get given over the season?

"Matt, Jim here, bit of a problem. Bo isn't in his room and he is meant to be driving me to the game."

"Great, typical. Can't you get the bus to the ground?"

"Could do, but not sure how to get there by bus. I'll give it ten minutes and give you a bell."

Ten minutes later he hasn't called back so I ring him back.

"Just about to ring you (yes, course you were). Bo got lucky last night and woke up at some bird's house in Chelsea. He is getting a cab to the flat and then we will drive to the ground, should be there by 10.15 at the latest."

I arrive to the ground at 9.45 and no one is here. We used to meet at 10.00 knowing that people wouldn't turn up till 10.15 so this season we decided to meet at 9.45 in the hope people will be here by 10.00. Gradually people start to appear and we head to the changing rooms. One of the joys of the changing rooms at Wandsworth Park is that six teams have to share three changing rooms and there is a good chance that the person you are changing next to will be the same person whose shadow you are chasing round the pitch fifteen minutes later.

I open the kit bag Nick has brought and can't believe we actually have six balls and new drink bottles this season as well as a new sports first-aid kit. Our previous first-aid kit had virtually nothing left in it. One game last season Danny got clattered on the ankle and went down in agony screaming for someone to go and get the first-aid kit as he thought he had broken his ankle. I went and got it but the only thing we had in it was wasp spray and I'm not sure how effective wasp spray is for injured ankles.

Danny blamed Calcio's slump in form last season on the fact that we had no decent first-aid kit and he couldn't play for weeks. I suppose I have to agree that wasp spray isn't too useful in February when it's snowing outside. However, I'm not sure him not playing resulted in our slide down the league; most of us thought the opposite would happen.

Tworty enters the changing room. "Alright Gibbo," he says. "I've been looking forward to the first game of the season for ages. I was so excited yesterday that I went and got pissed last night and only got in a few hours ago."

"Surely if you had been looking forward to the first game of the season so much," I reply, "you would have had a quiet night in with a healthy meal, a cup of cocoa and an early night?"

"Come on, mate. That's not what Sunday-morning football is about; it's not the same if you don't have a raging hangover, no sleep and no fast food inside you. We all play better with hangovers anyway."

Tworty's theory was proved four years ago when we reached a cup semi-final. We all agreed to stay in the night before and come the Sunday morning for the first time in years the changing room didn't reek of booze and everyone looked up for the game. However, I'm not sure if it was the inability of our bodies to play football without ten pints of lager inside us and a dodgy kebab a few hours earlier but we got stuffed 4-0. From that day onwards we decided that staying in before a game is a bad idea. We even had our Christmas bash at some ropey nightclub in London the day before a game last season and we won on the Sunday.

We have also come to the conclusion that playing football a few hours after downing your last pint is good for you as you sweat the booze out your system straight away and it means that you can go to the pub after the game and don't need to feel guilty as you have just done some exercise. The various sporting diet books also say that it's good to get some carbohydrates back into your body after exercise, although I'm not sure that a few pints of lager and a few packs of peanuts are quite what the doctors recommend.

The rest of the team arrive late in dribs and drabs and pretty much everyone looks shattered. Within minutes the whole changing room stinks of booze, the smell of which is occasionally worsened by the odd fart that creeps out of various team-mates. Most of the team have their head in their hands trying to piece together where they were and who they were with only a matter of hours ago. Jack is already on his second fag and has seems to have changed from Marlboro Light to Marlboro this season, so it looks like the giving up fags is working a treat. Everyone looks a stone heavier and with us all being a year older and none the wiser, judging by the state of the changing room, I'm not too confident about this season. And we haven't even kicked off yet.

We all slowly get changed in between discussing last night's escapades and venture out on to the pitch. I have heard nothing from Bo and Jim so I give Jim another ring.

"Just about to ring you mate, just approaching Wandsworth roundabout, will be there in five minutes." Yeah, sure.

"See you in about ten minutes then."

"Yeah, should be there by then if traffic isn't too bad."

"Yeah, traffic is murder at 10.15 on a Sunday morning."

"Too right it is. Sunday drivers, eh."

I fill in the team-sheet and we begin our warm-up which consists of a jog across the pitch and back again and a sprint for the last ten metres. You would think that the warm-up would be a bit more varied but no, this has been our warm-up more or less since we were founded. I once bought some cones and a book on warm-up drills with the view of varying our preparation but the book and cones are gathering dust under my bed.

"I'm knackered already and I was in bed by one last night which is quite early for me for a Saturday," Nick tells me whilst bending over trying to touch his toes. His hands can barely get below his kneecap.

"Don't worry, lads," says Phil. "I've got some jelly babies which are meant to give us energy and we'll running around like eighteen-year-olds with these in us. I read that several of the British rowing team used to take them during the Olympics and they won a load of gold medals."

Tworty seems unimpressed by the logic. "I know we're playing next to the River Thames but we're playing football mate, and I don't think the only reason they did well was because of the jelly babies. They also had talent – something we've lacked for a few years."

At 10.25 Jim and Bo finally arrive and the team seem more interested in finding out the vital statistics of Bo's conquest last night than listening to Danny's pre-match team talk, which basically consists of him just reading the team out.

"We've got two subs today, lads, so if you don't perform like Bo did last night you are off. I would also like to congratulate Nick and Gibbo on their performance in a five-a-side game last week. It was a close game by all accounts which went right down to the final whistle."

"How did you get on, Gibbo?" Bo enquires. "I sense you lost and you fucked up for their winning goal as Danny would not have brought it up otherwise?"

"Winning goal, Bo?" says Danny. "That should be winning goals with a capital 's'. They lost by twenty goals. Yes, twenty goals."

"Seventeen, Danny," I say by way of a red-faced correction. "Don't make it sound bad."

"Seventeen? Oh, that's alright then, Gibbo. That is so much more respectable. Seventeen makes it sound that so much closer. I'm surprised the ref didn't lose track of the score."

"I wish he had, Tom, anyway I'm well up for today. I fancy a good performance coming on."

We haven't played Wandsworth Milan before so I'm not too sure what to expect; if they're anything like AC and Inter I fear the worst. You should never try and judge your opponents by how they look, but I always do and they seem to have six or seven lads who are six foot or over and they seem to be built like brick shithouses as well. This immediately dampens my confidence and with me playing centre-back today I just hope that none of them are playing centre-forward. My ideal centre-forward would be the small lad I just saw miss a sitter in the warm-up.

The referee blows his whistle and asks for the captain. Real Calcio don't have a set captain and whoever is nearest the centre circle out of Danny, Nick, Damo and I tends to go up, lose the toss, turn around and shout out the ritual Calcio exhortation: "Switch on from the off, boys." Whether this has any effect is doubtful as we are prone to giving away a goal in the first five minutes.

The game starts and surprisingly enough after five minutes the game is still 0-0. What I find quite strange are our opponents' supporters at the edge of the pitch. They are shirtless and drinking cans of Stella at 10.30 in the morning. Fosters or Carlsberg fair enough, but Stella! Judging by the smell of the bloke I am marking he has had a couple of cans for breakfast and sadly he is also one of the big man-mountains I saw in the warm-up. I have stuck to my usual pre-match meal of a Mars Bar, a banana, can of Red Bull and today about six jelly babies.

"Big, muscular, fast fucker you're marking today, Gibbo – he'll kick lumps out of you," Danny tells me, grinning, as we await a throw-in.

"Thanks mate, you work wonders for my confidence."

"Apparently he banged in goals for fun last season. You know that small bloke we saw in the warm-up that looked about fifteen and seemed pretty shit? Well I'm marking him. Happy days."

"He is probably saying to his team-mates 'You know that fat, gobby Scouser who was out of breath after their warm-up? Happy days. I'm marking him'."

After about ten minutes I'm still waiting for my first touch of the season. Will it be a pass on to the pitch next to us, a pass to an opponent off my shin or maybe a thirty-yard screamer into the top corner? I have a good idea which one it won't be.

I do eventually get my first touch a moment or so later when I intercept a through-ball to their centre-forward. Rather than pass to a team-mate I decide to go for a bit of a dribble and beat the first player with a nice turn. I then seem to think I'm Pele and decide to try and beat another player only for him to dispossess me easily before passing to the forward I am meant to be marking, who shoots on goal. Luckily, Phil in goal makes a smart stop and spares my blushes.

"Fuck me, Gibbo, what are you playing at?" snaps Tom. "Remember you're Gibbo, not Maradona. Just because you beat a player for the first time in God knows how many years doesn't give you the licence to try and dribble through the whole team."

"Just got a bit over-confident, mate, though I did glide past the first player in some style, it must be said."

"Your turn, although not sure I can call it that for fear of getting sued by the Trades Description Act, on the second player was like a carthorse. It also had the end result of us being exposed at the back."

The first chance comes our way and I should have done better with a header from a decent free-kick from Tworty. The game is pretty even until their left-winger breaks down the left and crosses to the edge of the box. One of their midfield players seems to have the freedom of Wandsworth before picking his spot and scoring.

"Midfield, where the hell are you?" shouts Tom.

He has a fair point as most of them seem to be on the halfway line. Danny, who plays centre midfield, tends to take the 'centre' part literally and doesn't like to leave the centre circle the whole game. Hugh swears that the time he did leave the centre circle he got a nosebleed.

We then come very close to scoring when a cross from Tworty takes two deflections off defenders and ends up at Nick's feet about four yards from goal. However, rather than tapping the ball in the open net he somehow skies the ball over the bar.

"Concentrate lads," their captain shouts out to his team-mates. "They were a bit lucky it took two deflections."

"Well you were lucky it fell to Nick," I reply. "He can't hit a cow's arse with a banjo."

"Ha-ha mate," the guilty party pipes up. "It hit a divot as I went to shoot."

"Yes, your wayward right foot."

Half-time comes and we haven't mustered a shot on goal. Jack, who is one of the subs, takes the team talk and tells us to get the ball wide, keep the ball on the ground and all the other great half-time phrases most Sunday teams hear but never put into place during the second half. We have some more jelly babies (not that they did much good in the first half) and make a substitution, taking off Chris and putting on Bo who looks knackered. Even if he can play to half his potential he should be better than the rest of us.

Anyway, two minutes into the second half Tworty picks up the ball by the left touch line and from about thirty yards puts the ball in the top left-hand corner. We all initially stop in disbelief but soon run over to him to congratulate him.

"That's the goal of the season competition over," Tworty says and he is probably right.

"That is probably the best Calcio goal in our ten-year history," Nick tells me.

"You been practising those of summer have you, Tworty?" asks Bo.

"Natural talent, mate. I don't need to practice them. I'll show you how it's done after the game."

"That was so meant to be a cross, wasn't it, mate?" I say with characteristic generosity.

"Jealousy gets you nowhere, Gibbo."

The game continues and Phil pulls off a few good saves while I have to admit the man-mountain of a centre-forward I am marking is beginning to get the better of me. Yet whenever the referee isn't looking I'm getting digs in the ribs and being called all the names under the sun, especially as I am beginning to master the art of pulling his shirt without the referee noticing.

The game is beginning to become a bit dirty and Tom and Danny are having verbal battles with the guys they are marking. The atmosphere of the game isn't helped when Miles brings down the player I am marking with a late two-footed lunge.

"Fucking arsehole! What the fuck are you playing at?" yells their centre-forward as he jumps up and starts pushing Miles.

"Just mistimed it," our man responds. "It can't have been that bad, otherwise you would still be on the floor."

"Not the first dirty tackle you've done either," says the indignant centre-forward.

Danny enters the fray. "You boys can't talk, with your constant shirt-pulling, scraping down my Achilles and even scratching. Only kids do that."

The referee books Miles and tells us all to calm down before they restart the game with a free-kick.

Sounding slightly disappointed, Miles tells me: "I got him back for you, mate. Just wish I'd got him a bit harder."

"I'm glad you fucking didn't. A riot would have broken out if you had."

Finally, midway through the second half, we begin to apply some pressure and Paul misses a good chance to put us 2-1 up. It looks like the game could be heading for a draw until they pump the ball up front and their centre-forward, who is pretty fast (well, fast compared with me) outpaces me to the ball. To rectify the situation I bring him down. I protest my innocence knowing full well it was a foul and the referee justifiably gives a free-kick to them just outside the box.

"He's got to go for that, ref. Another dirty tackle from them," shouts their centre-forward in the general direction of the official.

"Fuck off, I barely touched you," I reply lying through my back teeth.

"Bullshit. And besides it's the closest you have got to me all day, you fucking carthorse."

"Remind me how many goals you've scored today?"

"Fucking son-of-a-bitch wanker you are."

"That's a new one, don't think I've been called that before and I've been called all sorts down the years."

"Calm down, Gibbo. He's twice the size of you," says Nick. "It's also nice to see you haven't lost your pace over the summer."

"I had no chance. It was either that or him through on goal in a one-on-one situation."

For some reason the referee gives an indirect free-kick and Jim mentions that as I gave away the free-kick as soon as the first player touches the ball I should charge out and close down the other chap. Great, I think to myself, knowing that there would be a good chance I'd get hit – and knowing my luck, straight in the nether regions.

After we've retreated 10 yards, they take a quick free-kick. As I turn around I see the ball nestle in the bottom left-hand corner. Wandsworth Milan all run over to their supporters, who are still drinking, and celebrate as if they've won the Champions League rather than scored a potential winner in the season's first match in London West League Division Five.

We kick-off and everyone piles forward searching for the equaliser. This leaves us heavily exposed at the back and a hopeful punt from their centre-back gives their centre-forward a clear run on goal. He calmly slots the ball under Phil in goal. Cue more wild celebrations. No sooner have we restarted than the referee blows his whistle and our first game of the season ends in defeat.

As we trudge off the pitch the lads start to take the piss out of me for giving away the goal. Rather than heading back to the changing rooms and bumping into the other team we get changed by the side of the pitch. I do though feel sorry for the old lady walking her dog as I imagine the last thing she wants to see on a Sunday morning is the lovely sight of a dozen overweight blokes getting changed out in the open.

Nick collects the subs, Jim blames his second half performance on the flavour of jelly babies he had at half-time and Danny, who collects the dirty kit, has his weekly moan that no one has turned the strip the right way round. Apparently the lady who runs the laundrette insists that he does that before he drops it off to be washed on Monday mornings.

We sometimes go for a drink after a game but no one feels like it so we say our goodbyes and head home. I get back to my flat and spend most of the afternoon on the sofa hoping that our season and my performance quickly improve.

Danny rings me early in the evening, saying: "Nice to see things haven't changed, mate."

"What do you mean, mate?"

"Well, you're just as shit as last season and seem to have lost even more pace which I never thought was possible. What the hell were you doing trying to beat half their team with your first touch as well? Only the likes of me can do that although I admit it is becoming less frequent now, perhaps just once a game rather than once a half. One more thing you also conceded the free-kick that led to their goal."

"Cheers mate for that vote of confidence; I wish I had put you in the wall as it would take some free-kick to get around you. Besides I can't say I saw you run round the pitch much today either."

"I don't have to, mate. I'm the creative force in our midfield whilst Nick is the ball-winner."

"It would be nice if you told Nick that, mate. I don't think he won a tackle all day and I'm pretty sure you created next to nothing today apart from your weekly moan about the kit."

"It also pissed me off that when I was giving my inspirational team talk that most of the team were more interested in the bird Bo pulled last night."

"Apparently she was a cracker, though, twenty-five-year-old Swedish bird with her own pad in Chelsea and with all her bits in the right places."

"When did he tell you?"

"When you were giving your inspirational team talk."

"That's my point. You should've been listening to me, not him!

Anyway she does sound nice. In fairness, I reckon if you pull a tasty, rich Swede that's an excuse for being late. I mean it rarely happens to any of us. At least I don't think it ever has."

"Think it only happens to Bo and I in all honesty. I have a queue of Swedes outside my flat most weekends."

"Fucking short queue, I bet. The only Swede you have a chance of pulling are the ones out the ground at the allotment."

"Getting back on to the topic of football, how do you think we will fair this season?"

"Not sure. We looked unfit, slow and off the pace today, which doesn't bode well."

"We also looked shattered at the end, which is worrying as it's only our first game."

"So relegation battle then?"

"Reckon so. Reckon we need twenty points to be safe."

"I can't believe you have worked that out already. We've only played one game."

"I actually worked it out last night."

"That's the spirit mate. Anyway, I better go as I need to move my legs from the sofa. I can feel them seizing up."

"We're probably the only team in the league sponsored by a multinational company"

When I wake up on Monday morning my legs feel as though they ran a marathon yesterday. I struggle into work and on arriving I get an email from Damo saying that Real Calcio are bottom of the league. I reply saying that we've only played one game and the only reason we're bottom is because ours was the only game yesterday but he insists that we'll need to improve on yesterday's performance and can't go giving away needless free-kicks in dangerous positions in the last five minutes.

Come Friday we're struggling to get eleven for Sunday and Bo is ignoring my phone calls. I can't say I blame him as it's only the second week and we are trying to rope him in again. We also have no keepers as both of them are on a stag do. Smithy emails me to tell me his mate who apparently used to play for Aldershot, when they were originally in the Football League, is up for playing for us on Sunday. I email Damo, Danny and Nick and we're all excited that for the first time in our history we have an ex-professional player in our side. However, I soon realise that Aldershot were originally wound up in the early Nineties so I call Smithy to enquire about his age.

"This goalkeeper – he sounds good, mate, but how old is he?"

"Not sure, mate, but he had a good fiftieth bash a couple of year's ago."

"Fifty? Christ does he keep himself fit?"

"No, mate. He's pretty overweight but he reckons the wider you are the smaller you make the goal."

The others haven't clocked on to the fact that our keeper is virtually a pensioner and still envisage him being an athletic youngster who would save everything that comes his way. Their hopes are dashed when the following day Smithy calls me on the way to the pub.

"Mate, we have to wait a bit longer for an ex-pro to play for us as my mate can't play now. He has realised it will take him ages to get over to Chiswick on Sunday morning and will probably involve about three trains and two bus journeys."

"Shit. Tell him I will pay his travel to get here and back if it helps."

"Mate, it's not the cost. I think he gets free travel at his age anyway."

"Oh yes, I forgot he was virtually an OAP and probably gets a free travel pass."

I'm Calcio's 'third keeper' and it looks like this Sunday I'm playing in goal. I've played a couple of times before and it's not as if with our defence I will get bored. I have a relaxed Saturday night, having the staple football diet of a curry and a few beers.

Jack sees our new kit in the changing room before the game. "Nivea for men! The other teams will have a field day when they see that splashed across our kit," he exclaims.

We had entered a competition sponsored by Nivea in a football magazine and won ourselves a new kit last week. The kit has their logo splashed across the front of the tops.

"Jack," I say proudly, "we're probably the only team in the league sponsored by a multinational company."

"Do we get any free moisturisers or facial products?"

"Afraid not, Jack, and anyway I think most of you lot need a lot more than moisturiser and facial products to sort yourselves out."

Paddy joins in. "I notice that there is one star on the back of our kits, does that symbolise the one cup I… I mean *we* won a few years ago."

He will never let us forget that he scored the winning (only) goal in the cup final. When it happened my initial reaction was one of joy but I soon wished that someone else had got it, ideally me, as we would never hear the end of it. He even enquired whether he was exempt from league fees the following season as he had scored the goal.

We let him keep the cup in his flat and I'm sure he bores people with the story of his goal. I bumped into one of his mates a week after the final and he said that Paddy had been telling him about how he dictated the game and scored a screamer from outside the box. The truth is Paddy came on for the second period of extra time and despite doing his best to head the ball wide from two yards it managed to squirm in at the far post.

Chiswick Chancers are today's opponents, a club we've had various battles with over the years. We seemed to beat them every season until about three years ago but since then they have tended to get the better of us. We usually score first, then think we'll thrash them so switch off and let in three or four goals.

They're a good set of lads, which can't always be said about the teams we play. And like us, they're one of the older teams in the league and also struggle with their waistlines and the ability to get the same eleven players each week.

Just as we leave the changing room the heavens open and being the professional team we are we decide to stay inside the changing room, thereby cutting short our warm-up. However, the torrential rain lasts only five minutes before the sun comes out and we all amble out to the pitch and are actually out before the home team, who must fear the rain more than us. For a change, we have a semi-decent warm-up. I'm in goal and manage to find two right-handed goalkeeper's gloves in the bag, but luckily Paul has a pair and Damo gives me some practice. Well, I say practice in the loosest term as all he does is hit the ball in the back of the net from ten yards, giving me no chance with any of them.

"Pity you can't do that in the game, Damo," says Jack.

"If only the keepers were of his standard, I would."

The referee arrives and he looks all of fifteen but he seems to look fit and should at least be able to keep up with the game. I wish all the referees were like this; we had one last season that looked half dead and was white as a ghost. Before and during the game we asked him several times if he was OK. We had visions of him collapsing on the pitch during the game and with our first-aid kit consisting only of wasp spray we would have feared the worst.

We have a brief pre-match talk which somehow gets round to us deciding on which pub we should go to after the game. Before we know it the referee blows the whistle and Nick, who is captain this week as he is nearest the centre spot, goes up for the toss. He manages to keep up his fine record of losing every toss and we change ends, which means I have the sun in my eyes first half.

"Anyone got a cap I can borrow to help me with this sun?"

"No mate, I have my beanie hat but I don't think that will be too helpful."

Great, I think, I haven't played in goal for ages and I also have the sun to contend with.

"Shoot on sight lads," their captain shouts out. "Their keeper's dodgy."

"Cheers mate," I retaliate. "I was surprised you were still in the team until your team-mates told me the only reason you are is because you're captain and run the team. From our point of view we just hope you continue captaining your fine side."

The first half goes along without much action. I don't have much to do, but then again nor does their keeper. The game is being played in a good spirit with no dirty tackles, no mouthing off between the teams and no one giving either linesman any abuse. The referee is also having a good game and has barely had to blow his whistle or raise his voice in the whole half.

Half-time finally comes and Nick gets the jelly babies out again and we take a breather. I try and give a motivational team talk but in typical Calcio tradition the rest of the team are more interested in a couple of pretty women wearing short skirts and knee-high boots, which you don't often see on a Sunday morning by a football pitch.

"Those two look like a couple of high-class prostitutes," says Danny edging closer towards the two women to get a closer look.

"They have come to the wrong place then," I say. "I struggle to get a fiver out of you boys each week for subs and reckon if they are high-class hookers they might charge more than a fiver."

Smithy tries to steer the conversation back to the match. "We still probably have more chance of scoring with those two than we do of scoring a goal today. We created nothing first half but then again the same could apply to our opponents."

The second half carries on much the way of the first. It's no football masterpiece and there hasn't been one decent chance for either team. The ball seems to be spending most of the time in midfield and when it breaks into the last third, nothing seems to come of it, with both defences standing firm. It's been so uneventful that if the *Match of the Day* cameras were here they would struggle to find enough action to fill twenty seconds of highlights. I also begin to feel sorry for some of the lads' girlfriends who've been dragged along, although most of them seemed to have disappeared to the organic market that is being held in the car park.

But with about ten minutes to go I punt the ball downfield. Their centre-back kicks the ball on the full, and to his and our astonishment the ball balloons in the air backwards and goes sailing over the goalkeeper into the net. I celebrate as if it's my goal.

"Here we go," shouts Danny.

"And don't even think about claiming that goal," Smithy adds.

"What do you mean? It's a definite assist – I'm the only one in this team who can create anything. I'm doing two jobs, stopping the goals and creating them."

Our opponents make a substitution and a youngish lad comes on. He seems quick, certainly compared with our defenders, and has the unique name of Spider. He is soon put through on goal and despite my best attempt of making the goal as big as possible for him he manages to screw the ball wide.

We bring on our sub Gio, who is actually playing under the name Graham Jones as we haven't got Gio registered yet. I sprint up to him before he gives the referee his name and remind him that today he is Graham Jones.

"Oh great. I have to pretend to be that angry Scouser," says Gio, a diehard Man United fan.

He gives his name to the referee and within seconds I hear Tom shout: "Go on, Gio, get stuck in."

The referee looks at me as if to say that he knows he is a ringer but is soon distracted as they bring on two subs.

"Who's coming on for them now," shouts Tom. "Batman and Superman to join Spiderman up front?"

Luckily for us they don't do much. The game peters out and we manage to record our first victory of the season.

"If I was in someone's fantasy football team they would think it's Christmas with my goal and clean sheet," I say to Nick as we walk off the pitch.

"There is no way you can possibly claim that goal," he replies. "I have just as much claim on that goal as you do."

The lads quickly get showered and changed to get away from me going on about my goal. They also want to get to the organic market and order a burger before Danny gets there and eats them all himself.

At the end of every game we have to text the result and goalscorers to the league secretary. After much, well no, deliberation, I text that we won 1-0 and I scored. Great, I think to myself, I'm joint top scorer.

We head back to Clapham to go for a few drinks and watch the live game on Sky.

"That was a good performance," I tell the lads. "A win *and* a clean sheet, which doesn't often happen. So, Danny, that's three points towards the magic twenty you reckon we need to have to survive."

"What?" a few of them reply.

"Danny, being the optimistic one, has set us a target of twenty points this season to avoid relegation."

Damo is suitably stirred. "Nice to see you're confident this season and already setting benchmarks on avoiding relegation," he says, "though I reckon we could get eighteen points and be safe."

"You are as bad as him, Damo," says Nick.

"It's all about stepping stones," says Danny. "After we hit twenty points we can then relax and concentrate on marching up the table and you never know we could end up with some silverware this season. Especially if I continue to boss the midfield like I did today."

"And I keep clean sheets," I say.

"Hang on, let's get a couple of things straight," says Nick, having evidently heard enough. "Gibbo, my gran could have kept goal – you had so little to do. Danny, the only reason you so-called 'bossed the midfield' was because I was doing all the donkey work, i.e. chasing back and winning the ball so that all you had to do was pass to Damo up front."

Danny isn't giving up without a fight. "Who contrived to miss every chance I put on a plate for him?"

"Don't think I had one chance all game, mate. You were about as creative as Carlton Palmer in his declining years before he retired," quips Damo.

"That's some insult as don't think Palmer created much in his formative years," I reply.

"Anyway, enough about our game and how I bossed the centre midfield with little help from Nick. Who do we fancy this afternoon?"

"The blonde bird in knee-high boots watching our game earlier," says Damo making us all laugh.

"No, the brunette was better mate," says Danny. "The blonde was nice from far but far from nice. Trust me, when you were getting bored by the crap Gibbo was coming out with in his half-time team talk I was mentally giving the birds marks out of ten on body, face and legs. The blonde scored nineteen, but her face let her down. The brunette – wait for it – scored a fantastic twenty four. She had legs to die for and was close to getting ten out of ten for them."

"Reckon if they marked you out of thirty on your football performance today you would've been lucky to get double figures, Danny," says Damo.

"Whatever, mate. Anyway, I'm going for City," he says, bringing us back to the Manchester derby on TV.

"United all day mate," I come back. "I put twenty quid on that yesterday and with my winnings I reckon I could buy someone up front to score us some goals, eh Damo, instead of you having to rely on your keeper to score goals."

The day would have been perfect if my bet hadn't been scuppered in the last minute. Not to worry: at least I'm off and running in the Real Calcio top goalscorer competition.

"It's Wednesday and we already have thirteen players"

These are Nick's words when he rings me on Wednesday in a panic. For the first time in Real Calcio's history we are thinking of having to tell people that they haven't made the squad for the weekend's game.

Most teams would love to have thirteen players come Wednesday but this is a strange occurrence for us. We are used to phoning people on the day before the match asking whether they know anyone who fancies a game on Sunday. We've never had to phone people and explain that they haven't made the squad.

Two years ago, however, when we somehow reached the cup final – and even more remarkably won it – our whole squad were available to play. Funny, that. Nick, Danny, Damo and I had lots of arguments over who we would pick and whether we would pick our best eleven or the most loyal players throughout the season. I think we took the right action and chose the latter. This also meant that us four were guaranteed to start.

We have a squad of around twenty and in September, when the weather is still OK, we are usually fine for numbers. But come October, when we have had a few defeats and the weather gets colder, numbers tend to drop and if we get twelve on Sundays we consider ourselves lucky. We have started a game with eight players – which by half-time had risen to ten with the arrival of two latecomers – but then due to my sending-off in the second half (a very harsh decision of course), we ended up with nine.

Nine times out of ten if you have thirteen players available on

Saturday you will be lucky to get twelve come Sunday. We had a lad called Dave who played for us last year who was renowned to saying he could play and then not turning up. If he did he would more than likely be late. Once I rang and asked him where he was and he said he was in his car five minutes away; this was despite the fact that I could hear his girlfriend in the background, asking him if he fancied a cup of tea in bed.

Come Friday we are up to fourteen and several emails are flying about between the committee about everyone's preferred team for Sunday. We're even discussing formations and tactics, which has to be a first. However, on Saturday Jim rings up and says that he has managed to injure his ribs. Although this is a blow, since he is one of our best players, at least it helps make team-selection easier.

I wake up Sunday feeling a bit ropey, with the taste of the kebab I had eaten a few hours earlier in my mouth, and set off to Clapham Junction station car park to meet the lads. I get my usual breakfast and also the *News of the World* for essential car-journey reading. I study my *London A-Z* and realise that I'm missing the page where Hounslow's ground is situated but assure the lads that I know the way before we set off in convoy.

"Christ, how did they get allowed to play in our league?" says Phil, aka Phaal, our Scottish custodian. "We've been driving for ages. Couldn't they have found a league nearer to them?"

"Well," replies Tom, deadpan, "our league is the London West football league and they are definitely west."

I study the *A-Z* again and realise I have mucked up with the directions. "Lads, I think I've got the A40 confused with the A4."

"Gibson, you are fucking hopeless. Don't ever become a taxi-driver," Phil shouts at me.

Tom piles in. "Have you seen him drive? I got in a car with him once and it was like a scary fairground ride. I can't believe we trusted you with the directions – we could end up anywhere in west London although wouldn't surprise me if we ended up in Wales."

We stop on the side of the road, nearly causing an accident, and wait for the other two cars. Nick comes out of one of the other vehicles and looks at me as if he knows that I have fucked up big-time. We spend about ten minutes trying to work out a way of getting back on track and Nick tells us that we have to head up the middle of page fifty eight until it goes to page eighty and then through the middle of page eighty until we get to page one hundred and six. Then it should be signposted.

What shit directions, I think to myself, until I realise that I'm in no position to criticise.

"Slight problem, Nick," says Tom. "Gibbo's *A-Z* doesn't have a page 106."

"I give up with him. OK, Tom, we'll lead."

"Hurry up and don't get us lost. Kick-off was ten minutes ago," I tell Nick, who gives me a look to say that I'm a fine one to talk.

I have to admit it is quite a big mistake on my part. I think I got distracted by reading about some Z-list celebrity getting another boob job in the *News of the World,* and to be honest they look pretty decent if you ask me. We used to play in a league in east London and on one away game we got so lost we gave up and had a pub lunch in a village in Kent where we had ended up. It worked out an expensive meal as we had to fork out about a hundred quid in fines. But we did get served extra Yorkshire puddings, so swings and roundabouts I suppose.

Smithy, who has driven straight to the ground, calls me from the ground enquiring about our whereabouts.

"Where the fuck are you? I've been here ages."

"Don't ask, mate."

"You got the team lost then, Gibbo."

"Well, could say that, although I'm sure my map is partly to blame as well."

We arrive at the ground at around 11.15, only forty five minutes late, and rush to the changing room.

"Sorry about that. Easy mistake to make, confusing the A4 with the A40. Anyway, it's the same team as last week apart from Chris coming in for Danny and, after much deliberation, Phil replacing me in goal. I will start as sub as punishment but will probably come on second half and dictate the game."

"Where's Danny?" Smithy asks, sounding concerned which is surprising considering Danny was shit in the first two games.

"He forgot his boots and he's gone back to collect them."

"Surely he could've borrowed a pair?"

"Yeah, but who has boots that can fit him? He's only a size seven but has wide feet."

I half fill in the team sheet and run out on to the pitch. I see that the referee is the bloke who is on the league committee and in charge of dealing out fines. Great, I think to myself, this could be an expensive morning. When he spots me he smiles and probably thinks to himself that with our team being nearly an hour late, my team sheet not properly filled in and some of our players' shirt numbers not corresponding to the team sheet, we have just paid for the league committee's Christmas piss-up.

A couple of years ago I never realised that this referee was also the fines secretary. When I was disputing a fine with him on the phone he asked me who refereed the game in question and I said that it was a tubby, tattooed bloke with a strange bleached hairstyle who couldn't keep up with the game. It turned out it was him and from that day on he has taken any excuse to fine us, although I have to admit he is a good referee and seems to have lost some weight.

"Sorry, ref. Roadworks, road closures and Sunday drivers, you know how it is."

"Your team-mates just said that you got the team completely lost."

"Bit of that as well, I suppose, but go easy on the fines, ref. I have a family of eight to feed at home and sadly we don't have an Abramovich bankrolling us."

45

Anton changes the subject. "Good pitch this, Gibbo." He's right; it has to be one of the best we've played on. Pity the ball will spend most of the time in the air, I think to myself.

"Matt, come here," the referee shouts out at me.

Oh shit. I find myself wondering what I've done now.

"Danny's signature is on the team sheet and he isn't even here. I would have heard him by now."

Every referee knows who Danny is as he's a mouthy Scouser who likes to be heard.

"Yes, he came and then realised he'd forgotten his boots so he's gone back home to collect them."

I'm sure he doesn't believe me and we will therefore get another fine which will probably help pay for their summer piss-up as well.

"Hounslow Hangovers," muses Paddy during our brief warm-up. "I love their name, Gibbo. I just hope they had a big night on the piss last night as I'm feeling a bit ropey today."

"This sun is pretty strong as well," I say, "which will sap the little energy we generally have most weeks."

"What are you like? If it rains you moan that the pitch will be a mudbath; if it's too windy you moan you won't be able to pass the ball straight; and if it's too sunny you moan you will have no energy. Is there any weather you actually like playing in?"

"When it's about twelve degrees, slightly overcast, dry and with no wind."

The game eventually kicks off just as Danny turns up. He enquires why we were so late starting, so I let him know that Phil got us lost. Hounslow start well and from their first corner after about two minutes their tall centre-back heads towards goal and rather than kicking the ball away Paddy ends up kicking it into the net.

Oh, great. Here we go, I think to myself.

"Head up Paddy, everyone makes mistakes," Danny shouts out.

"Especially you, Paddy," I add helpfully.

46

"Hounslow don't look too good, though, which is a nice bonus, Gibbo," Danny tells me.

"What does that make us then? This team that don't look too good are beating us and we've only played two minutes. At this rate we will lose 45-0."

"We will get back into it, trust me. I will come on and boss it later anyway."

The next half an hour or so is pretty end to end with both teams creating half-chances but not really testing the keepers.

"The referee has pretty much had nothing to do all game. He's barely blown his whistle," I tell Danny on the touchline.

"They seem a nice set of lads – no gobby shits, filthy fuckers, muscular, tattooed skinheads or moaners. I don't think they've even committed a foul yet."

Danny is right. They are a decent bunch and we like to think we are as well. The only people in our team who can occasionally get on other teams' nerves are firstly Miles with his mistimed tackling. He's only a slight chap but he never ducks out of a challenge. Sometimes you know he is going to be late but rather than pull out he just thinks: 'Sod it, I've run twenty yards to make this tackle, so what's the point of me pulling out now. Besides, it's only a seven-quid fine for a booking and I earn that in a second at work.'

Tom can also rile opponents with his constant carping and arguing with the bloke he is marking. He has a short fuse and there are times in games when you just wish he would shut up and get on with the game. He's one of our best players and doesn't need to get involved in most of the altercations he gets himself into. Off the pitch, though, he is one of the most pleasant chaps you could meet; he teaches children with behavioural problems, which you'd never know from watching him play. Out there you would think it's him needing the lessons.

Danny and I can be a bit gobby at times and give as good as we get. I'm not the biggest lad in the world and tend to stop just before

I might get punched. I'm sure Danny eggs people on half the time, hoping that it will end in a fight. It has to be said that he does pack a mean punch and I'm pretty sure he is undefeated in his scuffles on the pitch.

With the lack of fouls and real goalscoring opportunities, the referee is having an easy game. He is quite similar to Danny in that he doesn't like to leave the centre circle. I'm just hoping that he continues to have next to nothing to do. That way, at the end of the match I can have a laugh and a joke with him, buttering him up with the end result being that he doesn't put through our fines.

Danny and I begin to discuss substitutions. Making subs is one of the hardest things in Sunday football as no one ever wants to come off. You also have to think about whether you take the worst person off, even if you took him off last week, and what if you make two subs and someone gets injured. Half-time comes and Danny and I give the usual team talk of 'Get the ball out wide, play on the deck and look to play through the channels'. We don't make any subs although Paddy says he is carrying a knock.

"It's probably a knock of confidence after your howler earlier on," Danny tells him.

The second half starts well for us; Paul puts Damo through and he lobs the keeper well to equalise. Danny and I give it ten minutes and make a double substitution, Danny coming on for Paddy in midfield and me replacing Chris up front. I love playing there and although it isn't my best position nothing beats scoring a goal. Well, nothing on a Sunday morning anyway.

Within a few minutes we get a corner and Danny trots off over to take it and hits a pinpoint cross right on to my head and I bury the ball in the back of the net. I celebrate wildly and run back to the centre circle pointing at the number on the back of my shirt, not knowing that the shirt I have on has no number on it.

We continue to play quite well and miss a few half chances. One is a shocker of a miss. Nick tries his luck from thirty yards and their keeper spoons the ball on to the bar. I follow up and with the goalie lying on the ground I somehow head the ball over from all of a yard. I've missed a few, well loads of, sitters in my time but this has to be my worst ever. I hold my head in my hands and know that I'm in for all sorts of piss-taking.

"How the fuck did you miss that?" Damo asks me.

"Not sure mate, but I know I will never live it down."

"Too right you won't, mate. With that you've definitely retained the Miss of the Season award."

"For the fourth season in a row," asserts Nick with a satisfied grin.

"Not very good with directions today are you, mate," Paddy shouts out from the touchline, which makes me laugh.

At least we are still winning I think to myself although around five minutes later they draw level after a good move down the wing results in a tap-in for their centre-forward. Shit, I think to myself, if this ends a draw I'm going to get crucified by the lads.

The game enters the last five minutes and we get a corner and Danny delivers another good corner and this time Tom rises at the far post and heads it in.

"You legend, Tom. You've saved my bacon."

"You owe me a drink or two if we win this."

The game peters out and we hold out for the win.

"Talk us through your miss, Gibbo," Pete asks me on the way back to the changing room.

"At least I followed up Nick's shot. No one else did."

"Yeah, but most of Nick's shots never hit the target so no one bothers anymore."

"Anyway if you ask all the great centre-forwards – Messi, Rooney, Ronaldo, Gibson – they would be more worried if they weren't getting in the positions to score."

"And you sure got in a position to score today."

"Another thing, lads. With that goal I think I've completed the clean sweep."

"What do you mean?" asks Danny.

"Well I'm pretty sure I have now scored at every Sunday league ground in the league."

"The shit you come up with is unbelievable, Gibbo."

I jog up to the referee and say: "Cracking game, ref. Thought you played a blinder."

"I actually enjoyed refereeing that today," he replies.

"I'll be giving you a ten out ten today when I give the league the referee marks."

"Are you after something and hoping that I might let you off all the various fines?"

"To be honest, ref, I'd appreciate it if you could perhaps waive a couple or all of them."

"What was it you called me on the phone the other year – a fat, tattooed ref with a shit haircut who couldn't keep up with the play or words to that affect?"

"You know I was only joking."

"Get away from me and I'll have a think about today's fines."

"Cheers ref, you know it makes sense."

We head back into the changing room and everyone bar Nick gets showered.

"What is it with you and showers or should that be lack of shower," Smithy asks him. "Is it some kind of post-match ritual, mate?"

"Just prefer showering at home."

"But you're covered in mud, with sweat dripping down you. Is everything alright downstairs, mate? Come on you can tell us. Talk it through with your friends."

"Very funny, and besides, look at Danny now cleaning his boots in the shower. There's a good chance I'd come out dirtier than I went in."

In the afternoon I'm looking after my five-year-old godson,

who I'm trying to convince to become a Tottenham fan despite all his friends being Chelsea and Arsenal fans who are constantly telling him Spurs are rubbish. His Dad is a Charlton supporter and he realises that Jake will be in for a life of misery if he makes him support them, although being a Spurs fan won't be much better.

Anyway today is the day I'm buying him a football shirt. I tell his parents that I'll take him to a sports shop and let him choose a top with no pressure from me.

There is no way I can let him choose an Arsenal or Chelsea shirt so the only shop I can take him to is the Spurs megastore, where as promised I won't pressurise him at all as it's a win-win situation for me. There is less chance here of there being an Arsenal or Chelsea top than there is of Real Calcio going the rest of the season undefeated. His parents probably think I am taking him to some store on Oxford Street, but as I promised to them I let him choose a shirt under no pressure.

He chooses a nice blue number (Spurs' away shirt) which he probably thinks is a Chelsea kit and is really happy and we head off back to my flat. His mum doesn't know much about football and thinks it's a Chelsea shirt when she collects him later in the day. It's only when he wears it to a friend's party thinking he is Didier Drogba – when in fact he is Jermaine Defoe – that the secret's out. Call me cruel but I get my just desserts as he soon becomes a Chelsea fan, then a Man United fan before going back to Chelsea.

"It's Thursday and we only have eight"

It's Monday and Damo is having some leaving drinks in Clapham. He has been made redundant from his job and he's having a bit of a send-off.

He's been on the email all day telling us to get there early so we can get a couple of tables. So when I enter the pub at just gone seven and see just him and his girlfriend Amelia there I'm a bit surprised, but pleased as I can take the piss.

"Popular in London then were we, Damo? We could've had your leaving do in a phonebox, mate."

"Knew you would say something like that, anyway I've just been telling Amelia about your miss yesterday."

"Some miss that by the sounds of it, Gibbo," she says.

"Don't suppose you told her I scored as well."

"Of course not mate, why would I do that?"

The emails had been flying thick and fast in the morning about my inability to score the proverbial open goal yesterday. When I got to work on Monday morning I already had one from a mate of mine in Sydney taking the piss out of me after hearing about it from one of the lads. I know it is going to be hard to live this one down.

People begin arriving in dribs and drabs and before long most of the team have arrived. We begin talking about potential places to go on our end-of-season do next year. Various cities and their advantages are mentioned including:

Stockholm – gorgeous blondes.

Reykjavik – even better looking blondes according to Carl.

Sofia – fifty pence a pint.

Munich – busty women.

Amsterdam – where do you start?

Ljubljana – about the only place in Europe no one had been to.

Brussels – only fifty pounds on Eurostar.

Calcio – the town in Italy with the same name as us.

No one mentions anything about places where it's easy to get a game of football but then again the football tends to take a back seat on these tours. We all have a vote and it seems that Sofia is the favourite as you can get cheap flights on Easyjet, it's fifty pence a pint, locals are meant to be quite tasty and most of the team haven't been there before.

Another subject we discuss is our game this weekend. It's the first round of the Chopper Savage Cup which we won two years ago. Our opponents, Red Star Belowgrade, have won their first two games of the season 8-0 and 9-1 which seems to suggest their team name is wrong. According to Nick, who has just come back from the monthly league meeting, they are keen to get their cup back, as they had won it the year before we did.

Every month there is a league meeting held at a pub. Each team has to send someone to go, otherwise it's a thirty-pound fine. They last about an hour or so, in which time I usually have a pint, a packet of peanuts and a pack of crisps which ends up being supper.

The various secretaries all speak for about five minutes. The registrations secretary always complains that no one ever sends in stamped, self-addressed envelopes when they register players, and the fines secretary is invariably chasing up late payers and threatening to throw the clubs out the league. Last season the fines secretary managed to lose the details of every club who owed the league money and was asking for teams to let him know if they owed any money. Funnily enough, no one said anything.

The general secretary tends to have the most to say and today, according to Nick, he was telling everyone about the exciting topic of goalpost safety. There is also a publicity secretary and apparently one of the local papers will be running reports on certain games. God knows why they would want to report on the games in our league. Although these meetings can be boring, one thing our league can't be faulted for is a lack of organisation and it is easily the best-run league we have played in.

Nick is telling us that Red Star are all fired up for this weekend's game and despite us having a decent squad last game several people are unavailable this weekend which will result in us sending out a weakened team. Nick says he will send a chaser email tomorrow and we soon move on to the topic of the worst ever Real Calcio team in our ten-year history.

We've had some awful players in our time and we have a few dodgy ones playing for us now. We had one goalkeeper who used to keep his phone in his goal and answer it during the game which cost us various goals during the season, although by the time he had taken off his gloves to answer the phone it had usually stopped ringing. We also had one player – Dirty Del who, if he lasted ninety minutes without being sent off, it was a miracle – and Deadly Doug who played up front for us for about twenty times and never scored once. By the tenth game without scoring we used to tell him to aim away from the goal in the hope that his shots might hit the target. Sadly that didn't work either.

Another lad played for us once about three years ago and emailed us the week before saying he was Brazilian and had played to quite a high standard in Brazil. We all expected the next Pele to turn up but were sadly disappointed as he was pretty shit and also looked more English than most of us and had a Cockney accent to boot. I'm pretty sure the closest he had been to Brazil was Guanabara, which is the Brazilian bar in London.

One of my best mates, Banksy, played for Calcio once and I had been telling the team how good he was the week prior to him making his debut. The lads were pleased that I had found someone decent to play centre-back, but sadly he only lasted ten minutes before he got sent off. The forward he was marking was clean through on goal and Banksy brought him down from behind which was a clear penalty. The referee booked him but on producing the yellow card Banksy turned his back to him, bent over and told him where to stick his yellow card. The referee then had no option but to send him off and that was his first and last appearance. I'm pretty sure the swine still owes me thirty-five quid for the fine I got from the FA.

The last-orders bell rings at the pub and we begin to head out. A few years ago someone would have suggested going on somewhere else but since most of us are over thirty the thought of waking up on Tuesday morning with a steaming hangover isn't a pleasant one. We say our goodbyes and head off.

Nick calls me Thursday morning. "Gibbo, we still only have eight for Sunday, any suggestions?"

"At least we have no big decisions to make about whom to make sub."

"True, but who can we ask?"

"Not sure. But don't ask Phil – the two previous mates he has brought down have been woeful."

I send an email round to the lads and see if they know anyone who can play Sunday or whether there is a chance of them being able to get out of whatever they had planned. A couple of the team come back and say they would love to get out of seeing their mother in law on Sunday but sadly their other halves have other ideas. I am away on a ten-year university reunion (my God I'm getting old) in Leicester, and despite Nick mentioning that if I start drinking in the afternoon I would be in bed by 8pm and could still get a good few hours' sleep before heading back to London the following day, I have every intention of making a night of it.

Damo calls. "Gibbo I've got an idea, how about I put an advert out on Gumtree looking for players for Sunday?"

"Sounds good, mate, though I can't believe we're resorting to the internet to try and find players. Reckon we'll have much luck?"

"You can get everything on the internet these days, mate, from your weekly food shop at Tesco to a Russian bride. Even the dork from accounts with no personality got a date with a bird from some internet website, although apparently she didn't look anything like the photo. I'm not sure he did either as he put a photo that was five years old on the website. That was when he had hair and before he discovered the cake shop around the corner from work which has done wonders for his waistline."

"So in theory we could get a player but there is a good chance that if he says he's good, he'll be shit."

"Yes, and if he is shit he'll fit in perfectly."

By Friday Damo has managed to get someone to play who responded to our advert on Gumtree. Hugh has managed to persuade his girlfriend that a cup game is more important than a family christening. And Smithy has promised to take his wife shopping Sunday afternoon if she lets him play football in the morning.

We can't register players on the day for games so Damo's new recruit, like Gio a couple of weeks ago, will have to play under the name Graham Jones which is the name we give to most of our ringers whose names we have not registered. Graham is an angry, lanky and, if truth be told, pretty shit footballer who played for us once about four years ago and took the worst penalty I have ever seen. The ball ended up closer to the corner flag than the goal and in honour of his performance we name him in our squad every season. Whichever ringer we get along on the day takes his name.

We often meet Graham for a drink after the game on Sundays and the first thing he asks is whether he played. If we reply yes he will more than likely say that no doubt he was a handsome chap who banged in a hat-trick. "Graham Jones" scored a few goals last season and came second in the top goalscorer competition and Graham thought it was only fair that he came on the end-of-season do. In fact he was a bit pissed off though that we had no award for second top scorer.

"Gibbo we have eleven for Sunday. Don't worry, we can make do without a sub," Nick tells me on Saturday morning. "You just enjoy yourself in Leicester getting blown out by your old university birds and if someone gets injured we'll just play with ten."

"Don't try and make me feel guilty. I haven't missed a game for ages and at least I wasn't out for half the season last year with a bruised little toe."

Nick has a habit of getting injured and last season if he played two games in a row it was a miracle. Once he came on as a substitute in the second half just before our opponents had a corner. He ran on and managed to pull his hamstring before he had even reached our penalty box which led to us immediately substituting him. He must have been on the pitch for around thirty seconds. As you can probably imagine, he's never lived this down.

Paddy is another player who 'loves' an injury. One time last season he managed to get injured by two players who weren't even playing in our game. He was preparing to take a throw-in when two players from the next pitch, which was very close to ours, went for a challenge at the side of their pitch and managed to slide into Paddy causing him to fall over and injure his knee. This brought much amusement to everyone until we realised we had no more substitutes to bring on and had to play the rest of the game with ten men.

I spent the following week taking the piss out of Paddy but he got his own back on me a few weeks later when I managed to get injured within thirty seconds of a game. The opposition kicked off and their central midfielder played it back to the right-back. He had a bad first touch and I closed him down and slid in but managed to miss the ball and in the process I went over on my ankle. I was in terrible pain and had to hobble off without even having touched the ball. As I went I could see Paddy with a big grin on his face and knew I would cop a lot of shit from him after the game, which I of course did.

There was a game we had last year which pretty much sums up Real Calcio and our injury-prone players. We had twelve men including Nick and I, who were both injured. His back was bad and my ankle was playing up. In the changing room beforehand we were both putting forward our arguments to each other that we were more injured than the other and hence more deserving to be substitute. No one admitted defeat and we solved the situation by tossing a coin to see who would have the honour. I won and started on the bench, with absolutely no intention of coming on.

However, after about five minutes Nick gave me a look to say that he had damaged his back even more and that he wanted to come off. In fairness to Nick he was walking round like the Hunchback of Notre Dame. Alas, I was soon stripped off and on the pitch. I then lasted about ten minutes before rolling my ankle again. I ended up going in goal, barely able to walk.

Miles then got badly tackled and ended up with a huge dent in his shin which meant he had to go off and get a taxi to Casualty as you could see his bone. To cap it all off Anton soon pulled a hamstring which meant after twenty minutes we were down to nine men and we had a bloke with a dodgy ankle who couldn't kick the ball in goal. Needless to say we ended up getting thumped 8-0.

In Leicester I spend most of the Saturday catching up with my old mates, watching the football at the pub and then embarking on a pub crawl of all our old university hang-outs. We end up at the kebab house in the early hours of Sunday morning, devouring what used to be my staple diet at university. The bloke behind the counter even recognised one of the lads from ten years ago; he must have been a good customer as he got welcomed back like a long-lost brother. He promptly proved my theory right as he had a huge kebab, pie, large chips and a big bottle of Coke.

I head back to London on the Sunday and try to call the lads to get the result. I can't get through to anyone which makes me think they had been stuffed and don't want to answer the phone. Danny eventually calls.

"We won 3-0, mate. I banged in three thunderbolts."

"Bullshit, mate. There's no way in a million years that you would ever score a hat-trick and that we would keep a clean sheet without me in goal. Not sure which is more unbelievable. Even if you said you won 1-0 and you scored I wouldn't believe you. Remember a few years ago when I was away and you, Damo and Nick told me we had won 3-0 and it was only when I looked at the football mitoo website on the Monday I realised you'd lost 8-0."

"I remember that we had you hook, line and sinker. I think you even believed Nick had scored two goals and lasted ninety minutes without getting injured which we know never happens on both counts."

"So come on then, how many did we lose by?"

"OK, mate. The truth is we won't be winning the cup this year I'm afraid despite me orchestrating the play from centre midfield today. Red Star Belowgrade played a grade or two above us unfortunately."

"Shit, it's October and we are already out of a cup. So what was the score?"

"One-nil and it was a fluky goal that was meant to be a cross. We played alright, though, and got stuck in."

"Were they a good set of lads?"

"Seemed OK, though Tom was marking someone that moaned and was even more gobby than him, which surprised him."

"The league it is then. The league is, after all, the bread and butter."

"Yeah, suppose so. But I fancied a cup run this year and I can't see us going far in the other cup."

"At least I can tell my mates we lost in the quarter-final."

When I told them that we won the cup final two years ago a

lot of them said that it's a fine achievement to get to the final, let alone win it. However, what I didn't tell them is that there were only ten teams in the cup and that we entered at the quarter-final stage, as we did this time.

As I enter work on Monday, Rich shouts out. "How did your team get on in the cup, mate?"

"Lost 1-0, mate."

"What round was it?"

"Quarter-final."

"Not bad reaching the quarters mate. After all, you aren't spring chickens any more."

"Suppose so. It's further than Arsenal get in the Champions League most years and the same as England seem to do in all the major tournaments."

"Don't worry, Carl's back"

Nick's email to Danny, Damo and I on Wednesday before our game this weekend brings news of a 'new' signing. Carl didn't play much for us last year and hasn't had the honour of wearing our famous green shirt this season. However, he has told Nick that he is no longer working weekends and can therefore hopefully play most Sundays.

This season, albeit only four games old, we have struggled to score goals. Despite the fact that Carl, in his own words, hasn't played for over six months, is unfit and has a dodgy groin, Nick seems sure he is the answer to our goalscoring problems. After all, he is a Kiwi.

Come Friday it is clear that he isn't going to be the only one in the team. Chris is also available and is bringing along his brother, who is over from New Zealand. Another Kiwi lad, Wilky, is also available. He played for us last season but has been injured lately. Most games he manages to forget something. Last season he had forgotten his shinpads for one match but found a box outside the ground and broke off some cardboard which he used instead.

As it is an away game we have our usual 9.15 meet at Clapham Junction. Jack is already there. "Gibbo, I can't play today. Been shitting for England the last seventy two hours and have no energy at all. I've lost about a stone."

"Mate, you should let Danny know what you've been eating he's in dire need of losing a stone or two."

"Are we OK for numbers, though? I will drive you boys down there."

"Cheers, mate. We have eleven, including four people from that great football nation New Zealand."

The rest of the team arrive and most of them are pretty hung-over. I doubt it ever occurs to any of them at 2am in some ropey nightclub that they are playing football eight hours later.

Rapid Descent, who we're playing today, are based at Wormwood Scrubs – the pitches, not the prison – and I inform the lads that we have to go up the A40.

"Under no circumstance can we let Gibbo navigate today," insists Tom. "I'm meant to be taking my missus out for lunch and I don't want to be eating at 4.30."

"Where's Danny – thought he was meeting us here today?" asks Chris.

"He is playing but he's meeting us at the ground," I tell him. "He's in Manchester this weekend but despite the fact that he was going on the piss last night he has every intention of driving down at the crack of dawn to play. Fair play to him, I suppose. I told him that he has some dedication for someone that's going to be sub."

We arrive at the Scrubs and meet the rest of the lads in the changing room. Even Danny has arrived, although he looks awful and stinks of booze.

"Christ, Danny. Fair play. I never thought you'd make it."

"I'm a man of my word, Chris. I may be hung-over and have had no kip but I can't let Calcio down."

"How was last night anyway, mate?"

"Top night, mate. I fell in love with some Brazilian stripper at a dodgy strip club in Manchester and I'm pretty sure she loved me as well. Well she loved me when I kept giving her twenty pounds every five minutes for a dance. It's amazing what a big cleavage can do to one's bank account. She was telling me she's planning on going back to Rio this Christmas if she can afford it and I think I've paid for her to fly first class now. I just hope there's a space for me."

A grumpy lad pops his head in our changing room holding a can of lager. "Any of you lot got a pump I can borrow?"

"Got the Sunday morning thirst, eh. Thought our keeper's pre-match meal of two sausage rolls and a pint of milk was bad. Let me just pump up our balls and I'll bring it to you. Who are you boys playing today?"

"Calcio," replies the lager lad. "They could be in for an easy game as it was one of my team-mates' thirtieth birthday party last night and it is sort of still going on in our changing room. Anyway, we're in the one at the end if you can drop off the pump."

"So you're Rapid Descent. We're Calcio and we're renowned for giving opponents easy games."

"I have seen teams drinking lager after the game, usually in celebration of giving us a good tonking," says Wilky, "but don't think I've seen anyone have the urge to have a cheeky one beforehand."

I step into the corridor and hear loud house music blaring out from one of the other changing rooms, which funnily enough is theirs. It resembles a lock-in at a pub, with pretty much everyone in their changing room holding a can of lager in one hand and a fag in the other. There are even a couple of girls, or should that be WAGs, in there as well.

"The party is their changing room, lads," I tell the team as I arrive back in our changing room. "Music, beer, fags and birds all present."

"Birds? Are they fit?" Chris asks me, suddenly perking up.

"Could barely see them because of the smoke."

"Think this is the first time in our existence where we have come across a team more unprofessional than us," Danny tells us, which is probably true.

"You're right. We have to beat this lot, mate. We're playing a team who are still pissed, have had no sleep, are heavy smokers and a couple also look like they've had some disco biscuits. If we lose this we might as well retire."

No one fancies going in goal so Chris and I agree to do a half each. We all amble out to the pitch and actually have a productive warm-up although we can't do too much as we only have eleven men and don't want to get any injuries before the game.

Rapid Descent, who have eventually made it out on to the pitch, have lived up to their name the last few years and have gone down the leagues even quicker than us. Most of them, like us, are the wrong side of thirty although unlike us they always give one hundred percent. Everyone seems to put a shift in for the team, although whether they can today is doubtful.

They're a mouthy team and like to tell the referee how he should run the game. Being a big set of intimidating lads, who wouldn't look out of place in the prison a hundred metres away, referees in the past have tended to give them favourable decisions.

"Right, lads," says Danny. "Switch on. We only have eleven today and seem to have lots of players who play in the same position so we are going with a 4-3-2-2 formation with Wilky and Anton just off the front two."

"Hang on," Chris cuts in. "Isn't that eleven outfield players?"

"Four plus three… oh shit you're right, scratch that and we'll just go with the normal 4-4-2 then, with Anton and Wilky on the wings."

"You sure you're not still pissed, mate?"

"No, I've just got a big hangover now, though I imagine mine won't be as bad as their hangover's later on. Also lads, remember this lot are a right bunch of gobby wankers. They will moan and try to wind us up. Don't rise to it because if truth be told if we did, with them being a big set of lads, we'd come off worse and you'd wish it was a hospital over there and not a prison."

This brings out the sarcasm in Wilky. "Christ, can't fucking wait to start now. Sometimes I wonder why I get up at 8.00 on a Sunday as every time I play we seem to be up against a set of arseholes. This week, to top it off, I'm playing against a set of pissed arseholes."

We kick-off, just as the heavens open, and from the off the match is littered with errors from both sides. At a break in play I have a look at both sets of players and I'm pretty sure there is not one person who wishes he was here. If the referee agreed to abandon the game now and call it a draw no one would mind. It's pissing down with rain, it's cold and I imagine that at least eighteen of the people on the pitch were on the booze last night. Most of Rapid Descent still are. The first thing of note to happen is when Carl pulls his groin after twenty minutes – so much for him being our saviour.

"Carl can't continue but he reckons he can go in goal and you can go outfield," Nick tells me.

"OK mate, I'll take his place up front then."

"No. Danny and I think you should go to centre-back and put Hugh right-back and Chris up front."

Carl wanders over. "Gibbo, sorry about this, mate. I've tweaked the groin already."

"Unlucky, mate. Every cloud has a silver lining. At least I now have two games in goal and two clean sheets and I can now get out of goal."

"Any tips then?"

"Not really, mate. Just shout lots and stop the ball hitting the net behind you. It's not rocket science."

Wormwood Scrubs must have about a dozen pitches. It's very open and the wind is always really strong and today is no different. The ball spends more time off the pitch than on it and the match is continuing to be a poor advert for football; not that any of our games ever have been.

However, after about half an hour things take a turn for the worse when their winger clearly takes the ball out of play as he makes a break down the left-hand side, going on to whip in a cross for their centre-forward to bundle the ball in at the far post.

"Ref! The ball was miles out," shouts Chris.

"The whole ball has to go over the touchline," he replies. "And besides, the linesman never gave it."

Chris won't let it go. "But the linesman is from their side and have a look at him, ref. He's nowhere near the play and he's half cut from last night. There's no chance he'll give it. I doubt he even realises he is linesman."

Danny turns to me. "There's no chance of the ref not giving that goal. He's 5ft 5in tops and a fucking riot would break out if he disallows it."

Each team has to designate a linesman and due to the fact that we have no subs both linesmen are from our opponents. This means it's more than likely that any fifty-fifty decisions will go their way. I heard one opposing centre-back last season telling their linesman that if he ever shouted offside he was to raise his flag, whether the man was onside or not.

"Come on, Calcio. It's only 1-0."

"Heads up, lads."

"We can get back into this."

We kick-off and thankfully the rain is easing. Within a minute, however, the game turns into a nightmare for us and especially for me. Tom brings down their centre-forward just outside the box with a clumsy challenge, so they get a free kick in a good position.

"Fucking hell, ref! I was through then," shouts their tattooed centre-forward as he gets back on to his feet and eyeballs Tom.

"You made a fucking meal of it, mate. Get up you big girl," says Tom.

"Don't fucking call me mate. You are a filthy bastard. Ref, aren't you going to have a word?"

"Number four, come here," the referee shouts to Tom and produces the yellow card.

"Fucking hell, ref. You had no intention of booking me. Just because their mouthy centre-forward got on his high horse you are booking me."

"I was going to anyway. I was just letting the situation between the two of you defuse."

Carl positions our five-man wall, as well as a centre-forward with a dodgy groin who has never played in goal can, and their winger whips in a free kick. Carl hobbles off his line and misses the ball which their centre-forward heads towards goal. I am on the goal line and inexplicably jump up and tap the ball over the bar with my fingertips. My first thought is that's some save as their attacker was only a few yards out, but I then quickly realise that I'm now actually not in goal and could be in some shit.

"Ref, handball! Penalty! He has to go," most of their team shout out at him.

"Who me? I never touched it."

"Stone me, Gibbo," says Danny. "Good save but what the fuck are you playing at?"

"Thanks for confirming the ref's suspicions, Danny."

"Suspicions, mate? Nothing suspicious about that mate. See you back in the changing rooms and don't use all the hot water."

The referee calls me over. I think that I might have more chance with him by going for the sympathy option rather than denying the handball as I think everyone in Wormwood Scrubs saw me tip the ball over the bar.

"Sorry, ref. I forgot I wasn't in goal anymore and it was just instinct."

"There is good news and bad news," he tells me.

"Go on then."

"Well, I won't report your sending-off to the league so you won't get a fine and a ban. But I will have to send you off."

"Sounds fair enough, ref. I'd prefer you not to send me off but I think the other team would chuck you and I in the prison over there if you didn't."

I take off my shirt (like people do when they get sent off – I've never understood why) and trudge off towards the side of the pitch.

"Unlucky," a few of their players shout out.

I find this funny as these same players were baying for the referee to send me packing a minute earlier. I think about telling them where to go but decide it's probably best just to keep quiet.

With Carl's dodgy groin, Nick decides to go in goal to give us a bit of a chance with their penalty. Nick spends an age getting ready and eventually their centre-forward strolls up and strikes the ball into the net to make it 2-0. Nick didn't move an inch; Carl could have made more of an effort with his dodgy groin. Stone me, even my five-year-old godson could have done better.

"Glad we put Nick in goal. He made a real effort with that penalty. He was more concerned that his thinning barnet was looking OK rather than his positioning for the kick," Jack mentions to me on the touchline.

"Why are you off the pitch, Gibbo?" Pete's wife enquires.

"Sent off, I'm afraid. Deliberate handball."

"But you are allowed to touch the ball. You are goalkeeper, aren't you?" she persists, confirming my suspicions that although she comes to every game she never actually watches any of them.

"I was but had swapped with Carl as he had picked up an injury."

The boys are struggling and most of them looked pretty knackered but we hold out until half-time.

"Sorry about that, lads. Rush of blood and all that," I say as the boys come over.

"I'm knackered," says Danny. "It's hard enough today anyway with my hangover but now with us down to ten, well nine and a half with Carl, I feel half dead."

"Hangover?" says Nick. "Their whole fucking team is still half cut. We are losing to a bunch of pissheads who are still fucking pissed."

"This lot are fucking shit. We have to beat these. Get the ball on the deck and out to Anton and Wilky on the flanks – they have the beating of their full-backs," Jack tells the team whilst looking at Anton and Wilky, hoping for their approval.

"Let the ball do the work, cos I sure won't be able in about fifteen minutes' time," says Danny, who is now a worrying shade of red.

The lads troop back on to the pitch and start the second half quite well. Wilky should have scored when put through on goal and we have a couple of free-kicks in and around their box. Danny, needless to say, fires the free-kicks over the bar but at least we are getting in good positions. However, things take a turn for the worse when Carl has to come off, as he can barely walk, and it looks like any chance we have of getting back into the match against a set of alcoholics has disappeared.

Pete's wife has bought along their one-year-old son who is giving me and Jack much amusement on the sideline especially when we ask him to point to his daddy and he keeps pointing to Danny.

"Something you need to tell us?" Jack asks her.

"Not sure why he is pointing at Danny."

"It's not as if Pete looks anything like Danny, luckily for you and Pete."

The second half is another awful advert for football. Rapid Descent are tiring badly and so are our nine men. The ball tends to spend most of the time out of play which seems to suit both teams as no one seems to have any energy. The highlight comes when Nick takes a goal-kick and sends it straight to their centre-forward who responds to this act of kindness by scoring. Nick puts his head in his hands and Jack and I can't stop laughing.

"Unlucky Nick. Try and get some height on those goal-kicks though, mate," says Jack in between guffaws.

"Nice to see you boys are pleased to see us concede," grumbles Nick.

"Did he take you out for dinner last week and you're repaying the favour?" asks Jack.

"There was a divot by the ball which I noticed just as I kicked it."

"You shouldn't have fucking kicked it then."

They soon score another with a counter-attack before the game fizzles out in the last ten minutes and finishes up 4-0. The boys slope off back to the changing rooms.

"I suppose I can't have any complaints about being sent off today," I tell Nick.

"Well you did prevent a goalscoring opportunity."

"I prevented it very well, I hasten to add. Some save that was – my reflexes even surprised me."

"You're unbelievable with the crap you come out with."

"Talking of crap, tell me about your goal-kick at the end."

"I see it made yours and Jack's morning."

"Sure did, mate."

"Joking aside, we have just lost against a team who at 10.20 were all smoking and drinking. I doubt they even know the final score."

"It wasn't the best, I know, but we did only have nine men and some fucking doughnut in goal second half."

"To replace the doughnut we had at the beginning of first half before he got sent off."

We all get changed and showered – well, everyone gets showered apart from Nick – and head back to Clapham where Danny and I go for a few beers and grab some food.

"Today was hard work," says Danny. "The days of me being hung-over and being able to dictate games are long gone."

"What about them, though? They were all pissed."

"I know, but playing football pissed is easier than playing when you have a big hangover. Trust me, I've tried both now. When you're pissed you're confident on the ball and think you're Pele. Whereas when the hangover kicks in you have no energy and all you want is your bed."

"Perhaps we should go out on the piss all night and come straight from some dodgy nightclub to Sunday footy then."

"Could be a plan. Anyway you seemed to be having a long chat when with the referee when you got sent off. What were you doing – getting his phone number and arranging to meet for a drink afterwards? It would be your first date for a bit. After all he is blonde and you do like the blondes."

"Very funny. I was trying to convince the ref not to send me off but he wasn't having any of it."

"A bit like most of the birds you date."

"Whatever. But at least he said he wouldn't report it to the league which saves me a few quid and a ban. Mind you, a ban wouldn't be too bad as could do with a few Sunday lie-ins."

"Reckon the reason he isn't reporting it to the league is that he can't be arsed to deal with the admin side of it. Doubt he gives two hoots whether he's saving you a bit of cash."

"You're probably right. With the injuries today and how injury-prone we all are we really need fourteen players each week which seems to be impossible to get unless we are playing in a cup final."

"It's no fun playing with ten men, especially against teams that are ten years younger than us. We said this all last season and it looks like this season will be more of the same."

"Perhaps if we start training, people will take it more seriously and this might have the knock-on effect of more people wanting to play on Sundays. Tom and Anton mentioned they were up for a weekly training session. It also might help us recruit more players as they will see that we are an organised and a well-run team."

"Training? Stone me, that word is pretty much alien to Real Calcio. We've been playing for a dozen or so years and I don't think we have had one training session."

"Could be a good idea though if it helps us get more players?"

"When, though? I mean Monday everyone is shattered from the weekend, Tuesday and Wednesday the Champions League is on the box, Thursday night is the new Friday night and it's a good night to go on the piss, and Friday night is Friday night. We also have to fit in seeing wives, birds and mates. I just don't think we can fit in training."

Nick has just entered the pub and puts his oar in. "Think Danny is against training then, Gibbo. And to be honest a fair few of the team live and work outside London and I imagine if we did training we'd do it on Clapham Common as it's easy for us three to get to."

"Hang on, we can't train. What are we like?" replies Danny. "I mean, it's dark at 6.30 now so that's the Common out the equation and the only floodlit pitches available near here are in Kennington and the only times available are 9.00pm on a Monday and Wednesday. A lad from work who lives in Clapham was trying to get a pitch for his team to train on, and Battersea Park had no spare pitches. Kennington was the only available pitch and to be honest the astro pitch there isn't that great."

"That's sorted then," says Nick, who seems equally uninspired by the idea of training. "We can tell the lads we've spent time looking into pitches and despite all our hard work we can't find anywhere to train. Which of course we're all gutted about."

"We do need more players, though," I say, sensing that I will be spending most Saturdays on the phone trying to beg people to play the following day. "Any ideas how we can get any more seeing as the training idea has been quickly binned?"

"Not sure," says Danny. "We can all have a think about it this week, but at least we can tell the lads we have looked into training and it's impossible as there are no pitches available. I just hope someone doesn't find us a pitch that's available. Anyway where's that tasty waitress? I'm starving."

We enjoy a nice pub lunch – and a fair few drinks judging by my hangover on Monday morning.

"Are you sure you don't already play for us?"

Hi there,

My name is Steve and I am currently looking for a new football team. I have been playing for a team in another league and have become increasingly frustrated at the lack of organisation and total lack of effort in the side. It's like they just turn up for a kick-about every Sunday morning.

I am a central midfielder, I'm extremely vocal and don't mind getting stuck in. I'm always early, never miss a game and always give one hundred percent.

So if you are looking for new players then please mail me back and I can maybe come to a training session / trial session or something like that.

I'm 27 years old, left-footed and fit as a fiddle.

Thanks for your time.

Steve

This is the email that arrives in my inbox on Wednesday. He seems a good player, far too good for Calcio, but I ring Nick anyway during lunch.

"Sign him up," he says when I read out his description over the phone.

"He does sound pretty good, doesn't he?"

"Mate, he's fit as a fiddle, has a left foot, is twenty seven and gives a hundred percent, so get on the phone to him."

"I could get him down for a trial as he says."

"Trial? We don't even train and we said the other day we

wouldn't start any. We do need to get him signed up before he realises we're rubbish and besides, once he's signed up, he can't sign for anyone else."

"OK mate, I'll give him a call and try and sell us over the phone."

Nick seems to think that with him signed up we will win the league and from his description he would no doubt be an asset. However, I don't want to disappoint the lad. After all, the bad points from his current team tend to apply to us – and his good characteristics, well, they don't.

Lack of organisation – he complains that his team is badly organised. We are renowned for a lack of organisation. We're constantly phoning round, chasing people up to see whether they can play on Sundays and trying to get friends and friends of friends to play for us the day before the game. We also hardly ever arrive at an away game with more than ten minutes until kick-off. Our warm-up for our home games consists of putting the goal nets up and a jog from one side of the pitch to the other.

Lack of effort – we do try on Sundays (well, I like to think we do) but the fact that most of us are drinking four or five hours before kick-off at some dive in London, coupled with a kebab on the way home, doesn't do wonders for the quality of our football. To the outsider it would seem that our lack of box-to-box running was due to the fact that we didn't care when it's really the fact that we're still half cut from Saturday night.

Extremely vocal – this would be an asset for us as half the time none of the team knows who is marking who at corners and free-kicks. However, most of our team are half asleep on Sundays and he would soon lose his voice shouting at us.

Doesn't mind getting stuck in – he would when he realises he is the only person who does.

Never misses a game – he would be in a unique group of one.

Training – what's that?

Twenty seven – he would definitely bring down the average age of the team, and we need some younger legs in our team. But would he really enjoy doing everyone's running for them despite being so fit?

Left-footed – we're crying out for a left-sided player, but he says he is a centre midfield player and he can't play centre midfield as Danny and Nick play there and they are undropable as they are members of the committee. This would annoy him especially as they aren't having a good season.

My phone goes and it's Nick again. "Mate, been having second thoughts about this player. He sounds great, but do we really want an outsider to join us? It seems to me he takes his football far too seriously for us and anyway I've just realised he plays centre midfield and despite the fact that I'm having a bad season, I don't want to lose my place."

"Ah, mate, so the real reason that you don't want us to sign him up is because you're scared he'll take your place then?"

"Well you could say that, I suppose."

"The other day you were saying we needed new players and the first opportunity we have to delve into the transfer market and get what seems a cracking player on paper, you shun the opportunity. If this chap was a defender or attacker I'm sure you would have rung him yourself and got him signed up."

"Correct, mate. We could do with someone decent to replace you."

"Cheers. In theory, if the so called committee can't be dropped, we need wide players as we all play in central positions, which probably annoys other members of the team who reckon they should play in central positions."

"I didn't say you can't be dropped. It's just me."

"We do need to get some new players, though. If we have another season I want thirteen players each week and preferably ones that we haven't had to recruit at the last minute. Phoning round people all day Saturday isn't enjoyable. Anyway, better go and write back to Steve. Catch up in the week."

I write an email to Steve.

Dear Steve

Thanks for the email.

You sound like you would be a good addition to any team but I'm not sure we would be the right team for you as we sound far too much like the team you want to leave. Are you sure you don't already play for us?

I hope that you find a team soon and I also hope that they aren't in our league.

Best Wishes

Matt

Funnily enough, we are again struggling for numbers this weekend but Jack manages to convince one of his mates of the benefits of playing football for Real Calcio on a Sunday morning rather than enjoying a lie-in. I'm not sure how he did that but years of teaching kids PE clearly make him an expert at intimidating others into playing sport.

This weekend we're playing Real Sobad, a side who tend to blow hot and cold or should that be good and bad. They thumped us twice in the league two years ago – sadly, they weren't the only ones to do so – but we managed to beat them in the cup.

They're a good set of lads though which makes a change from the other week. One of their players is a doctor and he was invaluable when we played them last year and Damo badly injured his knee. They never question the referee and I'm pretty sure there isn't a member of their team with a tattoo, earring, skinhead or funny coloured football boots. I'm fairly certain their team is made up of doctors, lawyers, accountants and architects.

The game is at home (not that it makes a difference apart from the fact that we can get to our local pub quicker afterwards) at our fortress Garrett Park, in Earlsfield, and it's a 9.45 meet.

I arrive there at the appointed time and no one has arrived apart from the whole of Real Sobad and the referee. Our team finally arrive, one by one, at around 10.00.

"Lads, we've got to get here by 9.45. We need to fill in team sheets, put the nets up and have a decent warm-up," I tell them.

"Sorry, Gibbo, but with the clocks changing last night I lost track of time," says Anton.

"But they went backwards not forwards. You should've got here early, not late."

Paddy is rummaging through the kit. "Have we got any socks that don't have any holes in or any shorts where the elastic hasn't snapped?"

"Don't think so. They're ten years old, mate. What do you expect?"

Danny joins in. "I found a pair the first week and as I take the kit to the laundrette each week I've claimed them for myself. Perks of the job and all that."

"Lads, this is Darren," Jack says, introducing his mate, who is playing for us today. Like Jack he seems to enjoy a pre-match fag which doesn't fill me with confidence.

"Darren," I say, "today you are Graham Jones."

"What is this, *Stars in Your Eyes*?"

"Just that we haven't had time to officially register you so you'll have to be Graham if the referee asks. Anyway, Graham isn't a star, let me assure you. He would struggle to get in our team, and that is saying something."

We run, well, trot out on to the pitch, put up the nets and any thoughts of a warm-up and team talk are nipped in the bud when the referee blows his whistle and calls up the two captains. I amble up and actually win the toss for a change. A moral victory – we should have left it at that.

We start off pretty badly and how Real Sobad haven't taken the lead is beyond me. They seem to waste chance after chance, including one miss that was nearly as awful as mine a couple of weeks ago. I'm struggling to get into the game and it takes me about fifteen minutes to get my first touch which I put straight into touch. Damo urges us to raise our games but even if we did so by fifty percent we would still be some way off the pace.

The referee is probably having the best game and is by far the best we've had this season. He is keeping up with play, is authoritative in his decision making and doesn't award free-kicks judged on how loudly either team appeals. We have had some shocking referees over the years, ones that have booked players twice without sending them off, ordered off the wrong player and watched people punch each other on the pitch without even booking them. We even had one who awarded a goal when someone shot wide of the post.

Darren isn't having the best debut but then again no one is playing well and this is definitely the worst we've played this season. After about half an hour the inevitable happens and we concede. Their goalkeeper punts the ball downfield, both of our centre-backs let the ball bounce and their fast (at least compared to Jack) centre-forward nips in to score.

Here we go, I think to myself. The floodgates will open now. Somehow we manage to stay only one goal down until half-time.

"Bloody hell, lads," complains Damo. "This is awful. I'm not coming up from Brighton every week if people aren't going to give a hundred percent."

"He's right, lads," I reply. "We've been shocking. I will hold my hands up and admit I've been way off the pace but I'm not the only one. We need to change things quickly, and Jack do you really have to have a fag at half-time?"

"It's to calm my nerves. I might need a couple after our first-half performance."

"You must be the only PE teacher who smokes."

Damo, still sounding really pissed off, has the final word. "Back to the game, lads. We need to keep the ball on the deck, talk more, stick to the people we're marking and give an extra twenty odd percent."

They continue to pressure us in the second half with their central midfield player, who looks like a taller and fatter version of Paul Scholes, orchestrating proceedings. He is one of those rare and annoying players in Sunday football who always seems to have time on the ball and can pick out a killer pass. When he gets the ball in a tight situation, rather than panic and hoof it downfield aimlessly, with shouts from your teammates of 'get rid', 'Row Z' or 'anywhere will do', he manages to lay off a simple yet effective pass, a bit like Scholes. The Calcio player who occasionally seems like this is Jim, but sadly for him none of us is ever in a good position for him to play the simple ball to when he's in a tight spot.

Their second goal finally comes from a corner when no one decides to pick up their 6ft 4in centre-back and he has the simple task of heading it into the net to make it 2-0.

"Lads, who the fuck was marking him?" yells Phil. "It's not as if he isn't going to be a threat at corners. Paddy, who were you marking?"

"I was marking the ginger-haired lad."

"What, the lad taking the corner?"

"Ermm… shit, yeah him. Thought I couldn't spot him in the box."

"So you marked no one and left their big centre-back by himself."

Jack tries to defuse the situation. "Come on, Phil. Calm down mate. Even if Paddy had marked him the lad would've scored. It's not as if Paddy is much cop in the air anyway. He jumps like a heavily pregnant salmon at best."

The second half continues with the ball spending most of the time in our half, and it's clear that we are going to be in for a long last forty minutes or so. I've moved back to centre-back and have the joy of marking a fast, mobile striker. Things go from bad to worse when I go to pass it back to Phil from a wide position just inside my own half and don't see their centre-forward. He can't believe his luck – or my generosity – and easily beats Phil to the ball before rolling it into the empty net.

"Sorry, lads. I never saw him."

"Don't worry, mate. If only our wingers could play nice slide-rule passes through to me like that," Damo replies, making me chuckle.

Our heads drop and they soon score their fourth from a deflected free-kick and a fifth when one of their midfield players dances through what seems like our entire team before burying the ball in the bottom corner of the net.

Finally the referee blows the whistle and puts us out of our misery. I collect the corner flags and trudge back to the changing rooms.

"Put your hands up if their centre midfield didn't dribble past you on his way to their fifth goal, which was some goal," Danny says as I enter the room. Everyone puts up both hands.

"Think he beat me three times and tied me up in knots," sighs Paddy.

In walks Jack with customary fag in mouth.

"You took your time, mate," I tell him.

"Their centre-forward had me well and truly in his pocket and I've only just managed to free myself and get out," says Jack which provides a bit of light relief.

"I admit I was shit today," Nick adds.

"Tell me about it," Damo and Paddy both call out.

Nick collars me. "Meant to tell you, a mate emailed me Jose Mourinho's scouting report on Newcastle the week before Chelsea played them seven or so years ago and my God it goes into some depth. It was eight pages in all with diagrams and everything. Pretty much told you everything about each of their players, bar what they ate for breakfast."

"Eight pages? Surely all he had to say he is that they had a dodgy defence but a decent centre-forward in Shearer, who I imagine was playing at the time, who you can't take your eye off for a minute."

"Well, Gibbo, I think that's part of the reason, amongst hundreds of others, why your job isn't a scout or anything else remotely linked to football."

"The main reason, just so that you know, is that you are shit at football," says Paddy who is in no position to talk after his performance today.

"Imagine if a team decided to send a scout to watch us play the week before they played us. I think he'd just say turn up and they'll win," says Damo, spreading confidence amongst the team.

"Or say our defence is slow and prone to several lapses of concentration, our midfield rarely leaves the halfway line and our centre-forwards lack pace, shooting technique and, most importantly, goals," says Phil, who must think he is free of all criticism.

"Anyway, enough of this negative talk. Anyone fancy a pint or two?" asks Paddy. A few of us nod in agreement and head to the pub down the road.

"How did you do today. Did I play?" asks Graham Jones, who was already in the pub.

"Mate, we got thumped and you had a shocker."

"Me, a shocker? That's got to be my first bad game since I actually played for you."

"In fairness to Darren," says Paddy, "we weren't any better."

We soon forget about the game, I tuck into an overpriced and lukewarm roast and we stay watching a few good matches on television which were completely different from the crap game we were 'competing' in this morning.

We end up getting quite drunk and by ten it's just Danny, Nick and I left in the pub. Danny and Nick start playing Connect Four (rock 'n' roll), and I'm not sure whether it was the alcohol or boredom of watching them but I soon fall asleep on the comfortable sofa.

Nick and Danny, being great friends, don't bother to wake me when they leave the pub. I get woken by the bar staff at closing time and walk out the pub to much amusement from the other customers before flagging down a cab to take me home.

"I was different gravy today"

"How's it looking for Sunday?" I ask Nick on the phone on Thursday evening.

"Mate, if it was a five-a-side game we would only just be OK. We only have five definite for Sunday."

"Five? Christ, what's going on this season? We have a squad of around twenty."

"I know, mate. I've never known anything like it: people are either injured, on holiday, serving King and Country, at weddings or their better halves are pumping out kids like there's no tomorrow and they're banned from playing. Any idea how we can muscle up some more players for Sunday?"

"Not sure, mate. I'll ask my brother to see if he can drag some of his mates who play football on Saturdays."

This season has been hard getting players. Tworty seems to have retired after the first game and I suppose with his screamer of a goal it's a good way to go out. Del and Hugh are constantly injured, Jim and Bo's birds won't let them play Sundays as well as Saturdays. And after our thrashing last week, I suppose the thought of getting out of bed this Sunday isn't that appealing.

I decide to send an email on Friday to the whole team.

Lads,

We are struggling a bit for numbers on Sunday and with two days to go we have the ripe old number of five. Does anyone know anyone who wants to get out of bed ridiculously early on a Sunday to play at a ground which is an arse to get to with a team who got thumped 5-0 last week?

On the upside Danny won't be playing on Sunday as he is away and the forecast for Sunday is now just torrential rain rather than thunder and lightning like it was forecasted yesterday.

I know it's only November but we also need to start to think about next season. I for one can't be arsed to organise it if we don't have a bigger squad.

Please let Nick or I know as soon as possible.

Cheers

Gibbo

Surprisingly, the email seems to work and Chris emails me back to say that Tony can play. Tony is another Kiwi and used to play for us a couple of years ago but stopped as he kept pulling his hamstring and never seemed to last ninety minutes. However, beggars can't be choosers and I email Chris back and tell him that it is great news. We are now up to six.

Jim then emails me to say that he'll play and has managed to convince Bo and another mate of his Jamie to play as well. Bo is a great player, especially when not hung-over, and Jamie is meant to be useful as well. I email Jim back to say thanks and tell him to try and convince Bo the benefits of staying in on a Saturday night. Anyway, we're up to nine which is nearly a one hundred percent improvement on ten minutes ago.

Things get even better when Jack calls me later in the day to say that Darren is up for it and he will skip a christening to play. He makes it seem as if he is doing us a big favour in missing the christening but I'm pretty sure he is glad to get out of it. We now have ten; one more to go.

Nick calls me on the Saturday from his family get-together up in the Lake District. "How many?"

"Up to ten, mate, and I still haven't had to offer cash incentives yet and we still have a day to go."

"As much as I'd love to miss the big family lunch with my nan asking me the same question ten times, I'll be cut out the family inheritance if I play, mate."

"No worries, mate. I'm sure I'll be able to get two others – will keep you posted."

Carl calls me. "Gibbo, good news, mate. I'm around Sunday and will be there bright and early."

"Top news mate. We're up to eleven now. Just don't pull your groin as we have no subs."

"Can't guarantee that, but I will be there."

Just as I'm about to call Nick my phone goes. It's Anton. "Gibbo, sorry mate, haven't picked up my emails all week but can play Sunday."

"Twelve! Stone me, we even have a sub now. Good one, Anton. See you 9.15, Clapham Junction."

I give Nick a ring. "Mate, we have twelve. I even have to decide who is to be sub now."

"Excellent."

"I'm off to the pub now to have a few beers."

"Not too many, mate, although in all fairness didn't you say you had a quiet night last Saturday and you went on to have a shocker. So yes, go and have a big night – you might play better hung-over."

I take Nick's words out with me and wake up Sunday morning with a stinking hangover. It's hard enough getting out of bed at 8.30 on a Sunday but even harder if you have had the Sunday morning footballer's diet of ten pints of lager, a takeaway and no sleep the night before. The takeaway can't have been that great as most of it seems to be on sofa.

I head down to our ground and from looking at most of the team quite a few of them had been out late as well. With the amount of people playing today who haven't played before or haven't played for ages the pre-match team talk centres along the lines of everyone introducing themselves to each other.

We finally leave the changing room and head out to the pitch where a few dogs are running around. Having a warm-up is impossible because the dogs won't leave the balls alone. With me being scared of dogs, whenever someone passes it to me I quickly boot it away before I think the dog will bite my ankles. The goals also seem bigger than usual; I can usually just about touch the crossbar when I raise my hand in the air but with these goals I have to jump up and touch them.

"Fuck me, Gibbo, I'm sure these goals are bigger than they should be," Phil tells me, confirming my suspicions.

"Here you go, Phil," says Jack without a hint of sympathy, "making excuses before the game has even started on why you won't keep a clean sheet. It's the same for both sides, Phil. Stop moaning."

"You scared of dogs, mate?" Bo asks me, sniggering to himself.

"Yes, mate. Scared shitless. I'm convinced one of them is going to bite me and don't give me that shit that when they are charging at you they are only playing games because I don't find that game enjoyable."

The dogs are full of energy, fast, have good ball control and are constantly round everyone's ankles getting the ball back – all traits we could do with on a Sunday morning. Eventually their owners shout out to them and they leave the pitch having displayed more energy in our warm-up that we will in ninety minutes.

Juvictorious, who we are playing today, are not your stereotypical Sunday football team. They all sound very posh, have floppy haircuts and have names such as Rupert, Harry and Charles. They seem to me to be more suited to rowing at Henley which would no doubt be followed by a few gin and tonics. Most of their team are early-to-mid twenties and their parents tend to come and watch them with the chocolate labrador in tow.

Juvictorious are a good set of lads and play the game in the right spirit, meaning I actually feel guilty if I let out the odd expletive during the game.

The game starts and what amazes me in the first ten minutes is that we are playing well with the ball spending most of the time on the floor and not in the air. Bo and Jim seem to be orchestrating things in midfield and we are making the use of the wide pitch and are getting the balls out to the flanks. Our wingers, Anton and Jamie, are getting the better of their full-backs (mental note: get Jamie signed up after the game). Tony, who hasn't played for us for years, is overlapping Anton on the left wing, which has to be a first for a Real Calcio full-back. Damo and Carl are working well together up front and everything seems to look rosy.

Just when I'm thinking that it can be only a matter of time before we score our first goal, their central midfield player plays a ball between Chris and Jack and their centre-forward goes clean through on goal. However, Jack manages to bring him down very well just outside the box and the immediate problem is rescinded.

"Referee, that was surely a foul," their centre-forward politely enquires as the referee blows his whistle in agreement.

Jack is immediately called over to the referee, who produces a yellow card. I'm sure if the other team had complained more Jack might have been shown a red card as it was a professional foul. Jack's excuse to the referee is that he is forty five and surely it's OK to bring down a centre-forward if he is twenty years younger than you. Fair point, I reckon. Anyway, they waste their free-kick and we soon get the ball back up their end.

"Perfect timing, that was." Jack tells me with a grin on his face.

"What, your foul?" I reply.

"Yes, mate. I got him just outside the box so there was no penalty and just as he was about to shoot at goal. Textbook stuff, that."

"I suppose you've had years of practice of being outpaced by centre-forwards and bringing them down as a last resort."

Apart from that little glitch we are continuing to play some good football and we soon open a lead with a move that starts with a throw from Phil to Anton, who in turn passes to Jamie. He beats his man and plays a perfect through-ball to Damo, who in turn lobs their keeper.

"That's a first," Chris tells me. "A goal we've scored which started with a move from our own keeper."

"Think you could be right there. If only we had it on film."

Before too long we double our lead, this time with a lovely through-pass from Bo and again Damo is on to it and scores with ease. Damo seems to have found some pace today, I reflect, but on closer inspection the bloke who is marking him seems to look as though he enjoys a similar diet to Danny and seems to have his level of pace as well.

For once half-time comes too soon as we're playing well.

"This is superb," I tell the boys. "Keep it up, don't get complacent and we should be able to get a few more in the second half."

"I'm tempted to get the cigar out already but might just stick to the half-time fag," says Jack.

"I can feel a hat-trick coming on," Damo informs us, which, if successful, will mean weeks of him going on about it.

"Well, mate," says Jim, "if I keep putting the ball on a postage stamp for you, mate, you shouldn't have any problem."

"Suppose so. I'm not used to getting a decent service from midfield."

"Too right, mate. Anyway let's keep focused as we still have forty five minutes to go."

The game kicks off and within about thirty seconds Bo plays another through-ball to Damo who outpaces their centre-backs, rounds the keeper and scores. He then celebrates as if it's the first hat-trick he has ever scored (it could well be) and gives me a look as if to say it won't be the last I hear of it.

We decide to bring on Darren for Anton who seems to be carrying a knock, yet within two minutes Darren pulls his thigh and we're down to ten men. The grim reality is that we now have to play the last forty minutes with a man short. This isn't going to be great because we aren't that fit, most of us were out on the sauce last night and the average age of our team is over thirty.

Sure enough, they soon score with a header from a corner. Real Calcio have been playing for around ten years and every time we concede a corner there must be at least a fifty percent chance the opposition will score due to lax marking. This is despite the fact that with every corner conceded the first thing someone shouts out is 'Find a player and stick to him'.

"Cracking goal, Rupert. That was a marvellous header and what a beautiful corner from Richard," one of their parents shouts out.

"Fucking shit defending, Gibbo and Jack," Matty, a mate of mine, replies from the touchline, drawing disgusted looks from the other team's parents. "You were both marking each other, you fucking doughnuts."

"We weren't at our best at that corner and could be in for a long last half-hour or so," Jack tells me as we prepare to take kick-off.

"Yes and I can really feel the effects of last night now."

"Shit, they've just replaced their two forwards with two new guys, who no doubt will be full of energy," adds Jack.

"Which one do you want to mark?"

"Tell you in a few minutes."

"Great, so I will be getting the faster player then."

"Yep. After all, I am forty five."

They continue to pressurise our tiring team but Phil isn't forced to make a save the rest of the game and we manage to hold out for a 3-1 win. We head back towards the changing room.

"Some performance that, lads," Darren tells us all as we all collapse, exhausted. "Pity no one was videoing it – we actually played football today,"

"Think we actually lived up to our name today," Damo tells me on the way out of the changing room.

"What do you mean?"

"Well, Real means Royal in Spanish and Calcio means football in Italian. And I think we played some royal football."

"But what does royal football mean?"

"Not sure, but it implies something a bit special. The Brazil team of 1970, the Man United European Cup-winning team with Georgie Best pulling the strings or the current Barcelona side."

"Fuck me, Damo. What did you drink at half-time? One good, or should I say royal, performance and you are comparing us to Messi, Best and Pele. The only thing we have in common with Georgie Best is we like a beer and don't even think or describing your performance as Messi-like today."

"It was more Pele-like and being royal football, I'm sure if the Queen was watching today she would've enjoyed herself. She might even know Rupert, Tarquin and the other members of their team as well."

"I'm not sure she would have enjoyed the rest of the games we have played this season. We certainly haven't played royal football in any other game."

"It's days like this that makes the journey from Brighton worth it. A great performance and everyone seemed to play their part. Makes a nice change from the shambles it can be some weeks."

"If it was like this each week I'd definitely be up for another couple of seasons. It's just that days like today have been few and far between over the past few seasons."

"Tell me about it. I sometimes get the train up from Brighton and wonder why the hell I bother. The journey back after a win is always more bearable, though, and I think I might get a couple of beers to celebrate. One for the win and one for the hat-trick."

"It took you a bit of time to bring up your hat-trick, mate."

"I was different gravy today and what a great three goals they were. I also made them all look so easy."

"It did help having Bo in centre midfield today. He's too good for Sunday football but I'm not complaining. Hopefully after today's performance he will be up for playing some more."

"Luckily for Danny and Nick, though, he plays Saturday football and doesn't really want to play Sunday football week in, week out."

"Whenever we're short, Danny and Nick never mention calling Bo, funnily enough, as they realise that one of them would have to be shunted out wide."

"Can't say I blame them. Can you imagine them two taking on a full-back on the outside with their lack of pace? It'd be a good laugh watching them attempt it, though. Anyway, got to dash if I want to catch this train. See you next week. I'll email you all a run-down of the hat-trick tomorrow in case you forget about it!"

"I think I can only see two fingers on your hand"

This weekend we have another cup game, this time in the London World Invitation Trophy, which sounds grand but is just a cup that every team from all six divisions of our league is invited to enter. We've never managed to negotiate the first round but this season we have achieved it for the first time in our history. We have received a bye into round two.

Last season I was injured for our first round game and decided that I would put my football coaching badges to use and come down and manage the team from the sideline. I like to think I looked the part as I was wearing my new coat from Reiss, which I fancied gave the impression of a young Jose Mourinho, especially with my designer (couldn't-be-arsed-to-shave) stubble. However, unlike Jose used to have to do at Chelsea, I had to take public transport to our ground, and being the professional manager that I am I turned up half way through the first half.

Upon my arrival I had the pleasant surprise of us actually winning 3-0 and playing some good football. Come half-time the boys ambled over and after they took the piss out of my new jacket I like to think I gave a good team talk. Since we were three up I put on a couple of subs and made tactical adjustments to allow the two subs to play in their best positions.

What then happened in the second half was a nightmare. From leading 3-0 and coasting we then let in two soft goals (which were the fault of the two subs). Then in the last ten minutes our opponents scored two more and held out to win 4-3. To this day the team still blame me for this defeat and I've never worn the jacket again.

Our team for this week's game is looking OK. Bo can't play, sadly, but come Friday we have thirteen players; well, twelve plus Danny, who is flying in from Miami early morning and will come straight to the ground. He may have his faults but that is some dedication from the lad. The last thing I'd want to do after a long flight is play football, but that's the romance and pulling power of the London World Invitation Trophy I suppose.

I clamber out of bed on Sunday morning and manage to time my departure from the flat just as the heavens open, arriving at our ground soaked to the skin. Most of the team are already there, including Danny.

"Fair play, mate. Straight off the plane to footy."

"Dedication, Gibbo. If you cut me open you would see green Calcio blood, mate."

"Plus a lot of chocolate bars and fast food."

Anyway, Anton is late so Danny starts and we have Anton and Del, who is hardly ever fit, on the bench. Del, despite being in his thirties and a father, still loves an all-night rave and I'm pretty sure is still high as kite when he turns up on a Sunday. We head out to the pitch and it is heavily waterlogged with big puddles in the penalty boxes and corners, while the centre circle seems to be a mini-lake. You can barely see the lines and Nick has managed to forget the corner flags which will make it even harder for the referee. It also means that the pre-match javelin competition – which some of the lads are doing instead of an actual football-related warm-up these days – doesn't take place.

"Yesterday I was on the beach surrounded by a bevy of beauties," says Danny. "Today I'm about to play football in one big bath. I know which one I prefer, Gibbo."

"Just hope the referee doesn't call it off although not sure he has turned up yet. He probably put his head out the window this morning, saw the pissing rain and thought 'Fuck the thirty five quid, I'm staying in bed'."

However, the referee must be short of cash as he eventually shows up, gets changed and heads out to the pitch.

"I should really postpone this as it's unplayable but I want my match fee as I'm meeting mates for lunch and a few pints afterwards, and the thirty five quid should pay for it. I also think I have never refereed a game with two more bizarre team names," he tells River Saucer's captain and I.

Saucer are a youngish team who got relegated with us last season. They aren't the most talented team but they're all as fit as a butcher's dog. Their centre-forward was constantly dragging me all over the place when we played them last season, although luckily for me he seemed to panic when about to shoot. Their centre-back, who looks like a younger version of Carlos Puyol, with what appears to be a big perm, does like to provide a running commentary on the whole game.

We get the game underway but within a couple of minutes or so they break down the right and whip in a cross. Phil pulls off a blinding save.

"They're looking nervous, Saucer. Two minutes gone and we've already got them under the cosh," shouts their centre-back, who hasn't given up his commentating this season.

The game then turns sour when Nick and one of their players have an accidental clash of heads which results in blood gushing out of Nick's head and nose.

"Grab the first-aid kit," I shout out to Anton on the touchline.

"Please say you have got a new one and actually have some first-aid stuff in it now."

"Don't worry, mate. We've got a new one from Boots."

"Lads, I can't continue," says Nick. "I had a thumping headache anyway from going out on the piss last night, and this has made it even worse."

"It's rare you last ten minutes Nick, both on and off the pitch," quips Danny.

"Very funny, mate, though I've probably done more running in the short time I've been on the pitch than you will do over ninety."

We patch up Nick as best as we can with a ten-pound first-aid kit and he hobbles off the pitch as we bring Anton on.

When Nick goes off injured, which has been quite frequent over the last few seasons, we have tended to play better, but sadly not this time as River Saucer come on to us with wave after wave of attacks. Phil is playing brilliantly in goal; to this day I'm not sure if he has ever had a quiet game and I suppose all the practice he gets most weeks has made him into a decent keeper.

"It'll come, Saucer. It's only a matter of time till we score, trust me," their centre-back continues with his John Motson impersonation.

"Wish the arsehole would shut up," Jim tells me, and I'm pretty sure he isn't the only one who's thinking this.

"I might tell Miles to do one his trademark late two-footed challenges on him."

But just when we think the gods are smiling on us, after what seems like their umpteenth attack, Phil is finally beaten. Their winger outpaces Pete and crosses to the centre-forward, who I was marking. He taps the ball into an open goal at the far post for an easy goal. Well I say easy, though scoring open goals is still something I have not mastered judging by a couple of weeks ago.

"Sorry, Phil, he completely did me for pace," admits Pete.

"No worries, mate. You do have twenty-odd years on him, although you did make him look like Usain Bolt."

"Lovely move, Saucer," the dire commentary continues. "Told you it would come. Keep it up. No lapses of concentration. Let's push for a second."

We actually play quite well for the last twenty minutes of the half. Jim, who we've pushed into centre midfield, is playing well as is Danny, which is surprising considering he is meant to be jet-lagged. The half-time whistle blows and we head off to our bags by the side of the pitch. Nick has developed a hell of a bump above his eye and looks like the elephant man.

"Some bump you have there, mate," says Jim. "And are you sure your nose should be pointing in that direction?"

"Cheers, Jim. I feel awful, I've got a banging headache and I have a meeting with a key client tomorrow. God knows what he will think."

"He will think you have been fighting no matter what you tell him, mate, and will probably end up doing no business with you."

"Great. Thanks for the words of encouragement."

"Anyway, lads, enough of Nick and him losing his job," says Damo, addressing the team. "We're starting to play well, well for the last few minutes anyway and we can easily turn this around. Their keeper is dodgy. I also want to shut their fucking centre-back up. He thinks he's John Motson."

"I know," says Jim. "He's really getting on my tits. Anyway, how do you know their keeper is dodgy when we haven't even tested him?"

"I can just tell. And I also saw him fumble a few when he was warming up."

The second half kicks off and they pile on the pressure but can't get past Phil in goal. Our defence, or should that be lack of defence, is giving Phil no protection. Midway through the half, however, Jim begins to be taking a stranglehold on the centre midfield and up front Carl is giving their centre-backs a few problems. Our pressure finally pays off: Jim picks the ball up just inside their half, does a Gazza-style run and coolly slots the ball in the bottom corner before we all mob him.

"Always rely on a Gibson to pull us out of a rut," I shout to the lads as we pile on Jim.

"Yes but it's always me," says Jim, coming up for air. "You tend to get us in ruts."

"Lovely move, Calcio, I told you it would come," Danny shouts out to us, which results in most of us sniggering to ourselves. "Saucer are looking nervous now."

We carry on piling on the pressure and Miles is put through one on one but sadly scuffs his shot. Just as I'm thinking that we can beat this team a long ball goes over the top and their nippy winger and I set off after it. The winger seems to get up to fifth gear pretty quickly whereas I'm slowly getting from first to second. When I finally reach fourth gear (I don't have a fifth) their winger has reached the ball and plants a lovely cross into the box. Their centre-forward beats Jack to the ball and scores.

"What can I do?" I say to Danny. "The bloke is faster than me."

"No shit, Sherlock."

"Besides, the bloke I was marking told me they are all twenty three years old. When I was that age I had that kind of pace."

"Nice to see you're getting cosy with the centre-forward. You've built up such a great friendship that you're letting him have the freedom of London up front. Wonder what shit their centre-back will come out with now."

"Big ten minutes, Saucer. Keep switched on," he shouts out. If I was him I would have been tempted to take the piss out of us but I think he takes his football seriously.

The game kicks off and from looking at everyone it is now clear we're knackered. Our fitness, or rather the lack of it, is beginning to show and our opponents' heads seem to be up since the goal. To make matters worse Miles soon falls over and appears to damage his hand but vows to continue (or should I say is pressurised into staying on as we have no subs left since Anton has come on for Carl, who has pulled his groin).

With five minutes to go our Achilles' heel, the corner, leads to one of their players scoring with a header with no one anywhere near him. To add insult to injury, with the last kick of the game their winger shoots from distance and via a deflection off Jack the ball nestles in the bottom left-hand corner of the net. The whistle then goes as we kick-off to put us out of our misery. I collect the nets and head back to the changing room. This resembles Casualty on a Saturday night, what with Nick's two faces, Carl's pulled groin and Miles' fingers, which seem to be pointing the wrong way.

"Think I may have damaged my fingers," he says, which is a slight understatement.

"Christ, you get them checked out," says Pete. "I think I can only see two fingers on your hand. You should've come off, mate."

"Would've done but we had no subs left."

"Fair play. The lad plays with no working fingers for the love of Calcio," says Nick proudly.

Some of us – the ones that haven't gone to the hospital or been ordered to spend the afternoon with their girlfriends – head to the pub for a few pints and to watch the football. My phone goes later on in the day and it's Miles.

"How are you, mate?"

"Not great, mate. Got a couple of broken fingers and I'm in plaster."

"Shit. Sorry to hear that, mate."

"Got to have an operation as well, on Friday of all days."

"Weren't you meant to be going away on Thursday?"

"Yes, mate. I've just had to cancel my holiday to the States. I was looking forward to that."

"And with the new bird you are trying to impress?" I reply, rubbing salt into the wound.

"Yeah. She isn't too impressed with me now, though. It's her birthday and we were meant to be spending it with a trip to the Grand Canyon, not a trip to Epsom hospital."

"I'm off to Vegas in December, mate. Can get you some good photos of the Grand Canyon. It's meant to be great."

"You're hilarious. Anyway, not to worry. I'm sure the Grand Canyon's overrated anyway. It's only one of the wonders of the world. Besides it's only a holiday, a bird and a few fingers that I've lost. The things I do for Calcio."

"That's the spirit, mate. Calcio is another wonder of the world. I'll put you down for Sunday then – you should be alright to play with a cast on and you can bring the bird down to watch."

"No chance, mate, although there's more chance of me playing than my bird ever wanting to come and see us play especially after I have put paid to her dream holiday."

"Alright, mate, fair enough and sorry about the holiday. Worse things have happened at sea and all that."

"Suppose so, though I can't see it at the moment. Speak in the week."

We carry on enjoying ourselves in the pub taking the piss out of Miles, with his triple loss, and Nick, who has probably lost his job but gained a cracking extra forehead.

"That's a Calcio first, a player getting injured in the car on the way to the ground"

To: calcio squad
From: Nick

Lads,

Winning the cup is overrated anyway; the league is where it really counts. 4-1 was harsh yesterday and we got hit chasing the game. Man of the Match yesterday goes to Phil for a string of fine saves despite the ones that got past him. We get to take our revenge in the league this week as we have them again away from home. It's a 10.30 kick-off so a 9.45 meet at their ground in Mortlake or 9.00 at Clapham Junction.

Please let me know as soon as possible if you are playing and where you'll be meeting.
Thanks
Nick

P.S. Good luck to Miles who is having an operation Friday. I guess that means you aren't playing on Sunday… and aren't going on holiday.

P.P.S. I've got a closed eye and a massive shiner. Thankfully I didn't get my nose spread across my face.

Nick's weekly Monday-morning email comes out and, as luck would have it, we are playing the young whippersnappers again this weekend. I hope they rest a few players, especially the quick lads up front, but I don't think Sunday football teams do much squad rotation.

We, however, do a lot of rotation but that's usually due to the fact that most of the team can't play week in, week out due to injuries, being away or under the thumb from their other halves. We are therefore forced to change the team every week. I can't say I've ever taken someone aside and told them we're going to rest them this week as we have a big six-pointer the following weekend. Any half-decent players we have are the first names on the team-sheet.

The week begins to take on a familiar look and by Friday we're struggling for numbers again. However, after persuading mates the benefits of playing for us (I did struggle) we are back up to twelve by Saturday. The relief is short-lived as Carl now has to work and Jim is feeling unwell. Come 8.00 on Saturday night we're back down to ten.

I sometimes play on a Saturday with some mates from university if they're short and Rob, one of my mates from that team, is a self-confessed "football whore" who will play for anyone, although hopefully he won't be asking for any money on Sunday.

"Rob, do you fancy a game tomorrow up front with Damo?" I ask him on the phone.

Although really a right-sided midfielder, Rob loves playing as a striker and I hope that by waving this carrot in front of him he will bite.

"Definitely, mate. I'll do anything to get out of going to Bluewater shopping with the missus."

"Cheers, mate. You don't know anyone else from your team, do you?"

"Leave it with me."

I come off the phone a happy man although I wish I hadn't said he was guaranteed to play up front. Jamie is probably a better striker than him, and I reckon he would have even played if I said he was left-back, such was his delight at getting out of shopping.

He soon calls back. "Barry can play as well."

"You star. We can put him centre midfield with Danny, then."

"Sounds good. The missus is still keen for me to go to Bluewater in the afternoon but should still be able to have a couple of beers afterwards and hopefully she'll change her tune."

"We meet at 8.30 at Clapham Junction. See you tomorrow."

Rob is the worst time-keeper in the world and by saying 8.30 he should be there by 9.00. After all, he is the man who arrived at his wedding later than his bride.

I actually have a quiet night Saturday and am back home by midnight. I wake up Sunday feeling awake and not hung-over, which is a pleasant change. I head down to Clapham Junction and most of the lads arrive by 9.00 apart from Rob, who finally shows up around 9.30.

Anton, who wasn't even scheduled to play, has also turned up which brings us up to thirteen. That leaves me with the awkward decision about who we will make sub. I've been banned from navigating and luckily Barry is in a big lorry with a satellite navigation system, so we get to their ground in Mortlake by 10.00 with apparently no hitches.

This soon changes, however, when Hugh announces that he has managed to damage his contact lenses in the car and won't be able to play as he can barely see a thing from his right eye.

"That's a Calcio first, a player getting injured in the car on the way to the ground," I tell the lads. "Don't think either Nick or Paddy has managed to do that."

"Sorry lads, but I can't really play. I'll run the line if you want, though. Most linesmen are blind so I should fit in OK."

We get ready. Tom is happy to tell everyone who cares and doesn't care about his trip to Australia, and I introduce everyone to each other as per usual. I've also brought some energy tablets with me which I offer to the lads.

"He has been so bad this season he has resorted to taking performance-enhancing drugs," Rob says to the others.

"I mean, they can't make him any worse, can they?" Hugh asks the team.

Chris joins in the banter. "Do they also prevent you from missing open goals or do you need something stronger than drugs to ensure that?"

"So, lads, I take it you lot don't want any then."

"Not for me, mate, although if I see you running round the pitch like Steven Gerrard and scoring a hat-trick I will be having some."

"I don't think I'll be giving you any then, Rob."

Heading out to the pitch we have to pass a mobile food van. If I had any money on me I'm pretty sure I would have bought something. I turn around, though, and see that Rob has stopped and is buying himself a big bacon butty.

"Fuck me, Rob, we're starting in ten minutes. What are you doing having a bacon butty? You are meant to have a pre-match meal two hours before not literally pre-match. I told the lads you were a good player who takes his football seriously, but look at you now eating a butty with ketchup running down your face."

"Didn't have any breakfast this morning and besides it's a bacon and egg butty and it tastes heavenly. Pretty big for three quid."

"Go on, let's have a bite. Pretty sure none of the lads can see us."

"You've changed your tune, Gibbo," replies Rob as I try and take a big a bite as possible.

"Fucking hell, Gibbo. You've pretty much eaten half of it."

"Rob, Gibbo, hurry up. You're missing the warm-up," shouts Tom as we jog over.

"I can feel the butty already, mate," I tell Rob.

"So can I. It was worth it, though. Might have another afterwards; might even have one at half-time."

As we get to the pitch I notice that the two quick lads who

played last week are both playing again and they are probably pleased that I've kept my place. Their centre-back, who likes to provide a running commentary, doesn't seem to be playing, mercifully, so we will be spared his thoughts this week. We actually have a decent warm-up for a change and we have a couple of games of piggy in the middle which gets everyone's heart rate up and gives me and Rob indigestion.

"I'm knackered and we haven't even started yet," shouts Danny. "My body can't cope with warm-ups as well as ninety minutes."

"I wouldn't say that your body could cope with ninety minutes either," says Tom.

"Very funny. I might actually need some of Gibbo's drugs."

"Don't worry, mate," I say. "I have a few left. Just had my tablet now and am feeling full of energy."

The game finally kicks off and we are playing quite well for the first five minutes or so, passing the ball around nicely. I'm feeling full of energy, as well as full of butty, but sadly the tablets don't help cure my lack of speed. A ball over the top leads to their centre-forward outrunning me and slipping the ball past Chris in goal.

"Offside!" I shout to Hugh, who is running the line.

"Don't think so, mate, although to be honest I can't really see that far across. Think he just outpaced you."

"Those drugs are working well, mate," Danny says as I labour back to the centre circle with puffed-out cheeks.

"Don't think the tablets have kicked in yet."

"No shit. You sure it's not valium you have taken? Also have you cut yourself? It looks like their blood on your shirt," says Danny, pointing to the tomato ketchup I spilt on my shirt.

"Just opened up an old wound on my chest, mate. Don't worry about it, mate. I'm a tough lad and I'll get through the game."

The game restarts and they continue to pile on the pressure. They soon get a corner when Chris pulls off a good save.

"Front, back post."

"No free men, boys."

"Stick to your marker."

"Who's got the number eight?"

"Fucking hell, lads, whose man was he?" Chris says as number eight buries his header in the net. We all look round at each other and no one seems to admit guilt. Yet again a corner leads to a goal.

It soon goes from bad to worse. A quickly taken free-kick catches us all unawares and their winger crosses the ball to leave their centre-forward with a tap-in.

"Wake up, boys," shouts Chris. "Three-fucking-nil down and we've only been playing ten minutes."

It's going to be a long ninety minutes and when things can't seem to get any worse Chris pulls his groin while taking a goal-kick and has to go off. We bring Anton on and I end up having to go in goal again.

I'm not sure whether it's me going between the sticks but we begin to look more secure at the back and start to have a few chances, with Damo and Rob both going close. We eventually pull a goal back when Damo beats the offside trap and squares to Rob who has the straightforward task of putting the ball into the net.

"Good goal, butty boy," I shout out.

"What do you mean 'butty boy'?" Tom asks me.

"Surname is Butt mate," I reply, lying.

Danny gives a rallying cry as they kick-off. "Come on Calcio! We can get back into this."

We have most of the game up to half-time and I barely have a save to make. Pretty sure I could go and grab another butty I'm that unemployed. Just as half-time comes, though, one of their players gets injured and as they have no subs they are down to ten men.

"Come on, boys. They only have ten men now. Let's make the extra person count," I say to the lads at half-time.

"We can turn this around," says Danny. "We've been playing well the last twenty minutes or so."

We kick-off the second half and soon a good move started by Danny leads to a good interchange between Rob and Damo, who makes it 3-2.

"Come on, concentrate Saucer. Let's get back to how we were playing in the first half," yells their captain, trying to rally his troops as they kick-off.

Chris, who has come to stand by my goal with a bacon sandwich in hand, finds his exhortations amusing. "I swear I nearly pissed myself when he said 'Concentrate Saucer' with his high-pitched voice. He sounds like a redcoat in a *Carry On* film."

"Nice butty, Chris?"

"Hits the spot mate. The bloke in the food van said one of the players had one just before the game."

"Must've been one of theirs. Unprofessional, that."

We continue to apply pressure and another one of their players gets injured and goes down in pain. I'm not sure what to think here; part of me wants him to be injured so they go down to nine men but they are, in the Calcio vernacular, a good set of lads, so I hope he hasn't done anything too bad. I come to the conclusion that I hope he has to come off but his ankle is OK by lunchtime. The lad gets carried off in some pain which means that they are down to nine men, which is good. But I can't see him being OK by lunchtime, which isn't.

Luckily, in the dozen or so years I've played Sunday-morning football I don't think I have seen a really serious injury, which is quite surprising, especially considering some of the late tackles Miles puts in. There has never been an incident where an ambulance has been needed, the most frequent Sunday morning injury being a hangover, though I'm not sure you can really classify that as an injury.

You would like to think that we pile on the pressure after they have gone down to nine men. Sadly, the opposite happens and I have to make a couple of saves. Half our team can barely run now and look shattered; you would think that we had the nine men, not them. The game peters out and ends in a 3-2 defeat. We didn't manage a single shot on goal in the whole time they only had nine men.

"What happened, lads?" says Damo. "We didn't create a single chance."

"I know," says Del. "I was knackered the last fifteen minutes or so which didn't help. I really struggle now with an all-night rave and then Sunday morning football."

"Funny, that," says Tom.

Del has not finished. "Let's face it, Damo. Most of us are thirty plus and the last twenty minutes are always a mare."

"But they only had nine men," says Damo as we make our way back to the changing room.

"Fancy another butty, mate?" the bloke in the food van shouts out at Rob as we walk past.

"What? Don't tell me you had a fucking butty five minutes before kick-off, Rob," Damo asks him, looking pissed off.

"Nice, wasn't it, Gibbo?"

"I don't believe it, Gibbo," says Damo, determined to make me feel guilty. "You've had a fucking butty two minutes before kick-off. Not surprised you were shit. Butties, energy tablets, no doubt a skinful of beer and a kebab a few hours ago as well. You're meant to be setting an example."

"You fucking liar, Gibbo. That blood which you reckon you got from a chest wound, which I have to admit I thought was a bit strange at the time, is actually ketchup, isn't it?"

"Could be, Danny. Anyway, I only had a bite, though I was pleased with the size of it."

Back in the changing room Nick calls me from Iceland where he is spending the weekend with his girlfriend. "How did we get on?"

"We came second, mate."

"Score?"

"Not this week, mate, which will probably surprise you. I came close, though."

"I don't care about you and don't bullshit me that you came close to scoring. What was the final result?"

"Three-two."

"Better than last week, then. Did we play alright?"

"The usual, mate – shite in the first twenty minutes, then had a good spell pre- and post-half-time and then struggled in the last twenty minutes when our lack of fitness took its toll. Which was surprising seeing as they only had nine men."

"You lost and they only had nine men."

"You could say that. Anyway, how is Iceland? Have you seen Kerry Katona?"

"Good, mate. Fits one of our end-of-season tour criteria in that the local birds are fit, but sadly fails in another in the fact that pints are over a fiver."

"Gibbo had a fucking fry-up two minutes before kick-off," Damo shouts down my phone to Nick.

"What was that Gibbo, you had bangers, eggs, bacon, mushrooms and beans before the game?"

"Think your ears are playing up, mate. Besides, you know I don't like mushrooms. Anyway, best be off as I need to get changed. Catch up in the week."

Most of the lads head home apart from me and Rob. We go for a couple of pints at the pub just around the corner.

"Thanks for helping us out, mate. Think our fitness or lack of it meant that even playing a game against nine men still didn't end in victory."

"We're the same, mate. Every season we're getting older but the teams we play seem to be getting younger. It's always the last twenty minutes or so when we seem to concede most of our goals."

"We're considering making this our last season. I love the banter, the occasional win, the post-match drinks and end-of-season tour. But most of our players seem to spend half the season injured and we seem to pick up new injuries on a weekly basis."

"We are pretty injury-prone, too, though I don't think we've ever picked up an injury on the way to a game like Hugh did today."

"That sums us up, mate, and the annoying thing is that he's probably the fittest bloke in our team."

"Have you guys considered joining a veterans' league?"

"Not yet, but it could be an option at the end of the season, I suppose."

"We're thinking of joining one next season. I have to carry on playing because otherwise it will mean more trips to shopping centres and more DIY. The missus can't believe I'm still playing. If only she knew the main reason was to avoid her giving me more jobs around the house."

"Aren't veterans' leagues a pretty low standard and full of fat, unfit and pretty shit footballers?"

"Yes, mate, you boys would fit in fucking well. You might even win the odd game and you might even have more pace than the odd centre-forward you mark. Having a bacon butty before kick-off isn't frowned upon either. It might actually be encouraged."

"Cheers, mate. Haven't really discussed it with the other lads but it could be an option if we decide to make this our last season in this league. It sort of admits defeat if we do join one because it'll seem like we've admitted we can't compete in adult leagues. I like to think my football career isn't completely washed up and I can still compete against people in their twenties."

"You can, mate, although you would probably fare better against men in their forties. Anyway better go, mate. Just got a text from Sam asking me to say goodbye to Gibbo and leave the pub."

"She knows you too well."

"Would love to stay but better go to the joys of Bluewater. Thanks for the game, mate, and if you ever need a goalscoring machine you know who to ask."

"Yes I do, mate, and if he can't play I'll get you down again."

"You can't buy a finish like that"

To: calcio squad
From: Nick

Dear All

Hope everyone is well and enjoyed the weekend and made the most of having no game on Sunday. Judging by our performances in recent weeks, I think most of us make the most of our Saturday nights, game or no game, especially Del, whose Saturday night seems to roll into Sunday morning football.

Anyway, no doubt you have all been out training in preparation for this weekend's game against the lovely set of drunk individuals from Rapid Descent, where Gibbo let down the famous green shirt and got sent off earlier in the season. Let's hope he manages to stay on the pitch the whole game this time (if selected).

Meet 9.45 at home. Please be on time as we could do with a good warm-up.

Cheers
Nick

P.S. Thanks for everyone's concern about my injury a couple of weeks ago, I had no email from any of you arseholes asking how it is. However, you will be pleased to know it has more or less cleared up and I no longer look like the elephant man. Still waking up with headaches, especially this morning but that could be related to something else.

P.P.S. Miles – I hope Epsom Hospital the other week was a nice alternative to your planned holiday in the States.

From: Gibbo
To: calcio squad

Please get there on time lads. We need to put up the nets and have a good warm-up. I reckon half the reason we concede goals in first five minutes is because we rarely have a decent warm-up. Any latecomers should be prepared to start on the bench.
    Cheers
    Gibbo

From: Carl
To: calcio squad

You sure that us letting in early goals has nothing to do with our dodgy defence mate? It may be December on Sunday but it would be nice if the defence didn't hand out any presents this weekend.
    Cheers
    Carl

Come Thursday it looks like we will be lucky to get six players but after a bit of chasing up we are up to twelve which is a surprise considering the past few weeks.

I plan to have a few beers on Saturday but end up going out at lunchtime and not getting back to my flat till gone 2.00 Sunday morning. It would have been earlier but I fall asleep on the tube on the way home and instead of waking up in Clapham North I wake up in South Wimbledon at the southern end of the Northern line. The London Underground worker says there's one more train heading north, which pleases me, but I then fall asleep again and get woken up at the northern end of the line in High Barnet. I can't convince any black-cab drivers to take a pissed bloke south of the river and end up getting a dodgy mini-cab back home which costs me fifty pounds from virtually outside the bar I left two hours ago.

I get to the ground at 9.45 and sure enough no one has arrived apart from the whole of Rapid Descent and the referee. Rapid Descent seem a lot better than they did last time we played them, no beer can or fag in sight and if they beat us when pissed last time they could be quite useful sober and wide awake. They also all have matching club tracksuits which makes them look very professional.

"Any of your fucking players turning up today, mate?" one of their players politely asks me, "or are they running scared of us after we thumped you earlier this season despite the fact we were all half cut?"

"It was only 4-0. That's close in our book. Anyway good morning to you, too, and don't worry, they're all turning up."

"You may be shit but you seem to have a decent pitch and nice changing rooms."

He's right, we do probably have one of the best pitches in the league. It's flat, has clearly marked lines and has grass on it. The grass should be shorter but we like it long because it holds the ball up which is beneficial to a slow team like ours. Our pitch is also the only one in the park and each team has its own changing room that is heated and has semi-decent showers and toilets.

There is also somewhere safe to leave my bike. The changing rooms get locked which means you don't have to take your stuff out to the pitch and the chap who runs the facility is a nice lad who always asks how we get on after the match. When we say that we lost (more often than not) he seems generally disappointed for us. However, the best advantages of our pitch are that it is only a short bike ride from my flat and that it is right next door to a pub where we can go for a few pints after the game.

Finally the team begin to drift in at around 10.15.

"I'm taking a sweepstake on how long Nick will last today before getting injured," Danny announces as he enters the dressing room.

"What odds for less than five minutes," I reply.

"That's the favourite, I'm afraid. Can only offer evens on that."

Nick announces his arrival. "I actually feel up for today, lads. I fancy a goal as well."

"Your first for the season, Nick," I say. "How many goals have our centre midfield partnership of you and Danny scored this season?"

Danny weighs in. "Have to admit I haven't troubled the scoring chart this season, but must have created loads and would have made even more if half of you lot were on the same wavelength as me."

"Lads, listen up," says Nick. "We really need a performance today. We've been fucking shit recently; we should be called Rapid Descent, not them. We have had lacklustre performances from a lot of people recently, so let's really go for it right from the off today. If we all put in one hundred percent we can beat this set of arseholes."

"Are they sober today, Nick?" enquires Jack. "I might also need to grab a fag off them as I seem to have left my pre-match fag at home."

"What are you like. Yes, they are sober and they are also minus the WAGs this time, which is a shame."

We head out the changing room and have a half-decent warm-up, actually using the corner flags for some of the football drills which makes a nice change from using them as javelins. The referee today has to be the smartest I have ever seen. His boots are that polished I could probably do my hair in them, his kit is ironed and looks brand new, his socks are rolled up to his knees and it looks like he has spent half an hour doing his barnet beforehand.

I'm not sure if it is the shock of having an immaculately turned out referee or the shock of Rapid Descent playing football sober, but with their first attack their winger skips past Danny, Jack and I and then crosses for their centre-forward to touch the ball into the net.

"Fucking hell, lads! What happened there?" Phil shouts at the defence and midfield.

"Good to see you boys still can't defend for fucking toffee," their winger tells Nick as he runs past him on the way back to his own half.

"Good to see you boys are still a set of wankers. You boys should've gone to school, you might have enjoyed it."

"Fuck off, you cheeky sod. We all went to school. I probably earn more than you in a week than you do in a year," replies their millionaire winger to Nick.

Everyone looks at each other ashen-faced and we head back to the centre circle knowing that yet again we have conceded a goal in the first five minutes.

It then goes from bad to worse for me when I go for a fifty-fifty ball and come off second best and hit the ground in a heap in agony. The lads run over as I lie there writhing.

"You alright?" asks Carl.

I can barely breathe, let alone speak, and if I could speak I would feel like saying 'Yes Carl, I feel a million dollars, how are you, good night last night?'"

"Think he's badly winded," says Nick, stating the obvious.

"Stay still, Gibbo (as if I'm going anywhere in a hurry). Let me bend your legs to help even the breathing," Jack tells me, putting his first-aid course to good use.

"I'm in fucking agony, I can barely breathe." I manage to gasp.

"Take your time, Gibbo. Lots of deep breaths," Jack adds.

Eventually some of the lads help me to my feet and I hobble off. It's clear that I must have done something to my ribs as they are beginning to get really painful.

"What odds were you not to last five minutes?" Nick shouts out as I head off the pitch.

This makes me chuckle until I realise that laughing leads to more pain. I hobble back on and try to run but my ribs really hurt. We make a sub and I head to the changing room. I think to myself that I wished I had continued doing my hundred sit-ups a day as that would have given me some stomach muscles which might have eased the pain of getting winded. I'd started doing a hundred a day on New Year's Day and despite a good start, come January 4 I was down to fifty and then by January 6 I'd completed my last sit-up of the year.

One advantage of getting injured or sent off is that you're first in the shower and are guaranteed hot water. From the shower I can hear Danny scream in his high-pitched Scouse accent and I then hear a cheer which I reckon must mean they've scored another goal. The only people who are watching us today are Pete's wife and his one-year-old son, and unless Pete's wife's voice has broken in the last week the voices are most definitely from their ten or so supporters, which is quite a number for a Sunday League team away from home.

After a nice warm shower I head back out and sure enough we're 2-0 down but seem to playing some good football and create a couple of half-chances. Half-time comes and the lads head over to our kit bag.

"How are you, mate?" asks Danny.

"Not good. Ribs really fucking hurt but at least I had a warm shower, which was a bonus. Best showers I get are when I have been sent off or injured as there is hot water."

"What is it with you and this team-mate? You can't last ninety minutes; you either get sent off or get injured."

"I've never felt agony like that. I bet you've never been winded in your life. Must be impossible to wind you, mate."

"Yes, these layers of slight fat have some advantages."

"Come on, lads, concentrate," says Nick. "We can get back into this. We have had a good last fifteen minutes or so, their defence looks worse than ours and without Gibbo we're looking more solid."

The boys head out for the second half and I watch from the touchline hoping that I haven't done anything too bad to my ribs. I have become more susceptible to injuries in the past few years and usually have around a month out each season injured. The favourites the last couple of years have been swollen ankles, torn hamstrings and pulled calf muscles. The injuries have tended to come in January which is the best month to get injured as it's usually the coldest and wettest month. It's also mid-season so it gives me a chance to recharge my batteries.

What happens next, though, is a first for the season. Danny finds himself in acres of space alone up front (he had done the usual and not tracked back after our previous attack had broken down) and as the ball gets through to him, rather than run on with the ball, which is probably no bad thing as he has no pace, he strikes the ball with the outside of his foot from about twenty five yards and puts the ball in the top corner.

"Excellent goal, mate!" I shout from the touchline but soon realise that he will be going on about this one for months on end.

"I know, mate. You can't buy a finish like that," Danny replies, which confirms my view that I will be hearing about this finish for the rest of this and probably next year.

We continue to play well and are definitely on top, leading to an equaliser when Jim plays the ball out wide, Anton crosses and Nick, at the third attempt, manages to score. He then celebrates like someone would who hadn't scored for donkey's years, well this season anyway.

"We can beat this lot. They've lost their bottle. It's them that's running scared of us now," Danny shouts out just as they are about to kick-off.

"We'll see who's running scared at the end of the game, fat boy," retorts their winger.

"Calm down Danny, just concentrate on trying to get the winner," I say as I realise that if it's eleven of them against eleven of us in a fight we will lose pretty convincingly.

Rapid Descent are beginning to argue amongst themselves which is always a good sign for the opposing team. Their centre midfield player is moaning to their defence that they are bypassing the midfield to which their centre-back implies that he wouldn't if the midfield didn't keep giving the ball away.

We continue to pressurise them and Carl and Jim come close. Then in the last minute Damo is put through but the keeper makes a good save and the ball goes off for a corner.

"That's cost us two points mate," I shout out from the touchline.

"That's nothing on the amount of points you have cost us this season, mate."

"I can't believe you fucking bottled it."

Funnily enough, we create nothing from our corner and the referee blows his whistle to signal the end of the game.

"You changed the game today Gibbo," Nick tells me as he leaves the pitch.

"What do you mean?"

"Well, when you came off we suddenly looked a lot better. And what was that about me not lasting ten minutes, Gibbo? Pot calling the kettle and all that."

"You did do your best to miss your goal. Wasn't it the third or fourth attempt at trying to connect ball with foot before it went in?"

"Gibbo, you know last season I scored a few goals that defied physics. Well that goal today defied physics, chemistry and biology," Danny adds.

Before we go, I tell Jack I received a letter from the FA about him this week.

"Let me guess, Gibbo. They are considering me as the next England manager."

"Sadly not. You owe me seven quid for a booking from a couple of weeks ago."

"Can't believe the ref put it through. He told me he wouldn't at the end of the game."

"Sorry, but he did. Can't do the pub as I've got my parents up, and to be honest, I'm glad I have as no doubt Danny and Nick will be banging on about Real Calcio's goalscoring centre midfield."

"Shit! It's Babe Ruth!"

Not sure if it's the fact that we should win today – we're playing at home – or that there are two big games on Sky this afternoon at the pub, but we have, are you ready for it, fourteen today, yes four-fucking-teen players today. I can't believe it.

"The committee had to have a meeting in the boardroom last night, also known as the pub next door, to discuss who would go sub today," Nick tells the lads in the changing room before the game.

"We'll be using all the subs today so if you are shite you will be subbed," I say.

"But we can only make three substitutions, Gibbo," replies Wilky, who will now definitely be substituted.

Nick has an announcement. "Just like to welcome back Paul, who has literally flown straight in from Iraq to play today. I have to admit the last thing I would want to do after flying in from Iraq is to turn out for us. I would be looking for some relaxation, and with our dodgy defence there's no chance of that," he says, looking in the direction of Jack and I.

We all head out to the pitch and spend some time doing various pointless football warm-ups. Pete keeps trying to recreate his solitary goal from last season but can't seem to score even without a goalkeeper in goal. A couple of others are having a penalty competition, while Jim and Phil are continuing their season-long javelin competition with the corner flags. Damo, Nick, Danny and I are discussing our work Christmas parties whilst playing keepy-uppy – badly – and Paul is telling a few of the lads about his last couple of months in Iraq. The thought of actually doing a worthwhile warm-up doesn't enter anyone's mind.

Today has got to be the first time everyone arrives on time. Last season, Jack, Anton and Damo were late for one of our games and as we had already started our warm-up they warmed up by themselves on the other side of the pitch. This wasn't unusual, although to the outsider it would have looked as though we were a racist team. Jack, Anton and Damo were our only black players that day and people might have assumed we had a racial divide.

Today we're playing Hounslow Hangovers, who we beat earlier this season, although it looks like they've been in the transfer market as they seem to have quite a few new players.

"Been busy recruiting in the last month or so, mate?" Danny asks one of their players as he walks past us.

"Everyone's away today as it's a lad's stag do and we've had to get about eight ringers in," he replies, bold as brass.

"Ringers who I presume you've got signed up."

"Course we have, mate. How dare you question us," he replies, probably lying through his teeth before joining his team-mates warming up.

"Wonder if they call their ringers Graham Jones?" Danny says to me.

"If they do it sounds like they have around half a dozen of them playing today. Just hope they're all as shit as Graham Jones actually is."

The referee finally arrives at 10.45 and we must have had the longest warm-up in our history.

"My javelin-throwing is something else, mate," Phil tells me. "I've absolutely thrashed your brother in our competition."

"Good to see you've been having a productive warm-up. Have you actually touched a football in the warm-up?" I enquire.

"Be lying if I said I had but warm-ups don't seem to do much for us."

121

The referee arrives at last. "Sorry I'm late," he tells me as he jogs over. "Traffic was murder."

"If that was us turning up at 10.45, ref, we'd get fined," I say as he prepares to blow his whistle to signal the toss. "But don't worry, I won't tell the league. Just make sure you give any fifty-fifty decisions our way."

We win the toss and get the game underway. We start off well and come close through Damo within a minute or so when his shot is tipped over the bar by their keeper. It gets even better when from the resultant corner Paul scores after a goalmouth scramble.

"Keep the heads on the game, lads."

"Still 0-0, lads."

"Let's not give away a quick equaliser."

"Switch on from the off."

Things get even better when a fine through-ball from Wilky puts Damo through and despite doing his best to scuff the ball wide he manages to scuff it into the bottom corner.

"Two-nil after five minutes," I say to Nick as we make our way back to the centre circle. "That's a first for the season."

"Well, first time it's been us that are two up. If the league gets wind of this they will be sending round the drug-testers."

"True. I think we've even been 3-0 down after five minutes before."

This is probably the best we have played all season and leading 2-0 after five minutes is completely alien to us. In fact in my entire football career I don't think I've played in a team that has been 2-0 up after five minutes. I begin to panic and think whether we should perhaps make sure we hold out for the win and therefore shut up shop and become more defensive. Or do we continue as we are and perhaps score a few more goals? However, since we've never really had any tactics we might as well continue playing as we are, and if we let in a few goals due to the fact that everyone wants to get on the scoresheet, so be it.

It gets even better when, from a corner, Nick heads the ball goalwards. Despite it looking like it will cross the line anyway, I stab the ball in from a yard for my third goal of the season.

"You goal-grabbing bastard," curses Nick.

"Better to be safe than sorry. Besides, it might not have gone in."

"Oh yes, course not, mate, unless the Earlsfield ghost was planning to appear from the ground and stop it going in."

"You should've got some more power into the header."

"I'm surprised you didn't put it over the bar, mate."

"So am I."

The ringers they have signed up are a dirty bunch and the game is becoming increasingly niggly. A fair fifty-fifty challenge by Tom leaves one of their ringers rolling about on the floor in agony. A few of their players run up to Tom and start shoving him, and just when it seems to be calming down their goalkeeper sprints the length of the pitch and begins pushing a few of our players.

"What the fuck are you doing here?" Wilky asks him. "How can you see anything from the other end of the pitch?"

"It was a fucking awful tackle."

"It would be a free-kick if it was a bad tackle, and besides you should really concentrate on your goalkeeping, not pushing and shoving, as your goalkeeping sure needs improving."

The wounded party struggles to his feet. "Mate, you would never get away with that in the semi-pro team I play for on Saturdays," he says, which makes most of us laugh.

"I bet you play semi-pro because you're really good," Jim replies, taking the piss.

"I do, as it goes. And yes, I am good. I actually had trials for Nottingham Forest a few years ago."

"I bet they were gutted to let you go. And of course you play semi-pro – you can tell by the way you've been beating our left-back Pete every time you get the ball."

Nick cuts to the chase. "If you are semi-pro why are you so fucking shit and playing in this league, and in the fifth division at that?"

The referee tells us all to calm down. Their keeper heads back up the other end of the pitch to his goal and their "semi-pro" player returns to the wing, probably trying to work out how he can get round our forty-odd-year-old slow left-back Pete.

We have a few more chances before half-time but can't add to our tally of three.

"Keep it up," Nick calls out. "We can at least get another three by the end of the game."

"Too right, and let's try and keep a clean sheet," I respond. "After all, Phil hasn't had a clean sheet all season, have you, Phil?"

"Yes, and I know you have, Gibbo, blah blah blah."

Sure enough, as soon as they kick-off the second half, their winger whips in a cross that deflects off Pete and into the net, putting paid to Phil's clean sheet for another week.

"Shit, fuck, bollocks," comes the scream from Phil as he collects the ball from the net and boots it towards the halfway line.

Yet we soon add a fourth goal. Their keeper takes a goal-kick and the ball flies straight towards Danny, who controls it on his chest and volleys in from about twenty five yards.

"Never seen a goal where someone has controlled the ball by their cleavage before," says Nick as we go over to celebrate.

"You may have big breasts mate but they seem good for instant control," I tell him. "Some goal that, it might make it to the showboating section on *Soccer AM* next week."

Our opponents' heads have now completely dropped and the ringers they have this week probably wish they had stayed in bed. They look how we probably look most games, with their keeper slumped against the post, their two centre-backs miles apart from each other, their wingers looking uninterested (which isn't surprising as they have been starved of service) and their attackers bemoaning every decision and not passing to one another.

We make some substitutes and it's not too long until a fifth goal arrives when Jim makes a good run down the wing and crosses the ball. I score from about two yards, having not made it back from the previous corner.

"Two goals scored from a total of about three yards," snipes Nick.

"All about right place, right time, mate. And besides, how many goals did Gary Lineker get from outside the six-yard box?"

"Although in all fairness, you should have been about fifty yards further back."

"I could sense a second goal so I thought I'd stay up," I say less than truthfully.

I begin to have visions of a hat-trick and find myself gradually creeping up the pitch. However, I am made to pay as Tom is left with two attackers to mark during one of their rare attacks and a quick one-two leads to them scoring a second goal.

"Defence, where the fuck are you?" rages Phil as I try to hide behind Danny. "Gibbo, what the fuck are you doing up there? You won't get a hat-trick, believe you me."

The game then turns ugly again as their first half goalkeeper, who is now playing up front, gets himself sent off for raising an arm at Tom. He storms off the pitch with the words "I will be back," and I've never seen anyone run off so quickly after being dismissed.

Danny turns to me with a grin. "He must've heard that only the first person in the showers is guaranteed hot water."

"He will be back in a minute," one of their players assures us.

"But he's been sent off," I reply.

"Shit! It's Babe Ruth! Run!" Danny shouts out, and as I turn round I see the bloke who was sent off running back towards the pitch armed with a baseball bat.

Danny and the rest of us dash towards the other end of the pitch. Luckily, one of their players manages to appease Babe Ruth and heads back to the changing room with him.

"Thank God for that."

"I've never seen us run that fast before."

"First time we've showed any pace all season."

"Amazing what someone running towards you with a baseball bat can do for your speed."

The game eventually restarts with them down to nine men. Danny adds our sixth goal on the stroke of full-time with a tidy finish after a move that starts from Phil in goal. I would like to say the ball moves from defence to midfield to attack, but it is actually a punt downfield from Phil that their centre-back misjudges, allowing Danny to go on and score.

They manage a consolation goal on the break in injury time, when the whole of our team is in their half trying to get in on the act.

"Let's leave the pitch together," says Tom as the full-time whistle goes and we contemplate having to avoid a baseball bat before we have a shower.

"I came back from Iraq for some peace and quiet, not for this," says Paul.

"Perhaps you should sign him up for Queen and Country," says Wilky. "I mean, the bloke scared the shit out of us lot."

One of their players comes over to us. "It's alright, lads. He's gone home now. Sorry about that – it was his second and now last game for us. As you know we had to get a load of ringers in today and if I'd known they were like that we would've forfeited the game."

"Thanks for letting us know he's gone," I reply. "We were a bit apprehensive heading back to the changing rooms. Anyway, good luck for the rest of the season."

We get showered and changed but I'm still thinking about Babe Ruth. "So when that bloke gets ready for Sunday-morning football he must say to himself: football boots, shin pads, shower gel, towel, deodorant, underwear, hair wax and baseball bat."

"Yes," says Wilky, "although I think you are probably the only player who packs hair wax for Sunday-morning footy."

"That's because I'm about the only one who has a full head of hair."

"Yes, course you are," says Jack, who has long, thick dreadlocks.

Most of the teams we play in the league are decent lads but there has been the odd scuffle over the years. Last year one bloke I was marking was fouling me all game and constantly in my ear. Anyway, he was carrying a few extra pounds and in the second half I enquired whether he had eaten three or four doughnuts at half-time. He didn't take it too well and turned round and lamped me in the face. The referee never saw it and though I thought about hitting him back, knowing my luck I would have probably injured myself, so I let it go.

Another side we played last season ended up with nine men (we still only drew) after two of their own players started fighting each other and were sent off. The thing that amused us all the most was the fact that they were housemates. I doubt the atmosphere was too good in the house the following weeks.

We all head off to the pub to watch the football. If the two games are half as exciting as the game this morning it should be a good afternoon. Over a drink we discuss our season so far and although we haven't really set the world alight we are going to end the year in a position just below halfway in the table.

"We're a bit like Fulham," argues Tom, which doesn't sound as good as being told we're a bit like Barcelona.

"Suppose we are," agrees Anton, "although I don't think the Fulham lads would like to hear that. We never threaten promotion but should always just about escape relegation," he adds, suggesting he must have a short memory as we got relegated last season.

"Pity we have nothing really to play for after Christmas seeing as we only got to the last sixteen and quarter-final of the cups," says Nick, making us sound better than we are.

"Also known as the first round we played in," chuckles Hugh.

"I know, but last sixteen and quarter-final sound much better."

"Think lack of fitness and pace is our main problem," says Danny, who is probably the slowest and most unfit of us all.

Ever the optimist, I add: "And imagine what it will be like at the next game after the Christmas break after two weeks of eating and boozing."

"Well we can think about going for the odd run," says Danny.

"Thought about it and can't see that happening, Danny. I also can't imagine you will be dusting down your running shoes and going out running either, mate."

Nick changes the subject. "Anyone expecting anything exciting for Christmas? Miles, is Santa going to get you a couple of new fingers?"

"And you a goal that doesn't come off your shin," I suggest.

Nick warms to his new role as Father Christmas. "Anton could do with an alarm clock, Tworty needs a map of our ground as he hasn't been seen since the first game of the season, Hugh some contact lenses and Gibbo a map of London with our opponents' grounds clearly marked."

"I could do with a new defence," says Phil.

"Bad workman always blames his tools," I can't resist saying.

"I don't even have any tools half the time with you, Gibbo, and the other three muppets at the back giving most strikers the freedom of London most weeks."

"We all as a team could do with some pace, fitness, finishing ability and a book on marking at corners," adds Santa.

The first game on Sky eventually starts and thoughts of the festive season are replaced by shouting at the TV and drinking. By the time most of us leave at closing time we are the worse for wear but we all agree to go running every day during the Christmas break – and that we will go the whole of next year undefeated.

"Better than Gordon Banks in Mexico, that"

"Nick and I are getting to the ground at 9.15 tomorrow to have a decent warm-up," Danny tells me on the phone on Saturday afternoon. "I might've lost some fitness over the winter break."

"So you weren't out running and keeping fit during our two weeks off, then," I reply.

"Of course I wasn't. Were you?"

"Be lying if I said I was, although I have been cycling to work this week. Well, cycling to the train station and taking my bike on the train and cycling the other end."

"Yes, those five minutes must have done wonders for your fitness."

"Better than nothing. Anyway mate, decent warm-up sounds good. Planning a quiet one tonight so see you bright and early tomorrow."

Saturday night goes as planned and I feel nice and refreshed on Sunday. I jump on my bike and get to our home ground for 9.15 to meet Danny and Nick. However, when I get there I realise that I've forgotten my football boots and shinpads.

"Happy New Year and all that bollocks," Nick says to me as I arrive.

"Bit of a problem, mate. Seem to have forgotten my boots and shinpads."

"I mean it's a pretty easy thing to do, that," says Danny.

"What am I like? Any chance of a lift home as I'll never get there and back on my bike in time for kick-off?"

"What about our professional warm-up we were going to have?"

"It looks like we'll just have to have the usual warm-up of putting the nets up and a quick stretch."

We head off in Danny's car back to my flat to pick up my stuff.

"You know I said in my email to the team that we really need to get to the ground at 9.45 on Sundays and said how unacceptable it was blah blah blah," says Nick.

"Yes I know," I reply, "and you're going to look a right dick now, aren't you, turning up at around 10.00."

"You're fucking hopeless, Gibbo, and I can't believe I'm going to cop all the shit."

We arrive back at the ground just past 10.00 and already seven of the team are there. "I'm going to get some grief now," says Nick.

"What were you saying about arriving on time?" Wilky, who is actually on time for a change, asks him.

Miles joins in. "Didn't you say 9.45 and latecomers would be fined or start as sub?"

"Yes I know, although it was all Gibbo's fault. I was actually here at 9.15, but that fuckwit thought it would be a good idea to turn up without any football kit today."

"Don't blame me, Nick. You really should being setting an example seeing as you did write the email," I say before scarpering into the changing room.

"Christ it fucking stinks in here," says Paddy as he enters. He is right; the stench is unbelievable.

"Just popped my head in the cubicle and the toilet is blocked," says Tom, who looks like he is about to be sick. "Looks like someone has had a massive shit yesterday and the bastard couldn't get flushed down. I'm sure it winked at me as well."

"I need my Sunday-morning dump as well," Jim tells me.

"You can't, mate. We'll all pass out. Anyway why can't you have your Sunday-morning dump at home?"

"Don't want to ruin my nice clean toilet."

"Fair point."

"Who's in the toilet? I need a number two," says Nick as he enters the changing room.

"Another one," Tom tells him. "Fuck me, why can't you guys go to the bog at home? Besides, the toilet is blocked."

"Needs must and all that," replies Nick, "and I'll play better having released a bit of weight."

"I could do with starting sub today, been struggling with a cold this week," says Paddy.

"You mean, Paddy, that you've had two weeks on the piss and there's no way you can do ninety minutes today," says Nick.

"That as well. Well, that being the main reason."

"Not sure if you can as we only have ten at the moment. Where is Anton? He moans that he's sub but half the reason is that he is never here on time."

"Sorry I'm late, mate. Kid playing up and all that," says Anton as he walks in.

"If we told you that if you arrived at 9.45 you would be greeted by a naked Miss World for some pre-match fun, you would be on time," I say.

Tom's face lights up. "I'd be here at 8.30 with those promises, Gibbo. Anyway, is the referee here yet?"

"Give me a chance. I'm busy faking everyone's signature on the team sheet."

"I'll go and have a look then."

"So do we have one then, Tom?"

"Sort of."

"What do you mean 'sort of'?"

"Go outside and you'll see what I mean."

When I pop out and see the referee I understand what Tom's talking about. We've had this referee before, and he's a nice chap, but he looks eighty and he struggles to keep up with the play. Last time he refereed Calcio he managed to award a penalty when he was in the centre circle. But the league are really struggling for referees and as this one lives across the road, he fills in if anyone drops out. In all honesty, though, I think it would be better if we refereed the game ourselves as he has to be the worst in the league. He can barely walk, let alone run.

"Are you alright for the game, ref?" I ask him.

"Sure am. It's the first game I've refereed all season," he replies, which fills me with confidence.

"Lads, the ref we have today is alright but he struggles to leave the centre circle," I tell everyone as I walk back into the changing room.

"Is Danny the ref then?" more than half the team reply in unison.

"We can't complain, though. Our original referee pulled out at the last minute and the league secretary got us a referee last night which is good of them as we could have easily been left with no ref today."

"Where's Darren?" someone asks.

"Not sure. Looks like you're starting right-back then, Paddy."

"Their left-winger will have a field day," says Anton. "He'll think it's Christmas again."

"Thanks for the confidence-booster, mate."

"Who's in goal today, any volunteers?" asks Nick, and the whole changing room falls silent.

"Gibbo said he would do a half," says Danny.

"Did he? And who did I tell?" I reply.

"Cheers, Gibbo," replies Nick, presuming I will.

"Alright. If we want a clean sheet I suppose I'm the man, then. But if I'm in goal today I'm going up front next week."

"You sound like a twelve-year-old, mate," says Nick.

"Christ, how can I play in goal with these gloves? They have holes in and one of the gloves is torn down one side."

Today we're playing Red Star Belowgrade, who are the top of the league. We have no pump so I go into their changing room to borrow one, and it looks so different to ours. There is no smell of fags, alcohol or shit; all their players are changed; it looks like they have all polished their boots; and I'd bet they all had a quiet night last night. They were probably wrapped up in bed at 10.30 with a hot chocolate whilst most of our team were on their way to some shoddy nightclub.

We finally head out of the changing room and spend the usual ten minutes trying to put up the nets which is harder than something on *The Krypton Factor*. It must be the only time Tom regrets being 6ft 4in; with him being the tallest lad it tends to fall on him to hook the net on to the crossbar and then tape the net to it. Today is made even harder as we hardly have any tape, which is making Tom's job more difficult and leads to a stream of expletives. Anton and Miles are trying to tape the net to the posts but are struggling as the net doesn't seem wide enough for the goal, and Danny is trying to bend our pegs back into shape so he can peg the back of the net.

Yet they are all giving one hundred percent, which they don't always do on the football field and if Danny had as much strength in his tackle as he does in bending back pegs he would be a better player.

"Fucking hard work that – thank God I'm a strong lad," he tells me. "Think it's my turn to be captain this week."

"And mine next week."

Danny wins the toss and for some reason he decides to swap ends.

"Mate, what you playing at? The sun will now be shining directly into my eyes first half."

"Yes, but we have the wind first half. Your kicks will seem quite long this half, which will make a nice change."

"Pity I won't be able to see the ball, though."

"Anyone got a hat for Gibbo for the sun?"

"Got my beanie hat again for you mate," replies Tom.

"He'd look like a dustman with that and his gloves with holes in," says Paddy.

"And with the rubbish I have at right-back in you, mate, it's probably quite appropriate."

Red Star Belowgrade kick-off and the first twenty minutes or so is pretty uneventful with no real chances for either team. Considering that we're missing quite a few players, and with their position in the league, we're playing well, with Jim and Miles combining well down the left-hand side. I barely touch the ball – I can barely see it – but finally do so when their left-winger cuts inside Paddy and shoots at goal. It should be a relatively comfortable save but I fumble it and push the ball round the post.

"Why didn't you just catch it?" queries Nick.

"Lost my bearings, mate."

Luckily the corner doesn't lead to a goal, mainly due to the fact that the chap who took it managed to kick the ball directly out of play behind the goal. But we aren't really creating much up front and just as I think that we will hold on until half-time they score when a deflected cross off Miles leaves me stranded and the ball hits the back of the net.

"Shit. We didn't deserve that," Jack tells me as I kick the ball back towards the centre circle.

"And a deflected goal at that."

We kick-off and within a minute we're level. A good move involving Jamie and Paul leads to Anton having the simple task of tapping the ball in from six yards with our first chance of the half. This breeds some confidence in the team and for the next ten or so minutes we have a couple of corners and Anton hits the bar with a cracking first-time volley from just outside the box.

Half-time comes just as they kick-off and we head towards our kit bag for some much-needed liquid refreshments. It has to be said we've had a good half and are playing well, with everyone getting stuck in and giving a hundred percent. Jamie is pretty much running the show for us with some fantastic passing and great tackling. He rarely plays for us but when he does he really stands out; it's a shame that his girlfriend lives in Newcastle as he tends to go and see her most weekends.

Sadly, according to his best mate Jim, the relationship is going strong so there's little chance of him being able to play more for us.

"Anyone fancy going in goal second half?" I ask tentatively.

"No thanks," reply virtually the whole team.

"Sod it. I'll do the second half. Anyway lads, we're playing well with Jamie winning most of the tackles in midfield. Let's get the ball out wide to Jim and Miles as they're causing all sorts of problems down the left side."

"I swear you must say the 'Get it out wide' line every week at half-time, Gibbo," says Miles.

"Let's just stay switched on and try not to get injured as we have no subs, which at least means we won't have the awkward decision to decide who to take off," says Nick, who seems happier playing with no substitutes.

"It wouldn't be an awkward decision today, mate," says Paddy. "I'll be knackered by seventy minutes but I'll just have to battle through."

"Good lad. You haven't been too shit today either," replies Miles, offering some words of encouragement.

The second half begins with constant pressure from Red Star Belowgrade although their forwards seem to be having an off day and most of their shots are going wide. A draw would be a good result for us and I'm taking my time – some would call it time-wasting – when fetching the ball and taking goal-kicks.

"Ref, he's time wasting – can't believe you're playing for a draw," shouts their centre-forward (who has an Afro that Tottenham's Benoit Assou-Ekotto would be proud of) as I walk off to collect another wayward shot from him.

"If you're so worried about the time you can go and fetch the ball. Or how about trying to hit the ball on target for a change?"

I take a goal-kick and slip just as I kick it which produces another chance for their centre-forward. Sure enough he manages to hit it wide and vents his frustration at me.

"You can't kick for toffee can you, mate?"

"Yes, mate, we make a good pair. I can't kick and you sure as hell can't shoot."

He is strong and fast and has a fantastic range of passes. However, he just can't seem to hit the target which he is finding increasingly exasperating. If he could, he would be some player, but he seems to panic just as he shoots. I'm not sure why as it doesn't take much to beat me in goal and with our defence being the slowest in the league he has enough time to pick a spot each time he is through on goal.

They continue to search for the winner and I pull off a couple of saves. One I didn't know much about, but the second was a good reflex save from a header from about six yards.

"Better than Gordon Banks in Mexico, that," I inform everyone.

"You just stuck your leg out and luckily the ball hit it," Paddy replies.

I'm soon called into action again when Paddy passes the ball to their left-winger, who is through on goal, but I manage to come out, narrow the angle and make the save.

"Sorry, Gibbo. Don't know what I was doing there, mate."

"No worries. Only five minutes to hold on before we can go for a pint. Think the winger was so surprised you passed it to him he fluffed his chance."

We find some energy from somewhere in the last five minutes and Jim and Anton both test their goalkeeper. Then, from a corner, Tom rises above their defenders to send a header crashing on to the bar and over. That would have been an excellent finish to the game but I can't really say we deserve to win. From the resultant goal-kick the referee blows the full-time whistle.

"Top performance, Calcio," Danny tells everyone as we stroll off the pitch.

"You're right, we really dug in. Any idea who we can make

Man of the Match?" Nick asks me and Danny as we enter the changing room.

"Got to be Jim, Jamie or Miles," replies Danny as I cough rather loudly.

"I could never vote for you, mate, even if you were Man of the Match," says Nick.

"Think it has to be Miles," I say. "He got stuck in, combined well with Jim and he has never been Man of the Match."

"Plus I could do with a lift home from him, and even though my flat is out of the way giving him Man of the Match could work in my favour," replies Nick, deciding his nomination on non-footballing reasons.

"Lads! Committee's decision for Man of the Match today is Miles," Nick tells the team.

"Cheers, mate, first one of the season," says the award-winner.

"Any chance of a lift home?"

"No worries, mate," says Miles, which brings a smile to Nick's face.

"Lads, their goal difference is minus thirty four"

My phone wakes me up at 8.00 Sunday morning and it can only mean that someone is dropping out of football today. None of my mates can understand how I can get up early on a Sunday and there's no chance of any of them being awake for them to call me.

"Matt, sorry mate, been up all night ill and feel like shit today," says Jim as I answer the phone.

"Was it a big night, then?"

"Yes, big night on the bog. Think I've got one of those twenty four-hour bugs."

"No worries, mate. We have eleven – let's just hope that no one gets injured."

We are playing away today so I head off down to Clapham to meet the rest of the lads.

"You look shit, mate," are Danny's kind words as I jump into his car.

"Cheers, mate. I didn't even have a huge night last night."

"How are we looking for numbers?"

"Got eleven. Jim pulled out this morning."

"He was on the piss last night then?"

"Pretty sure he wasn't. He did sound shit this morning on the phone and he was dying for a game today. Anyway, where's Anton?"

"He said he would be here in two minutes… ten minutes ago."

"Think club funds will have to get him an alarm clock. He's never on time," I reply just as Anton taps the passenger window.

"What was that, Gibbo?"

"Nothing, mate. Just saying that we have get the ball out to you quickly today as you played a blinder last game."

We reach the ground just as it starts to rain and from previous encounters the pitches here are pretty muddy at the best of times. I dread to think what they're like today.

We get changed and trot out on to the pitch and my preconceptions are confirmed as the pitch is a complete mudbath. The centre circle is under water and you can barely see the lines of the penalty box.

"This has to be the worst pitch I've ever played on and I've played on some shit holes in my time," Danny tells me while trying to rugby-tackle me in the centre circle.

"Tell me about it. Pitch is certainly a bit heavy and we will look even slower than normal today," I reply, oozing confidence.

"Lads, come round," says Nick. "Right, we can see the pitch is fucking awful so let's get the ball out wide straight away. I swear I saw at least a couple of blades of grass out on the wings."

"Let's get three points as well," says Danny. "We played well last week, and lads, Hottingham Topspur, who we are playing today, have a goal difference of minus thirty four. They haven't won all season and they sit bottom of the league by some distance," he adds, bringing a smile to everyone's face.

"Hottingham Topspur," shouts Miles. "Not surprised they're shit being named after Spurs. Do they have a cock, I mean cockerel, on their shirt as well?"

"Very funny, mate. They play good football like Spurs but are struggling a bit this season, again like Spurs have been recently," I reply.

"Isn't Hottingham Topspur how Ossie Ardiles pronounces Tottenham Hotspur?"

"It could be and whenever I hear one of their players shout out 'Come on you Spurs' during the game, I'm tempted to shout it out as well."

"It's probably the closest you get to playing for a Premiership team when we play them each season."

"Enough about Gibbo's infatuation with the other team. Let's not have the attitude that all we have to do is turn up and we will stuff Spurs," says Nick, bringing some realism to the game. "With the awful pitch we might have to grind out a result."

"We only have eleven today so everyone is guaranteed ninety minutes. Carl and Damo can't play today and I'm going up front with Jamie."

"But you're a defender, Gibbo, and a pretty ropey one at that," laughs Miles.

"Albeit a slow one who is prone to lapses of concentration," says Nick who in all honesty is probably telling the truth.

"I've had thirty minutes up front and scored one goal; if all goes to plan today I should bang in a hat-trick."

Hottingham Topspur are a good team and how they have not beaten any other team in our league is a mystery. They are also a good set of lads and play the game in the right spirit. They always win The Fair Play award the league gives out each year and if all teams were like them it would make the pain of getting out of bed each Sunday a lot easier. We have even, on occasion, gone for a couple of drinks with them at the pub afterwards.

The referee today is a bloke called Rich who we have had quite a few times over the years. We get on well with him. Before the game you are meant to give the referee your team-sheet, show him your first-aid kit and the match ball, otherwise you will get fined. With Rich refereeing we know we don't have to do any of this. He must be the only referee who has never fined us.

We were playing one league game and were losing 1-0 and he must have played about fifteen minutes of injury time to help us get the equaliser. In the end, though, he said he had to blow the whistle as he had a flight to catch. He reckoned he could have refereed all day and we wouldn't have scored.

"Happy days. It's Rich today, Gibbo," Danny tells me during the warm-up.

"I know, mate. A ref that likes us – it's like starting 1-0 up with him refereeing."

"Two-nil mate."

"Alright, Rich, how are you mate?" I say. "You haven't had the privilege of refereeing us all season."

'Alright Rich, how are you mate' – you two sound like best mates," says their captain, mimicking me as he comes up for the toss.

"Don't worry sunshine, he only knows me as I seem to book him every match," Rich tells their captain. He has never booked or sent any of us off in ten years of refereeing Calcio.

"You must have cost me fifty quid this season in fines," I reply, lying.

Hottingham Topspur kick-off and the first ten minutes or so is pretty awful stuff with the ball getting stuck in the mud and the wind disrupting both team's long-ball game. So much for us getting the ball on the deck and playing it out wide, and so much for Hottingham Topspur playing the Spurs way.

I have a half-chance when I manage to get round my marker by tugging his shirt, which Rich pretends he doesn't see, but then proceed to scuff my shot and the keeper makes a comfortable save. He then kicks the ball downfield and from just inside their half Danny kicks the ball on the full and sends it over their keeper's head into the top corner.

It is some goal and as much as I hate to say it, it is probably better than Tworty's on the first day of the season. If only someone else had scored the goal I would have run over and probably planted a smacker on their cheek. As it's Danny I can't bring myself to celebrate.

"We're never going to hear the end of this goal, are we?" Nick says to me as I trot back to the centre circle.

"Too right, mate. I'm denying that I saw it."

"See that Gibbo, pure class. You can't buy that mate. I should insure my right foot," Danny tells me, confirming my suspicions.

"Never saw the goal, mate. I was doing up my shoelaces. What happened?"

"Don't worry, mate. I'll talk you through it in fine detail after the game. I won't let you forget about the goal of the season."

Last season Danny scored a similar goal and he was unbearable for a week. In the afternoon following that game I received numerous text messages saying things like:-

'You can't buy that'

'Eat your heart out David Beckham'

'Best goal ever'

'You can't coach that'

'Thank God for Danny'

I have an awful feeling that this afternoon will be Groundhog Day.

They kick-off and rather than pushing on we seem to be playing rather lethargically and soon pay the price. Darren, at right-back, tries to play the ball to Pete to left-back but the ball gets easily cut out by their centre-forward who rounds Phil before tapping the ball into the empty net.

"Offside, ref," shouts Danny, but not even Rich can award this as he was a good ten yards onside.

"Fucking hell, lads," I call out.

"That was so Sunday league wasn't it?" Jamie replies.

"What the fuck was Darren thinking?"

"Not sure, mate, but don't think he meant to pass the ball to their centre-forward."

"If only we got service like that up front, eh."

It soon goes from bad to worse when a failed clearance from a corner leads them scoring their second. Rich looks at me as if to say there is no way he can disallow the goal.

"Concentrate, lads," bellows Nick as we prepare to kick-off.

"This is fucking shit. None of us is giving a hundred percent at the moment."

He is right: the whole team bar Miles is playing poorly. I'm struggling to get in the game, our midfield's passing is all over the place and our defence aren't picking up their forwards. Phil is doing his nut in goal and I will be surprised if he can talk in the second half, which will probably please our defenders. Rich blows his whistle for half-time which puts us out of our misery.

"This is fucking awful. I can't remember a time when we were this bad," Nick tells us all.

"Come on, lads, we should be thrashing this team," says Danny. "They haven't won all season and we're making them look good and they're making us look shit. We even have Rich fucking refereeing, it's like having twelve men, and he wants us to win as well. We're losing and we've got a bent ref on our side."

We head out for the second half determined to change things round and within a few minutes we are level. A good move leads to Nick hitting the bar from outside the box and Paul, following up, heads it into the net from an offside position.

"Offside, ref!" their centre-back shouts out.

"He was level, goal counts," says Rich, running back to the halfway line.

"We're getting no decisions ref," their centre-forward tells Rich just before he restarts the game. In all honesty he is probably right.

It is getting a bit embarrassing now with all the decisions that Rich is giving us. We're getting awarded free-kicks when they fairly tackled us, corners when it should be a goal-kick and every offside call is going in our favour. Hottingham Topspur are also a good set of lads, named after my favourite football team, which makes it feel even more wrong. I'm tempted to tell Rich to give a few dodgy decisions in their favour, but with the game delicately poised at 2-2 I decide against it.

We should make it 3-2 when Paul goes on a mazy run down

the left-hand side, beats two defenders and draws the goalie towards him.

"Paul!" I scream as I'm standing on the edge of the six-yard box with an empty net in front of me.

Paul ignores me and shoots at goal from an acute angle. The ball goes wide which pisses me off immensely.

"Why the fuck didn't you pass rather than try and do it all yourself?"

"Oh fuck off. I never heard or saw you and I think you were offside," he replies, not that it would make any difference if I was with Rich being the referee.

"Bullshit. I was screaming for it and had a simple tap-in, you selfish git."

Their keeper takes the goal-kick and I hope to God we don't pay for that but we soon do. Five minutes later an attack of ours breaks down and from a punt downfield their attacker, who is in acres of space, delicately strikes the ball past Phil. What makes it even worse is that Jack, who is meant to be centre-back, is up in their eighteen-yard box.

"What's Jack fucking playing at?" I ask Nick.

"God knows. Sometimes he thinks he is Franco Baresi and can dribble the ball out of the back and join the attack."

"Frank Carson, more like. He's forty five. There's no chance of him getting back and he's a defender."

We kick-off and for five minutes or so play some better football, Anton comes close and I hit the bar. We continue to pile on the pressure but a long kick from their goalkeeper is missed by all of our defence and their centre-forward runs on to score. Four-fucking-two to the bottom of the league, I think to myself. Times like this I do wonder why I get out of bed at the crack of dawn to play the 'beautiful game', although there has been nothing beautiful about this performance.

Rich eventually puts us out of our misery and I walk off the pitch pissed off with the team's performance, not to mention my own. There is no way the lads will let me play up front again, and to make matters worse my new boots seem to be letting in water. The only plus point is the fact that we lost to a team named after Tottenham Hotspur.

"Lads, that was fucking appalling," Danny tells everyone in the changing room. "We were an utter disgrace. I'm lost for words for a change, and just don't know what to say."

"We were fucking shit and one of our goals was blatantly offside," I say. "Sometimes I do wonder why I do this and lads, another thing today, no one was on time and it really pisses me off. Anton, you haven't been on time all fucking season."

"Bullshit, Gibbo. It's only been once maybe twice this season. Anyway, I was probably about the only one who tried today, so don't pick on me. You were fucking shit today, just because they are named after your beloved Spurs and wear a similar kit doesn't mean you aren't allowed to tackle them."

"Bullshit. You're late every week."

"And you're fucking shit every week."

"Jack, what you were doing today?" says Phil, joining in the post mortem. "For one of their goals you, our centre-back, was our furthest player forward. You are fucking centre-back."

"I'm fifteen years older than you. I couldn't get back from our corner quick enough,"

"We didn't even have a corner."

"Come on, lads, calm down," says Nick. "Let's not get personal. We win as a team and lose as a team. We were all shit today, but we can't just think that all we have to do is turn up and we will win against some teams. Sadly we aren't as good as that."

We all get dressed in near silence and head out to the car park and make our way home. Today is without doubt the first time I haven't enjoyed the game in the slightest. We were shit, didn't seem to try that hard and argued with each other both during and after the match. In hindsight I shouldn't have singled out Anton, and we do, as a team, get on really well and have good banter amongst ourselves most Sundays.

We very rarely argue with each other as it's obviously bad for team morale. However, last season we did have one unsavoury incident when me and Tom had to be pulled apart after we let in a goal, with him blaming me for the goal and with me blaming him. No fists were thrown but I felt I let the team down afterwards and in hindsight we were both lucky not to get sent off. We did settle our differences after the game and apologised to the team, but it should never have happened. I'm still convinced the goal conceded was Tom's fault, though.

Real Calcio have been going for a long time and we are a bunch of mates first and foremost. This is how it has always been from the moment Nick set up the team with some of his work colleagues. Damo and I then joined the company – hence the team – and we were quickly joined by Danny, who I met in Australia. The rest of the team are made up of our mates, mates of mates and, in Tom's and my case, our brothers.

One chap who played for us a few years ago was one of our best players but he was always having a go at our players on the pitch and also gave the referees and other teams unnecessary stick. Despite the fact that he was an excellent player we had no hesitation in telling him mid-season that we didn't want him to play for us anymore. This probably cost us points in the league but the fact that he disrupted the changing room and had become a right wanker made it an easy decision for us.

What happened today should never happen and I hope I don't have to experience a changing room like that after a game again.

.

"He had trials for a few clubs when he was younger"

To: Calcio squad
From: Nick

Lads,
A bit of a shambles last game, giving Hottingham Topspur with their minus thirty four goal difference their first win of the season. No Man of the Match, I'm afraid. We were all shit and I hope everyone made the most of the free weekend and went for a run, like I nearly did.

We have the chance to get back on track and keep ourselves out of the relegation zone on Sunday against that famous name in football Richmond Common Eileen. It's a 9.45 meet at our home ground, so please let me know as soon as possible if you can play or not.

Thanks
Nick

To: Nick, Danny, Gibbo
From: Damo

What the f★★k went wrong last game? Looks like I was badly missed.

To: Nick, Danny, Damo
From: Gibbo

Mate, we were awful. Pitch didn't help but our defenders couldn't defend and we had nothing up front which was surprising as I was playing up front yesterday. Got to be one of the worse ever Calcio performances and we have had a few in our time. What made it even worse was that Danny apparently scored a blinding goal although I never saw it as I was doing up my shoelaces. We also had Rich refereeing!

To: Nick, Damo, Gibbo
From: Danny

You could have been doing up your shoelaces all game mate you were that useful yesterday. Damo, before you ask I will give you a lowdown of my goal. Their keeper punts the ball down field and from just inside their half, yes you heard me right just inside their half, I volley the ball first time back over his head and into the top corner. Their keeper must have been pushing seven foot which makes the goal even more remarkable. Sometimes I amaze myself.

You will be pleased to hear I can play Sunday so that's probably another cracker scored then! Have I scored an average goal this season, I think not.

Goal one – outside of the right foot from edge of box into top corner.

Goal two – chest and volley from outside area, what an execution.

Goal three – powerful finish from outside the area, the keeper never saw it.

Goal four – first-time volley to lob their eight-foot keeper, only a genius would think of catching the keeper off-guard and only the likes of me and maybe Messi could score that. Well, in hindsight I think young Lionel might struggle.

Genius is a word too often used as is the phrase 'world-class'. Now I'm not saying I am there quite yet but I am definitely knocking on the door.

To: Nick, Danny, Damo
From: Gibbo

What a painful email to read. Surprised it took you until 9.20 to tell Damo about your goal.

To: Nick, Danny, Gibbo
From: Damo

He did leave a detailed message on my answerphone yesterday describing the goal, though the keeper seems to get taller every time I hear the story.

To: Gibbo, Danny, Damo
From: Nick

OK, credit where credit is due, your goal was slightly above average yesterday but your fitness is certainly way below average.

To: Nick, Damo, Gibbo
From: Danny

Is that all you can come back with? I was all over the pitch on Sunday and besides the first five yards is in your brain, I've got to be the hottest property in Sunday league football this season.

To: Nick, Danny, Damo
From: Gibbo

If you are so fit how come you are carrying about nineteen stone then?

To: Nick, Danny, Gibbo
From: Damo

To be fair to Danny he's always all over the pitch!!
Goals record:
Danny played 12(?) scored 4
Damo played 7 scored 6 or 7 (I begin to lose count this time of year)
Gibbo played? Scored three (all two-yarders)
Nick played 12 scored... oh well
The facts don't lie.

To: Gibbo, Danny, Damo
From: Nick

I scored one and an important one at that as it was

against second in the table. Have also hit the bar a couple of times; one time I hit the bar the person who followed up managed to hit the ball over the bar from a yard. Who would have been inept enough to do that then eh, Gibbo?

As per the norm by Thursday we are struggling for numbers until an email enters my inbox from Damo.

To: Nick, Danny, Gibbo
From: Damo

Lads got an email from a lad today through my website www.play4ateam.com and he is up for playing Sunday morning football. Apparently he used to play to county level and had a few trials for some professional clubs when he was younger, though he did say he is lacking some fitness. Shall I get him along?

To: Damo, Danny, Gibbo
From: Nick

He will fit in well then (the unfit bit, not playing for the county).

To: Nick, Danny, Gibbo
From: Damo

He can't be any more injury-prone than Nick, slower than Danny, older than Pete, worse at shooting than Gibbo and I doubt he is as handsome as me.

To: Damo, Danny, Nick
From: Gibbo

Had trials before, a bit unfit now, this bloke could be fifty for all we know. Has Smithy's mate resurfaced again?

To: Gibbo, Danny, Nick
From: Damo

No pretty sure he isn't. I am going to get him down on Sunday and we can see how good or unfit he is. With him we are now up to twelve.

I arrive at the ground on Sunday and Damo is already there.

"No sign of Pele then yet, Damo?" I ask him as I enter the changing room.

"Not yet, but he said he would be here for about 10.00. He sounded good on the phone."

"How can someone sound good on the phone?"

"Not sure. He just did; he had an air of confidence about him. Trust me, Gibbo."

"Did he also sound like someone who isn't the most punctual?"

"Good one. It's the first time he's playing. We'll let him off."

"Phil, did Damo tell you that we've got a new star player today donning the famous Calcio shirt," I ask as he trudges into the changing room. "Apparently he used to be a pro."

"I never said that. He used to play for the county and he had trials for a few clubs when he was younger."

"Mate, I had a few trials for clubs as well when I was younger, too."

"Mate, trials for professional clubs, I should've said."

"I can't remember if I had a trial for Celtic," says Phil. "Actually,

I think I might have just missed out on that one. If I had who knows what would have happened to me, I doubt I would be playing with you doughnuts every week, that's for sure."

The rest of the boys arrive and there is still no sign of Pele.

"Lads, just want to let you know that we have a new star player playing for us today, don't we, Damo?" I tell them.

"Where is he then?" replies an intrigued Paddy.

"Think he's coming now," I say as I stick my head out the changing room door.

"I knew he'd come," replies Damo.

"Only joking, mate. It's 10.15. Let's face facts: this bloke isn't turning up, is he?"

"Looks like it's eleven again today, boys," Danny tells everyone as we get changed and head out to the pitch. "No injuries then, lads, and make sure the little energy we all have lasts ninety minutes."

"Are this Eileen team we've got today useful?" Paddy asks me as we stroll out.

"Richmond Common Eileen are second in the league, mate. Could be quite useful."

"Great. Can't fucking wait to get started then?"

"By the way I'm centre midfield today," I add. "Nick's away, and after last week's performance up front, Danny and Damo have banned me from there for the rest of the season."

"After today you will probably be banned from centre midfield as well, mate."

"Thanks for the vote of confidence."

Danny runs through the team as I go up for the toss and win it. Well I say win it, the other captain called heads and it came up tails so in a roundabout sort of way I do.

Today's referee is recently qualified and the league secretary called me in the week and told me that we were to go easy on him as they didn't want to lose him, especially as there are a shortage of referees in the league at the moment. He also told me that he wanted to give him a game between two teams who are a nice set of lads, so the fact that he gave the referee our game is a compliment I suppose.

He does seem nervous, though. When he tossed the coin his hands were shaking but then again that could have been down to the cold or the fact that he had a big night on the booze last night and therefore has the shakes this morning.

We have enjoyed some good battles with Richmond Common Eileen over the years and they are all in all a good set of lads. They have the full set of Sunday-morning footballers — an overweight lad, a tattooed lad, a skinhead, a lad with dreadlocks, a lad with about five earrings, a lad with bleached hair, a lad the size of a second-row rugby player, a mouthy lad, a bald lad and someone who thinks he is the best Sunday football player in London as he has won the golden boot the past two years.

We kick-off and start pretty well. We're getting the ball out wide to Anton and Miles who seem to have the legs on their full-backs, which makes a nice change. Paul has an early chance which he puts over the bar and I have a shot from outside the box which just skims the post. What makes it even more remarkable was that it was with my left foot. Normality is soon restored, however, when a good free-kick from Danny results in me heading the ball over from about six yards.

Our promising start is soon shattered when a good through-ball dissects Tom and Pete. Their centre-forward, the one who thinks he is the best Sunday footballer in London, calmly strokes the ball past Phil, perhaps therefore proving he is. He celebrates like Eric Cantona used to; he stands still, lifts his shirt collar up and barely raises a smile, but then again I suppose being the self-appointed best Sunday footballer in London he scores every week, so there's nothing that much to celebrate.

The contrast is very different to whenever I score. A big grin comes across my face; I hug or even kiss any team mates near me;

and then I spend the next day going on about it even if it was a goal from two yards that came off my backside (which to my mates outside the team tend to get described as a twenty-yard curler into the top corner). Luckily for my team-mates I don't score many goals. The only other person they dread scoring more than me is Danny.

"Come on midfield, you have to pick up these runners and track back." Tom shouts in the direction of Danny and I.

"Think Tom is talking to you, mate." I tell Danny as we trot back to the centre circle, from just outside the centre circle; Tom was right.

"Let's push for a second now. Come on Eileen," their centre-forward shouts out as we prepare to kick-off.

"Toora loora toora loo rye aye," Danny whispers to me which gives me the giggles.

Anton spots me laughing. "Gibbo, we are fucking losing 1-0. Why are you looking so happy?" In all fairness he has a point.

"Come on, Gibbo, get in the game mate. Stop pissing about, you Dexys Midnight Runners fan," says Danny, the cheeky sod.

They soon nearly have a second but Phil pulls off a great save. We immediately take the ball down the other end of the pitch and Miles comes close from a good cross from Anton. The game is pretty much end to end and the referee, who is having a good first game, finally brings the half to an end just after Tom sends a header over the bar from the corner.

"Heads up, lads. We can get back into this. We're showing some Calcio passion which makes a nice change," Danny tells us as we take some much-needed water.

"Yes, we're doing well," I respond, looking to instil some confidence into the lads. "Eileen are second in the league and we're matching them out there. We just have to take our chances. Yes, I know I missed a sitter, before anyone says anything. There are big gaps between their centre- and full-backs and if we can try and exploit those I think we are in with a chance."

"Is anyone carrying an injury… Paddy, you must be due one?"

"Hamstring is feeling tight but I'll struggle on seeing as we have no subs — unless Pele has turned up, eh Damo."

The second half starts really well with everyone giving a hundred percent and a good through-ball from Miles puts Damo through, who in turn lobs the goalkeeper to draw us level. We continue to press and Anton and Miles both come close with half-chances before our pressure finally counts when an aimless hoof downfield from Paddy ends up at the feet of Paul, who goes round his marker and beats the goalkeeper at his near post to give us the lead.

Having taken the lead we all seem to think we can score and rather than sitting tight and keeping the score at 2-1 to secure a win against a decent team, we all think we can win the game 4-1 or 5-1. This leads to our formation becoming just Tom in defence, a four-man midfield and five up front. Soon enough, a big kick from their keeper ends up at their winger's feet who has about six team-mates he can cross to, Tom being the sole Real Calcio player in our penalty box. The inevitable happens and their centre midfielder, who seems to have a new tattoo every time we play them, buries the ball into the back of the net. Cue a lot of expletives from Tom and Phil's mouths directed at the nine of us attackers.

We decide to go back to our normal formation in fear of Tom and actually come close to a winner through Paul but their keeper, who must be the first I have seen with full-length dreadlocks, makes a fine fingertip save. They also have a couple of chances and Phil pulls off two cracking saves both from the so-called best Sunday footballer to keep the score at 2-2.

"Good performance, lads," declares Danny as he enters the changing room.

"We played well," replies Tom, "but when we went into a 2-1 lead why the fuck did everyone suddenly decide they were going to play centre-forward? It's the sort of thing that happens in my school playground with the ten-year-olds I teach. I don't understand the logic. If we're losing we should push up and try and equalise, but if we are winning we should consolidate. I give up with half of you. No, make that all of you."

"Chin up, Tom," I say. "Apart those five minutes everyone played well and gave one hundred percent today. It will be hard to pick a Man of the Match but that new ex-county player was great today, eh Damo."

"Piss off, Gibbo. You should be glad he wasn't, mate, as it would have been you that got subbed for him."

"Cheers, mate. Let us know if you hear back from him anyway. It's not as if a football pitch off a main road is hard to find. Anyway I better go as I've got a christening this afternoon."

Today was such a nice contrast from last week when the team was arguing with each other. On days like today I love playing Sunday football. We had some good banter in the changing room before the game and everyone got stuck in. Richmond Common Eileen are no mugs either, being second in the league, but I like to think we gave them a good game.

However, we still have the same problem of getting enough players on a Sunday. I would be happy with just one substitute each week to run the line and come on for the last twenty minutes, most of our opponents have two so it's not as if I'm asking for much.

With our team getting older compared to most other sides, and more injury-prone too, we really do need substitutes each week. I'm shattered halfway through the second half most weeks; trying to keep up with people ten years younger than me after a night out on the booze is really hard in the latter part of the second half. In all honesty it's actually pretty difficult from the beginning of the match as well.

I suppose in theory I could have quiet Saturday nights in for a change but I'm young(ish), free and single and live in London so there is no danger of that happening. Anyway, as already mentioned, we as a team have tried staying in on Saturday nights and we have lost the following day. To be honest I wasn't too bothered about losing as it meant that the 'staying in the night before a game would work wonders for your game' theory wasn't true.

Which means I can get drunk Saturday night without an ounce of guilt.

"He hasn't played football since primary school"

"Damo, how many have we got for Sunday?" I call and ask on Friday.

"Not many, nine at the moment, and I also forgot to tell the lads on the email that it's a 9.45 start on Sunday."

"Great, so Nick is away and your only job all week is to get eleven players and send the email out and you've failed with both of those, then?"

"Could be down to eight as well as Jack's missus is about to drop any moment."

"Hope she can hold on. Surely if he tells her the current situation she can hold off till at least Sunday afternoon."

"Don't think it quite works like that. I'll send an email out to say it's a 9.45 start and see if anyone knows anyone who fancies a game Sunday."

"I look forward to the huge interest, 9.45 start as well. You need to prepare a good sales pitch, mate. You said you were looking to get into recruitment and this could be an acid test to see if you're up for it."

I have no luck convincing any of my mates to play on Sunday but luckily Damo calls to say he has turned up trumps.

"Gibbo, I think recruitment could be the career for me. I've got eleven players."

"Well done, mate. Who have you got?"

"Anton can now play and Tom's mate Gio can play, and so can his other brother Leonard."

"Good on you. Gio is alright. What about Leonard, is he the next Pele like the bloke you brought along last week?"

"Very funny. He is more of a Jonny Wilkinson. You see he's a rugby player and he hasn't played football since primary school, but most people who can play rugby can play football."

"You've sold him well, mate. Anyway I don't care; we have eleven now."

"Tom also said he was really fit."

"Where does he play?"

"Flanker, mate."

"Whatever. Anyway, see you tomorrow bright and early."

Danny meets Damo and I at Clapham Junction and we make our way to Roehampton for the game. I nearly faint when I walk in the changing room and see everyone there.

"Fuck me, I can't believe it. Early kick-off away from home and everyone is here. Is everyone feeling OK?"

"I know," says Pete. "Can't believe I'm here on time. If I'd known it would only take me twenty minutes I wouldn't be here."

"So you're early by default then?"

"You could say that, I suppose."

We are playing Red Star Belowgrade for the third time this season, and having lost one and drawn one, surely it's our turn to win today. We head out to the pitch a good ten minutes before kick-off thinking we are professional but Red Star are already out and look to be midway through a mini training session. They are wearing bibs, there are training cones and poles out and it looks like they have a manager and a coach.

"Have you seen them?" Pete asks me. "They're only playing us, for God's sake."

"I know and we have one bloke playing who hasn't played football in donkey's years."

In all the years I've played Sunday football I don't think I've seen a team with a manager and a coach. If you asked most of the lads in our team they would say we had neither. When I see other teams warm up it bugs me that we don't make more of an effort. Jack, Danny and I are all UEFA-qualified coaches but we have never conducted a session, which is a disgrace; fourteen odd years and pretty much no training sessions. Danny and Jack are at the moment seeing how many headers they can head to each other before the ball hits the ground, and Jack has his mobile phone in the one hand and a cigarette in the other. He reckons he coached Jack Wilshere in his youth but I just can't quite picture him telling Jack how to make the killer pass with a fag in his mouth and his mobile ringing in his pocket.

Phil has the rest of team taking three penalties each against him and I'm tempted to tell everybody that we should perhaps have a decent warm-up. However, as I approach him he throws me the ball and the thought of me scoring a hat-trick against him is too good to turn down. I actually manage to get three out of three, much to his annoyance. I then take a few against Damo and manage to miss the lot.

"Either Phil's shit or I'm superb mate," Damo shouts out to both of us.

"Just giving Gibbo a chance. After all it's been some time since he has scored."

"And that's not just on the pitch."

"Actually seen this bird a few times over the last couple of weeks," I reply. "But she texted me yesterday saying I wasn't creative enough for her. I mean, what does she want me to do, draw her a picture or make her a dress whilst singing her a song?"

"Reckon she must've seen you on the football pitch as I've never seen you creative on one before either, mate."

"So predictable, mate. Anyway, also been seeing this tasty blonde who seems a nice girl although she has a daughter which makes it hard to see her as much as I would like."

"How old is she?"

"Thirty five."

"Thirty five? How old is the bird you're dating then? She must be seventy-odd. Christ, Gibbo, that is sick, I know you like an older lady, but seventy…"

"*She* is thirty five, not the daughter. Anyway, I'm surprised you're playing today because the game is away and it's also a team from the top half, and we know you only usually play against teams in the bottom half and at home."

"Only reason I am is because I stayed up in town last night as Amelia had a work event and they put us up in a five-star hotel for the night."

We have a quick team talk and introduce Gio and Leonard to the rest of the boys just as thunder appears and a torrential downpour starts.

"Glad you're playing now, Damo?" I say.

"Why the fuck did I leave my five-star hotel and breakfast in bed with the Sunday papers, which was going to be followed by a jacuzzi and steam room? It's now pissing down, I'm cold and I'm soaked through."

"For the love of the game."

"Big game this, lads, and they're going well, so no silly mistakes and no injuries as we only have eleven today," Danny tells the team, every one of whom has his head pointing downwards probably wishing he was still in bed.

"Today? It's been every week this year," says Pete.

"I know, mate. I don't know what's happening. People's other halves seem to be dropping kids, people are constantly injured, away on holiday and Smithy is forever away with work in Vegas."

"Away with work in Vegas," says Tom, sounding jealous. "Smithy always makes it sound such an ordeal as well. Flies out first class, stays at a five-star hotel, all expenses paid with meals at lovely restaurants and I imagine he spends his spare time either gambling or chucking twenty dollar notes down some bird's bra in one of the lap dancing joints."

"It sounds better than my work trip last week which was a two-day conference in Hull," says Damo. "I stayed in a ropey hotel that had dirty pillows, the couple in the room next door were at it all night and the birds at the strip club were all over forty and fat. I was paying them money to keep their clothes on by the end of the night."

Our non-productive warm-up, which now consists of us sheltering under a tree with just Leonard stretching, comes to an end. The referee blows his whistle to signify the toss and I amble up to the centre circle. Their captain is the guy who couldn't shoot straight last time, who I took the piss out of, and after he wins the toss he virtually breaks my hand shaking it. The referee tells us not to question any of his decisions and that he will make the odd mistake but not as many as we will, which is probably true. He also tells us that bad language will not be tolerated, so it could work out an expensive Sunday morning for us as well.

I look at their team and they all look up for it: no one is fooling around or worried about the rain; they are all busy stretching or jumping up and down to keep warm. I turn around with dread to see us and sure enough, half the team are still under the tree and the other half are either by the goal smashing the ball at Phil or behind the goal collecting the balls they have hit too wide or high.

However, we actually start off brightly and for someone who is used to the sport of egg-chasing, Leonard is doing OK. Well, he hasn't picked the ball up or rugby-tackled anyone. The wind and rain, though, is playing havoc with both teams' passing and the ball seems to spend a lot of time off the pitch, which is no bad thing as it gives us several frequent thirty-second breaks to catch our breath back. The game is pretty much being played in our half but we seem to be doing well containing them and Phil easily saves any shots that are coming in.

After twenty minutes or so we squander our first real chance when Paul, after a good run, blazes the ball over from just outside the box. We soon get a free-kick from a similar position and despite my efforts to take it, Danny decides it's his.

"Mate, I saw Ronaldo's in the week and I'm pretty sure I know how he scored it."

"Yes, so am I. He put it in the top corner and the keeper didn't move."

Danny takes the free-kick and hits it straight at the keeper, but just as I'm about to turn and berate him the keeper lets the ball slide out his hands. It bobbles out to Anton who has the easy task of tapping it in.

"It was the swerve that got him, Gibbo."

"Swerve? I'd put it down to the keeper making a right fuck-up, mate, due the rain."

"How did you not catch that?" their defender shouts to the keeper, which pleases me.

"Think he agrees with me Danny."

They kick-off and shortly afterwards a fair fifty-fifty between Tom and their centre midfield player leaves their player injured and unable to continue. It was one of those tackles where both players didn't duck out and both put their full body weight into the tackle. Most normal people would probably duck out of it – well I certainly would – and I imagine their player now wishes he had. To his credit he doesn't complain, which is surprising as he spent most of the last game we played them moaning, as he hobbles off and is substituted. He was beginning to run the show, so in all honesty, I wasn't too upset to see him leave the field.

"See that, mate, the bloke I was marking has left the field after half an hour mate," Danny tells me. "He couldn't cope with me bossing the centre of midfield."

"Yes right, mate. He must be gutted because he was having a field day in the centre of the park you couldn't get anywhere near him. I'm surprised he didn't continue. I mean, even with one leg he'd still be able to cause you all sorts of problems."

The replacement for him turns out to be quite useful and continues to run circles round Danny but their forwards, as per last time, seem to be having an off day and we reach half-time still winning. We also have the added bonus of that the rain has stopped.

"Cracking half that, lads, and Leonard, for someone who hasn't played football you are having a blinder, mate," says Danny.

"Only been close to picking up the ball and running with it once," he replies.

"Defence also looks solid, and Miles, you are having a field day on their right-back. Let's just not switch off and I reckon we can bang in a second as I'm pretty sure their keeper isn't a keeper."

We head out and I'm not sure what they had in their half-time cup of tea but our goal is besieged in the first ten minutes and only a few good saves from Phil and some wayward finishing from them keeps the score in our favour. After ten minutes Phil pulls off one of the best saves I've seen this season when he somehow dives full stretch and manages to flick the ball over the crossbar.

With their lack of luck Red Star are becoming increasingly frustrated with themselves, us and the referee. They are beginning to leave their feet in when tackling us and are also constantly pulling our shirts, although the referee doesn't seem to be doing anything about it.

Just when we think we can hold on for the win we eventually let in a goal when a cross from the left eludes our defence and their winger has the simple task of tapping the ball in the net. It was definitely coming but we soon pick up our tempo and Gio and Miles both come close to scoring. The game is end to end and it looks like we can hold out for a draw until Damo fouls their centre-forward in the box and the referee points to the spot.

"Never a penalty, ref," Damo shouts to the referee, pleading his innocence.

"You took away the striker's legs. Clear penalty."

"I have to be honest and that was pretty much as clear as they can be," Danny says to me as their player hobbles off the pitch in pain.

"And we were looking as though we could hold out for a draw."

Our negative thoughts though soon disappear when their player manages to send the spot-kick high over the bar and into orbit. This has the added bonus of another minute or so of rest as the ball won't be coming back quickly, especially as Phil seems to be walking very slowly to collect it. In the last five minutes we continue to defend like Trojans and manage to hold out for the draw in what has been a cracking performance from us.

"Man of the Match will be tough to decide today," Danny says as he and I head towards the changing room.

"It certainly won't be you, mate."

"Nor you. Has to be Phil, Miles or Tom."

We get changed and the referee pops in to say that he enjoyed the game. In all fairness he had a fantastic game and like he said before the game he made fewer mistakes than both the teams. He let the game flow and didn't blow his whistle unless he had to; he also booked no one and had the respect of both teams. In the changing room he goes through a couple of decisions he made and wishes us luck for the rest of the season. At this point Phil bursts into the changing room and doesn't see the referee.

"Just seen the referee wish the other team all the best for the season. Can't believe he's so pally with them. I mean, he's the ref for God's sake. Not surprised he wasn't awarding us free-kicks in the second half for their constant fouling."

"And I would like to wish you all the best for the season as well," says the referee much to Phil's embarrassment and our amusement.

"I'm only joking, ref. I knew you were in our changing room."

We all get changed and I grab a lift home from Danny.

"That was a cracking performance, Gibbo. Two good games in a row, which has to be a first."

"I know. Like last week we all got stuck in and really played for each other. I just wish it was like that every week."

"Thought Leo did alright for a rugby player and that save Phil made was out of this world."

"Not that I would tell him, but he must save us a fair few points over the season."

"To make up for the points you and Jack lose us at the back."

"Cheers, mate. But I bet you were glad when their centre midfielder came off. He did look as though he was bossing the midfield."

"I was pleased for about a minute until I realised that his replacement was decent and pretty much left off where the other one ended."

"Running rings round you."

"Yes mate, could say that I suppose. Even if I did manage to boss the midfield there isn't a chance that you would appreciate the fact is there?"

"You're right there, mate, and I imagine if I ever bossed the defence, which I agree is more infrequent as the years go by, you would never acknowledge the fact. And if I scored a hat-trick you would somehow find an argument that the goals were nothing to do with me."

"I know, mate. My missus doesn't understand the fact that you, me, Nick and Damo are really good mates but we can never admit to each other that one of us played really well."

"In fairness, mate, I don't think there have been many games when one of us has."

"What about my goal, I mean goals this season. Two or was it three from in my own half and another one from the outside of my right foot. I had no congratulations from you three for any of them. I know I won't get goal of the season despite the fact that I should get the top three. The first goal from inside my own half is better than anything I have seen in the Premiership this season."

"You can drop me off here, mate."

"But we haven't reached your flat yet."

"I know but I need to go to Sainsbury's, and I feel that I am about to get an in-depth description of your goal again so I want to get out."

"The thought of playing centre midfield with you drives me to drink"

This week's game is Carl's last before he heads back to New Zealand and I can't say we will miss his goals because he hasn't scored all season. However, he is one of the longest-serving members of the team and if it wasn't the fact that every girl he falls for either lives in Sweden or Denmark he would have played a lot more for us.

"Carl, seeing as it's your last game in the famous dodgy faded green Calcio shirt we have decided to make you captain on Sunday," I tell him over the phone on Thursday night.

"Mate, I'm made up. I mean, just thinking of the famous captains we've had in the past i.e. you, Danny, Damo and Nick, makes me a proud man," he replies, taking the piss.

"Cheeky git. One thing, just get there on time on Sunday so you can give a rousing team talk in front of the lads."

"Anyway, who are we playing?"

"Hottingham Topspur, named after the greatest team in the world. They're bottom of the league and have a minus thirty goal difference. It was more than that a few weeks ago but they then beat us."

"Don't worry, mate, I fancy myself to add to my tally of zero goals this season and if their defence is like Spurs' I'm pretty confident I will."

"Yeah, I mean you must be full of confidence with that total."

"Are they a good set of lads? Could do with playing against a nice set of lads in my last game."

"Of course they are. The other week especially so, considering we had Rich refereeing who might as well have been wearing a green shirt."

"The lads tell me you might as well have been wearing a white shirt that game you were so shit."

"I might take the captaincy back if you aren't careful."

I arrive at the ground at 9.50 on Sunday and as usual I'm the first to arrive. Damo, however, assures me that this week the chap who logged on to to his website is definitely turning up and sends me a text to say to look out for him. I text back saying that I have no idea what he looks like and he replies saying nor does he but for me to just look out for someone who looks like a Sunday league footballer. I'm not sure what the stereotypical Sunday league footballer looks like; after all, we have fat, thin, lanky, short arses, bald guys and people with dreadlocks all playing for us this season.

The rest of the team arrive in ones and twos apart from Carl, who is still nowhere to be seen in his last-ever appearance. I decide to give him a ring.

"Mate, where are you?"

"Sorry, mate," he replies just as Damo comes in the changing room with the chap who signed up through his website. "Been up all night on the piss, I mean preparing my captain's speech. Literally just round the corner mate."

"Lads, this is Mark."

"Heard a lot about you, mate. Apparently you used to be an ex-pro," I tell him.

"Our hopes rest on your shoulders, mate," adds Paddy.

"Ignore them," says Damo. "They're just worried that they'll lose their place to you."

"You haven't seen me play yet."

"You can't be worse than most of this team, mate, trust me."

"Big night on the piss ref, straight from a late-night bar to come here?" I ask the referee – who has arrived late and bleary-eyed – as I make my way outside the changing room trying to spot Carl.

"Could say that. Give me five minutes and I'll be ready. You boys got eleven today?"

"Thirteen, mate."

"Christ, don't think I've ever reffed a game with you boys before when you have actually had subs."

"Better late than never eh, captain," I tell Carl as he finally arrives.

"Sorry lads. Public transport, alarm not going off, too many beers last night and all that."

"Mate, we are all waiting for your Winston Churchill-style speech for your last-ever game."

"Anyway what are this Spurs team like? I hear they're bottom of the league but we got turned over by them a couple of weeks ago."

"Mate, their defence is hard to break down. I was up front that game and even I didn't score."

"With their minus thirty goal difference and position at the foot of the table it does sound as though they're hard to break down."

We head on to the pitch and our pre-match warm-up consists of the whole team trying to put up the net, which doesn't seem to be big enough. The referee blows his whistle and the two captains go to the centre circle for the flick of the coin.

"Carl, what about your pre-match captain's speech?" shouts Jim.

"Shit, lads let's put in one hundred percent today. It's my last game and I know it's been a few weeks since I last played, but if we score more than we let in I'm pretty sure we will win today. I mean it's Spurs after all."

"Thanks for that rousing speech, mate," says Del. "Anything on tactics or how we should play the game?"

"Tactics? That would be a first for us. Just stick to the tactic I just mentioned i.e. scoring more than we let in. We can't fail with that one, mate."

Carl wins the toss and we start with Mark on the bench with

Del, who has been out raving all night, as per usual. I dread to think what kind of substances are in his body at the moment. The game starts off quite well and after about five minutes a shot by Damo rebounds back to Carl who manages to miss the target completely from about twelve yards with the keeper nowhere to be seen, bringing him an avalanche of abuse from us all.

"When are you off, Carl?"

"Thank God it's your last game."

"Think it has been three years since you actually scored."

"What happened to the Carl of last year?"

"Hang on, he was shit then as well. Make that the Carl of three years ago."

"Sorry, lads. The magnitude of the occasion got to me."

We continue to play quite well and keep the ball on the deck rather than just hoofing the ball up front. However, the longer the game goes without us scoring the more I think that we will screw up and end up losing. Phil is having a relatively quiet morning in goal and we are creating a fair few chances, but Damo and Carl appear to have left their shooting boots at home as they can't seem to hit the target.

"So much for us going out on a high for Carl's last game," I say to Danny as one of their players receives attention for an injury.

"Tell me about it. I'm creating a fair few chances with some sublime passing but there's no one on the end to put the ball in the fucking onion bag."

Phil is finally called into action and does well to save when a Spurs corner ends up on the head of their centre-forward. This is the last activity of the half as the referee blows his whistle as Phil punts downfield.

"The goal will come," says Danny. "We're playing decent football but can't seem to put the ball in the back of the net, eh Carl and Damo."

"Yeah, have to admit my final game isn't going quite as I planned it, but there is still time for me to finish with a hat-trick."

"You taking bets on that, mate?" I say. "Could do with some easy money."

"Don't want to take your money, Gibbo."

"Danny you forgot to fill up the water bottles," Jim tells him as he finds five empty bottles in the kit bag. "I'm dehydrated and dying of thirst."

"Sorry, I forgot, though you shouldn't be out on the piss the night before a game."

"I have to go on the piss the night before," retaliates Jim. "The thought of playing centre midfield with you drives me to drink."

"Come on, lads. Let's keep switched on and get a goodbye victory for Carl," Damo tells us as we jog out for the second half.

We really should be winning the game and if it wasn't the fact it was Carl's last game I would be a lot more pissed off, especially as no one, myself included, seems to be taking the game at all seriously. You would think that as the years go by we would become more professional in our approach and that people would arrive on time, we would warm up together and that during the week we wouldn't have a battle to get eleven players out on the pitch. Yet as the seasons have gone on, the more unprofessional we've become.

Hottingham Topspur are a good set of lads, but in truth they're pretty hopeless, so God knows what that makes us. Three or four years ago we would be beating them 3-0 or 4-0 at half-time without breaking sweat. Their goalkeeper can't seem to catch the ball and can barely kick it out of his own half; their defence just hoof the ball upfield whenever they get it; and if their hoof finds one of their players it's a bonus. Their midfield can barely string an accurate forward pass to their strikers, who are slow and look more like prop forwards rather than centre-forwards.

The second half gets underway and we soon pay the price for not taking our chances in the first half. Tom fouls their centre-forward in our box and the referee points to the spot.

"Never a penalty, ref. I played the ball."

"But you got the man first I'm afraid," replies the referee, which is a fair point.

Phil gets close to the penalty but not close enough as their centre-forward buries the ball in the bottom corner.

"Why do we always concede just after half-time?" Danny asks me.

"Don't know, mate. Perhaps the fact that we never have any water in the water bottles at half-time could be a factor."

"So all the goals we concede just after half-time – that's down to me forgetting to fill up the bottles most weeks then?"

"Yep."

"Come on you Spurs, lets have another," yells one of their supporters from the touchline.

"Look at you – as soon as he said that you looked so happy," sneers Danny. "You're playing for Real Calcio and we've just let in the first goal. I swear anytime anyone mentions Spurs a big smile comes to your face."

"Sorry mate," I respond, knowing he is probably correct. "But 'Come on you Spurs' is the start of the Chas 'n' Dave song and I'm almost tempted to start singing it."

"You are thirty-odd, not fucking ten. Now switch on and let's get back in this game."

For the next fifteen minutes we have most of the possession, but like the first half we can't hit the back of the net. Carl has definitely forgotten his shooting boots today as he sends shots into the playground, bushes and he also nearly hits Pete's wife with one effort that ends up closer to the corner flag than the goal.

However, following a free-kick from Danny, we finally get our equaliser when Anton flicks the ball across goal and I have the easy job of tapping the ball into the net from all of two yards.

"You nearly missed that, Gibbo. I swear you sliced that," Damo says to me as we walk back to the centre circle.

"They all count, mate. It's just that I wasn't sure if I wanted to score against Spurs. Anyway, that's me up to four goals this season, second top scorer now – not bad for a centre-back."

"Four goals and I would say the total yardage for them can't be any more than ten."

"All about right place, right time, mate. You can't teach that. You should count your lucky stars that I've scored, mate, as we could be playing all day and there would be no danger of you and Carl scoring."

My joy though is short-lived. Five minutes later a shot from their centre-forward takes a deflection off me, wrong-footing Phil, and the ball ends up in the net.

"That's you back down to three goals then," says Damo.

"Piss off, Damo. I couldn't help that, mate."

"Getting out the way of the ball would have helped no end."

"At least I can now say I have scored for Spurs."

The referee tells us we have ten minutes left, but we don't look like scoring and increasing Hottingham Topspur's minus thirty goal difference. The situation becomes even worse in the last minute when their slow, fat right-back goes on a mazy run from just inside our half and scores with a shot that bobbles along the ground and slips under Phil's body.

Everyone in the team is speechless for a change trying to comprehend how this fat, slow non-footballer somehow danced past half our team and put the ball in the net. Nothing about him points to the fact that he is a footballer yet somehow he has just made us look completely ridiculous.

"That was probably the most embarrassing one minute of my footballing career," says Danny. "That bloke is so shit it defies belief, yet he has just gone and taken the piss out of us and danced round half our team. I'll need something stronger than beer in the pub."

"It was like a slow-motion replay," I reply, "but it was actually real as the bloke is that slow, if that makes sense."

Luckily the referee finally calls a halt to our embarrassment. The league's bottom team have collected their second win of the season, both of which were against us.

"How can we draw with the two top teams of the league and lose twice to this lot?" Jim tells me as we head off the pitch. "I swear half our team just thought they could just fucking turn up and we'd win easily."

"No, it wasn't the best performance, was it? They must love playing us."

Phil continues the theme in the dressing room. "Lads, that was fucking awful. We should all be really pissed off with ourselves, especially with the last goal which will probably give me cold sweats for years to come. But enough about that: let's all get down the pub to give Carl a good send-off. After his performance I'm not too disappointed he's off, eh Carl."

"I didn't really go out in glory today, I have to admit," says the temporary skipper.

"No shit, mate," says Phil. "Let's try and get a centre-forward who can score goals now."

"I've banged in a few this season," says Damo getting all defensive.

"Lads," says Carl, having his final say. "Remember about four years ago, when we needed to win away against the team that were third to win the league and I banged in a hat-trick?"

"Yeah, I remember that game, Carl," says Damo. "It was the last one you scored in, mate. That was when you were fit, fast and a goalscoring threat, mate."

"Anyway, lads," I say. "As a leaving gift for Carl, can everyone sign this shirt?"

"You sure we have enough shirts, Gibbo?"

"It's the number fifteen shirt, Damo. There's no danger of anyone wearing that shirt as I don't think we've ever had three subs before."

We all sign the shirt with remarks such as:

'We will miss our centre-forward who hasn't scored all season.'

'A centre-back's dream, a striker who can't hit a cow's arse with a banjo.'

'I have enjoyed seeing you get progressively worse every season.'

'You can't even score against Spurs.'

'To Carl's mates back home who read this – he is really shit at football; all the statements on the shirt are true; don't believe anything he tells you.'

We end up having a big day at the pub and spend ages trying to remember the last time Carl scored. We also discuss the ropey bird he pulled in Amsterdam and whether he slept with her (which he still denies), why he doesn't play rugby like most Kiwis, and the fact that although he's had a shocker of a season we will miss him – albeit in the pub more than on the pitch.

"They only had nine, though"

We have a free weekend after our awful performance against Hottingham Topspur and I have to admit I enjoy it. I have a big Saturday night knowing that I don't have to get up in the morning, a lovely lie-in and a greasy full English breakfast from my favourite dodgy cafe with the Sunday papers. I then watch the lunchtime game on TV and finally meet some mates for a nice, late, long Sunday lunch.

This makes a pleasant change from my usual Sunday mornings of waking up before it's even light, cycling in the rain to football, filling in the team-sheet whilst taking phone calls from members of the team saying that they are running late, putting the nets up and then spending the next ninety minutes getting shouted out by Tom.

I go for a few drinks with Nick in the week and we are now seriously considering making this our last season. We're constantly struggling for numbers week after week and seem to spend all day Saturday chasing people up and trying to convince ringers the joys of playing for us the following morning. This, coupled with the fact that the team is getting older and progressively worse, all seems to point to the fact that this should be our last season.

There are certain parts of playing Sunday football I enjoy, however, such as the banter in the changing room before and after the game and the joy of scoring. OK, I admit that I don't get loads of goals but I still always get a buzz whether it be a sliced tap-in from two yards or a thirty-yard volley (although I can't remember the last time I scored one of those; not sure if I ever have). It also gets us fit, though judging by the amount of running we do it can't get us too fit.

The pub after the game is always good fun with us all taking the piss out of each other. Last Sunday, for instance, was a great afternoon. The Monday-morning hangover was awful, but it was well worth it. The end-of-season tours are always very enjoyable, too, with the weekend we had in Amsterdam two years ago probably the funniest I've ever had.

As mentioned a couple of years ago we somehow reached the Cup Final, which was probably the best football match I've ever played in. We played at a proper stadium with a stand and floodlights, my mates were there to watch, we had more than enough players, proper linesmen, a decent referee, and a flat pitch with grass on. To top it all off, we won, which ended up with a huge piss-up. The only downside was that Paddy scored the winner.

We do, however, have to do some serious thinking to do; to work out whether the positives outweigh the negatives. We can still go out on the piss and go abroad if we don't play football – but would it be the same as we were no longer all playing football together?

The phone call I get from Nick on Friday certainly leans towards the idea of making this the last season.

"Mate, only got eight for Sunday against Rupert, Tarquin, Sebastian and the rest of Juvictorious, the poshest team in football. This is becoming a fucking joke now. I can't be arsed to constantly chase people. Any ideas, mate?"

"Don't know really. See if Damo and Danny can get any ringers. I'm off to Madrid in a minute and can't really help I'm afraid."

As I'm away this weekend I have to admit I'm not too arsed about whether we get eleven players and perhaps this is a sign that my heart isn't in it as much as it was in previous years. We don't have anything to play for as we should just about escape relegation and there's no chance of us getting promoted, so it won't be the end of the world if we don't have eleven. I leave for Madrid and have a big weekend drinking, seeing the sights and watching Real Madrid play.

It is only on the journey back to my flat from Gatwick that I think about the lads and how they got on so I ring Nick.

"*Hola* mate, did we get eleven for today?"

"No, mate, we got ten, though that was two more than we had on Saturday evening despite the fact that I spent pretty much the whole day on the phone trying to get players."

"How did we get on then? I fear the worst."

"We won 2-1."

"With ten men?"

"But they only had nine, though. There must have been some posh society event that most of their team had to go to."

"So we aren't the only team to struggle with numbers then."

"In all honesty, though, we were shit. We scored the winner in the last minute, or should I say they scored the winner for us with an own goal."

"Why, what happened?"

"Don't know, mate. It just seemed that half the team couldn't be arsed today. I mean, the team we played were awful and had nine men, yet we created hardly any chances."

"How did you play, mate?"

"How most people play after spending the last ten days on the piss in New Zealand."

"You were awful, then?"

"Yes."

"How did Danny play?"

"He was very creative today. He set up two goals, one for us with a good through-ball to Anton, who scored, and one for them when his cross-field pass in his own penalty box was blocked by their centre-forward who scored."

"Sounds like I missed a classic then."

"How was Madrid?"

"Great, mate. I saw Real Madrid play. Ronaldo was on fire."

"We could do with a Ronaldo or eleven in our team."

I dread to think how Nick would have sounded if we had lost. He seemed down in the dumps having won and victories are pretty rare for us this season. However, spending all Saturday on the phone trying to get players isn't enjoyable and it isn't helped by people not returning your calls and texts. Most weeks Nick and I will ask teammates to see if they can get some of their mates to play and I'm pretty sure that despite them saying they will have a ring round, they never actually do.

You also begin to look stupid phoning the same people most weeks seeing if they fancy playing. Half my mates don't understand why I persevere with it. But folding the club after all these years would be a hard thing to do. As much as this season is becoming a hassle each week, if we fold the club and quit that's the end of Real Calcio. Surely it can't come to this.

"This weekend Richmond, next week Hollywood"

My alarm clock wakes me up at 8.30 and the thought of getting out of bed to play football isn't a great one. It is not helped by my quiet few drinks last night turning in to a big session in the pub. I also have a bad cold and I could quite easily turn the alarm off and sleep another six hours. However, we only have eleven men and I can't let the lads down so I crawl out of bed, chuck on some clothes and head to Clapham Junction.

"Big night on the piss then, Gibbo?" is Nick's greeting.

"You could say that. It isn't helped by me having the 'flu all last week."

"How bad is the cold?"

"It's 'flu, severe man 'flu."

"You're such a bird."

"I could really do with going in goal today. Can't believe I've just said that, but the thought of running round for ninety minutes scares me."

"Bad luck, mate. Jack has done his back in and can't run and has already asked to go in goal."

"Can't believe that. The one day I actually want to go in goal, I can't."

"Cheer up, mate," says Nick. "I fancy a win today. We have quite a good team today, which makes a nice change."

"Good. You sound a lot chirpier this week than when I spoke to you after we won the other week. I dread to think what you would have been like if we'd lost."

"I know. It just got to me the other week. Getting ten players was a fucking hassle and then half the players just couldn't be arsed. Today is a different week and with the team we have, we should put in a good performance."

Most of the team soon turn up, including Chris, who despite the fact that he is injured and lives in east London, has driven here to help ferry some of the lads to the ground in Richmond.

"Have you had a big row with the missus, mate?"

"Why do you say that?"

"It's just the fact that you have driven all the way here at the crack of the dawn on a Sunday and you can't even play."

"It's for the love of Calcio, mate."

"Good on you, mate."

"Do you know where their ground is anyway?"

"Somewhere in the Richmond area, I think. Just waiting for a few lads to get their essential journey reading and pre-match meal from Sainsbury's and we can leave."

We eventually head off towards Richmond with people eating Mars bars, crisps, pasties and sausage sandwiches, which I'm sure no professional player would ever dream of having an hour prior to kick-off, before meeting the rest of the team at the ground. The ground we're playing at today is probably the worst in the league. The changing rooms are always filthy and full of sweet-wrappers, empty beer cans, fag butts and copies of yesterday's *Sun*. I'm pretty sure they're cleaned only once a week, so the only people guaranteed a semi-clean changing room have to play half an hour after the cleaner leaves.

The showers, if they can be described as that, are disgusting. I refuse to shower in them now as a couple of years ago I picked up verrucas on one foot, cut my other foot on some glass and due to the fact that the bloke next to me was washing his boots in the shower, I came out dirtier than I was before I entered.

The toilets are foul with a leaking urinal. Last year Jim had the misfortune of needing a dump before the game and came out the cubicle a different colour to what he went in. Half the toilets have no seats and if you find one with paper you have done well. As Jim likes his pre-match dump, whenever we play here he makes sure he takes Imodium beforehand.

"Lads, hope everyone is feeling one hundred percent," Nick tells us in the changing room. "Because you guessed, it we have no subs as per usual."

"My back is pretty screwed and I can barely move, so be careful on the back-passes today, lads," says Jack. The others follow suit.

"I'm 'flued up."

"Pulled groin."

"Tight hamstring."

"Hung-over."

"Dodgy calf."

"Fucking hell, lads," I say. "It sounds like a doctor's surgery and we haven't even started yet. Think positive, lads. We can beat this lot; we should've won a few weeks ago and let's put on a performance for our fans."

"Fans?" a few of the team shout out.

"Well, when I say fans we have Pete's wife and kid, Chris and Danny who are both injured, and Matty, which by my reckoning is the biggest away support we've had all season."

"Can't believe your wife and son still come and watch us, Pete," says Damo.

"I wouldn't say they come and watch the football. Nine times out of ten she has no idea of the score when we've finished."

"Probably no bad thing, that."

"The toilets are as foul as ever," says a pale-looking Chris as he enters the changing room.

"Just go by the pitch, mate," advises Danny. "I've bought some bog paper if anyone has nature calling."

"We don't want people dumping by the side of the pitch, mate," says Jack.

"Well perhaps make sure you're at least ten metres back."

When Matty mentioned he was coming to watch us today I was a bit surprised until I found out that a girl he met a couple of weeks ago lives round the corner and he was meeting her for lunch.

Having any kind of support is a bonus. Most of my mates keep promising to come down and watch but never seem to, and to be honest judging on how well I've been playing this season I'm not upset about it. I can't say I would get up before it's even light on a Sunday in the pissing rain to watch my mates play Sunday football. Can't say I would even if it was twenty five degrees and sunny either.

My mum and dad have been down occasionally to watch me, but not this season. Mum says she prefers watching Jim on a Saturday as there is less swearing and the standard is better. Thanks, Mum. Last time Dad came down he spent the whole journey home telling me that ever since I turned eighteen I have slowly deteriorated over the years and I might as well pack it in. He also said that Jim was a much better player than me.

We head out on to the pitch and I notice that the referee is actually warming up which I haven't seen before. He firstly jogs with high knees across the pitch and then with his ankles up. After doing this a few times he then starts running backwards before finally turning and sprinting ten metres. He then stretches before finishing with keepy-uppy and he must have got to at least fifty before the ball touched the ground. I am tempted to go over to him and see if he fancies swapping his pristine black referee's top for a faded green Real Calcio top next week. He would certainly be the quickest man in our team.

The referee blows his whistle and I jog up to the centre circle and shake his and the Richmond Common Eileen captain's hand.

"Some warm-up, that, ref. Ours was literally walking from the changing room to the pitch."

"Well I have heard that your defenders basically hoof it

downfield whenever they get it and bypass the midfield. So I have to be fit to keep up with the play."

"Cheers, ref. I'm usually centre-back, so that's a small dig at me, but you're probably right."

Our opponents, who we drew with a month ago, are currently hovering around mid-table and today seem to have four substitutes, which is virtually unheard of in our league. I have a look round their team and spot the tattooed lad, the keeper with dreadlocks and the self-appointed best Sunday morning football player who is that good he is still playing in this division.

We start really well and within the first minute Damo has a good chance, with their keeper doing well to turn the ball round the post. However, from the resultant corner Damo flicks the ball in from a tight angle to give us the perfect start.

"Good goal, mate," I tell Damo. "What a start! Champagne football, this is."

"Champagne football? Hold your horses, mate. We've only been playing a minute and you know it won't last."

"Probably true, mate."

Champagne football is probably a bit over the top, but we continue to pass the ball around well and Anton is beating his man every time down the left wing. Damo and Jamie soon both come close and I send a header over from a corner.

Jack, playing in goal, hasn't touched the ball in the first twenty minutes but he is soon woken up and embarrassed when a hopeful punt from their blue-haired winger, his hair is a different colour every time we play them, sails over Jack's head and into the net.

"He'll blame his dodgy back for that," I tell Jim.

"What was he doing? Typical of us this season: just when it looks like we're about to increase our advantage we go and shoot ourselves in the foot and concede."

To our credit we continue to look for a second goal and are still playing some nice football, with Jack again having little to do in goal, which is no bad thing. Anton comes close to scoring and soon after sends over a lovely cross to Nick who tries his luck with a bicycle-kick, which he executes completely wrong and has me in stitches of laughter. He barely touches the ball and ends up in a heap on the floor with the ball rolling slowly towards the corner flag.

"Close that, Nick," I tell him between laughs. "Close to the fucking corner flag."

"The execution wasn't the best I have to admit."

"No shit, mate. The technique wasn't the best either."

"Don't think there was a technique, and I seem to have hurt my back."

"You should be bossing it today, mate. The bloke you're marking must be about fifty."

"He's quite useful, though."

The lad, or should that be old gentleman, Nick is marking has grey hair (what's left of it), is overweight and really slow. When I'm fifty there is no chance I will be playing Sunday-morning football; I will be happy enough just to be alive. Nevertheless, he's playing well and always seems to have time on the ball, spreading it round the pitch really well. In all fairness he is probably showing Nick up a bit.

For the next ten minutes our free-flowing football of earlier in the half is a distant memory as the ball seems to spend more time off the pitch than on it. There is an allotment over the fence next to the side of the pitch and the ball seems to spend a lot of time in there. I'm not too unhappy about this as last night is beginning to catch up on me, and I'm not in the opposition's good books when I thump the ball in there when I could have just tapped the ball out of play. However, I'm running on juice and the ensuing three-minute breather does me the world of good.

The bloke I'm marking today, who wasn't playing in our previous game, must be at least 6ft 6in. I have marked him a few times over the years and although he looks good – I was very apprehensive the first time I marked him – he is actually pretty shit. For someone so tall he is rubbish in the air and he also seems to be slower than me, which is a welcome bonus. The only reason he is probably in the team is that he can hold the ball up quite well and he is also the brother-in-law of the bloke who runs the team.

Half-time comes and some much-needed liquid refreshment. Danny comes over and gives the half-time team talk.

"Lads, despite not having the midfield maestro playing today we are doing well. We battered them in the first twenty minutes and the only reason they are back in this is due to a fluke of a goal. We can't lose to a team who has someone with blue hair, a man who must have a hundred tattoos, a granddad and a basketball player."

"Come on, boys," says Pete. "Let's start the second half like we did the first and get the ball on the deck and out to the wings. Simple passes, boys. The last fifteen minutes or so some of us were trying the Hollywood pass."

"Do you want to talk us through your bicycle-kick, Nick?" asks Anton. "It was the most immobile bicycle-kick I have ever seen."

"You will have the trades descriptions people on to you calling it a bicycle kick," says Jim, adding in a bid to boost his confidence: "But Nick, have to admit you aren't looking as screwed as you usually do at half-time."

"The bloke I'm marking being fifty helps. He does about the same amount of running Danny does most weeks. It's also nice having Paul, a box-to-box central midfielder, playing alongside me rather than Danny, the so-called midfield maestro."

"Paul, you're having a blinder in centre midfield," says Paddy. "Keep it up, mate, and you'll nail the position as yours."

"I agree," says Danny. "Nick might have to step aside next week when I return."

We head back out to the pitch, and rather than starting the second half like we did the first we start it like we do most second halves. A ball from their evergreen centre midfield player does Jim for pace and their blue-haired winger bursts into the box before Jack hacks him down. The referee points to the spot.

"He has to go, ref," their beanpole of a centre-forward shouts and he has a point as Jack was the last man.

"I wasn't the last man, ref," pleads Jack, and as I turn back to the goal I see Pete on the line. He must have run there after the foul was given.

The referee, to our surprise, produces only a yellow card which annoys their centre-forward.

"They had a man on the line," the referee tells him while pointing to Pete.

"Never knew you were there when I brought him down, Pete," says Jack.

"I wasn't. I was ten yards behind the centre-forward."

"Ref's had a mare, then. Not surprised the centre-forward is pissed off."

Our joy is short lived though as the blue-haired winger strikes the ball into the net and we are losing 2-1 despite the fact that we've dominated the match.

We apply more pressure and from a corner I somehow send a header wide from about six yards.

"How the fuck did you miss that?" Damo asks me.

"I wish I could answer that, mate. Can't even think of any bullshit excuses."

"Because there aren't any."

Yet we are soon back on level terms. Damo plays Paul in from out wide and he beats two players before scoring from a tight angle.

"Come on, lads, concentrate."

"Keep switched on."

"Big ten minutes, boys."

We continue to press and Damo, Paul and Anton all come close to giving us a deserved lead. We get another corner and rather than

Jim taking it, Damo decides to and sends in an awful corner which doesn't clear their first defender, who slices it out for another corner.

"Damo, why the fuck are you taking the corners?" I shout. "Let Jim take them. You're one of the few people who can head the ball, and besides, that was a shocking corner."

Damo ignores me and takes the second corner. To his credit he sends over a beauty and I rise from the penalty spot and send a header crashing against the bar and over the top.

"That's why I take them, Gibbo. I put them on a sixpence and you still miss."

Jim nearly scores with a good shot from outside the area. But within minutes, a goal-kick from their keeper is flicked on by one of their midfield players and their overweight striker buries the ball in the back of the net from outside the area.

"Fucking hell! How did that happen?" says Tom. "Losing 3-2 now to a team we should be beating 4-0."

"How much longer, ref?"

"Two minutes."

"Right, I'm going up front then," I tell Tom.

There's still time for a through-ball from Paul to put Damo through on goal and he lobs the keeper, the ball slowly creeping over the goal line for the equaliser. I chase the ball after Damo has lifted it over the keeper and do my best to try and touch it in order to claim my fifth goal of the season and pull one away from Anton and Danny. Sadly I can't and just end up a heap in the back of the net.

"I can't believe you tried to steal my goal."

"Too right, mate. Each for one and one for all and all that."

No sooner have Richmond Common Eileen kicked off than the referee blows the final whistle and the game ends in a 3-3 draw.

"I can't believe we didn't win that," Danny tells me as we head to the changing room.

"Nor can I, but I'd have settled for a draw with two minutes to go."

Matty soon strolls over to us. "Gibbo, last night you were telling me you were the best player in Sunday football at heading the ball," he says. "But even I could have scored those two missed headers today, mate."

"He is full of it, mate," says Damo. "Him and his heading ability, rising like a salmon and all the other shit he comes out with."

"Tell me about it, Damo," says Matty. "No point rising like a salmon if he can't hit the target. And how fucking slow is he these days?"

"Cheers, lads. I won't be inviting you down again, Matty. Anyway, the first five yards is in the head."

As we approach the changing room a couple of blokes with cameras make their way towards us.

"Excuse me lads but we're from Lucozade. Would you mind if we took some photos of you for a potential advert?"

"I thought my modelling days were over," says Damo.

"They never started, mate," I reply.

Tom, tucking in his shirt and tidying his hair, joins us. "Feel free to fire away, mate," he says. "Are you just taking photos of us?"

"Sadly not," replies one of the guys. "We've spent the last few weekends taking photos of Sunday league players from all over London and next week we are going to come up with a shortlist of eleven for the TV advert we're doing."

"How much do we get if we're selected?" asks Danny.

"Look at you," says Jim, injecting a dose of reality. "What chance have you got of being selected? I'm amazed someone as ugly as you only has one face."

"You get one hundred pounds plus some free kit."

"Is the hundred quid negotiable?" enquires Damo.

"No."

"That's OK. One hundred will be fine."

"Why, don't you get out of bed for less than ten grand then, Damo?" says Tom.

"Correct, although I make an exception on Sunday mornings."

We all pose for our shots and try and look as good as we can for the camera, which is hard considering we are all filthy and sweaty. After our five minutes of fame the photographers go and find some better-looking lads as we head inside.

Since it is Mothering Sunday the pub is out of the question this week. Jim and I get changed and head back to our parents' via a petrol station to get her some dodgy flowers and a card.

"What lovely flowers," she tells us politely.

"Well, you know, only the best for you, Mum."

"Well, the best you can get for under a tenner anyway," adds Jim.

We enjoy a lovely roast which, despite it being Mothering Sunday, Mum has cooked. The day is topped off when Dad, for the first time since I was at school, agrees to clean our football boots while Jim and I drink his lovely French wine. He soon regrets this when he realises I haven't cleaned the boots all season and that we've drunk his favourite bottle of red as he was hard at work cleaning or boots.

On the way back to London the thought occurs to me that I can really stitch up someone from the team and convince them that they have been chosen for the advert.

Damo is the person that immediately springs to mind as he stitched me up in January last year. At my work Christmas party at around 2.00am a few of us ended up in Cheers bar (we're really classy) and ironically enough I met a girl from Boston called Sarah, who was classy as well. After failing to convince her of the benefits of coming back to my hotel for a coffee (I can't say I blame her as I could barely stand, let alone communicate), I got her number and we left separately.

The following day I flew on holiday for two weeks and arrived back on Christmas Day. During the afternoon I received a text saying: 'Great to meet you at Cheers bar hope your holiday was good honey, let's catch up soon love Sarah xx.'

The text put a smile on myself and certainly brightened up the Queen's speech I was watching. I also realised that I must have taken down the wrong number when I met her as I had another number in my phone for her. This didn't surprise me considering the state I was in and I deleted the other number I had for her.

I didn't want to come across too keen so I waited all of two minutes before texting her back saying it was great to meet her, and we continued to send texts to each other throughout the next few days and agreed to meet on the Friday.

On the Wednesday I tried to call her but it went straight through to her voicemail, but she soon texted back suggesting a pub to meet in. The following night I played football and a few of us, including Damo, went to the pub for a few drinks. While I was in the pub Sarah rang and we finalised the plans for Friday. One thing that struck me was that she didn't sound that American but she seemed nice enough on the phone. After putting the phone down I realised that perhaps I should have suggested 7.30 as I was in a meeting out of London on Friday afternoon. So I rang her back.

I dialled the number in my phone and just as I rang the phone, a phone from Damo's bag rang. I then stopped ringing her and sure enough Damo's phone stopped ringing. I now realised that the lovely Sarah was in fact Damo, and we looked at one another and burst into laughter. The little swine had just acquired a work phone and it was him that was sending me all the texts. He had no idea I had met someone at my work Christmas do called Sarah and just thought he'd send a text from a girl who ironically enough he called Sarah. The girl that rang in the pub was the barmaid, who was in on the prank and had rung from out the back.

Needless to say, I was the butt of most of the team's jokes for a week or so. Damo had no hesitation in showing the lads all the texts I'd sent him over the previous week. It also resulted in me not contacting the real Sarah as I had deleted her actual number from my phone when I received the first text.

Anyway, this was my chance to get Damo back, so on Monday at work I begin to set about my plan.

"Rich, you don't fancy helping me stitch up my mate, do you?" I ask him on Monday at work.

"Course not, mate."

"To cut a long story short, can you call my mate Damo from your phone and say that you're from Lucozade, and that he's been selected for the advert and has to meet at Richmond Common at 9.00 on Sunday morning."

"No worries, mate."

Rich calls Damo and I can hear the excitement from his voice as Rich tells him he has been selected. It takes all of ten seconds before Damo rings me on my mobile.

"Mate, I may be in my mid-thirties but I still have it. Lucozade have chosen me to be in their advert. The bloke there said my photos came out really well and I definitely have the face for TV, unlike you with your face for radio. He also said that only eleven out of around two thousand people were chosen, so don't hold your breath, Gibbo."

"The bloke said you were chosen from two thousand people?" I reply looking at Rich, who said no such thing.

"Might even have been three thousand, I can't remember."

"Anyway, Damo, they must think I have the look as they also chose me. Some bloke called Rich called me earlier."

"Shit, can't believe he called you as well."

"Glad you are happy for me, mate, me and my so-called face for radio."

"I suppose they have to make it realistic. I mean, most teams have the odd ugly bloke in."

"Nine o'clock Sunday then."

"Yes, I might just call Rich back in a minute and see what I have to wear."

I come off the phone and me and Rich are laughing to

ourselves. I tell Rich to change his mobile answer machine and say he is Rich from Lucozade in case Damo tries to ring. Sure enough a minute or so later he calls Rich, who lets it ring through to his voicemail. I soon get another call from Damo.

"Mate, just called that Rich bloke and good thing is that he is definitely from Lucozade as it went through to his voicemail. At least it's not one of Danny's wind-ups."

"Good news, that. Anyway, mate, see you Sunday."

Rich rings back an excited Damo and tells him what to bring on Sunday and within two minutes I have an email in my inbox from Damo.

To: Real Calcio
From: Damo

Just to let you know lads that this Sunday could be the start of a new career in TV for me as I have been selected for the advert. Apparently they took over four thousand photos and no one came close to being as photogenic as me.

This weekend Richmond, next week Hollywood…

Laters

Upon reading this I realise that it is now four thousand, at this rate it will be one hundred thousand by Friday. At least he is happy I think to myself.

To: Real Calcio
From: Nick

Mate it can't have been done on looks as Gibbo has also been selected.

To: Real Calcio
From: Miles

Kept that quiet Damo eh about Gibbo being selected! Anyway I wish you both the best in your new careers; it can't go any worse than your footballing careers.

"Mate, I'm taking this seriously, I've turned down going to watch Man United play and a night on the piss afterwards," Damo tells me over the phone on Friday.

"Blind me, mate, it's only one hundred pounds," I reply feeling a bit guilty as he has turned down going to see his beloved United.

"Yes, but this one hundred pounds could lead to me earning thousands more in weeks and months to come."

"Don't run before you can walk, mate."

I hang up and am tempted to let him come all the way from Brighton on Sunday morning to Richmond for no reason. But on Saturday the guilt gets to me and I give him a ring.

"Mate, something to tell you."

"What?"

"Your TV career is over before it's started."

"What do you mean?"

"Well, you know that nice lad Rich from Lucozade? He's actually Rich from my work."

"You bastard! And I turned down going to see Man United today."

"Sorry, Sarah."

"OK, you've got your own back now. One-all, you git. You've shattered my dream of going to Hollywood."

"You can still go on holiday there and get a photo of yourself next to that Hollywood sign. After all, that's the closest you'll ever get."

"I've never seen the opposition clap before"

Today we're playing away on Tooting Common which is both a good and a bad thing. The pitches are close to my flat which means I can cycle there and the changing rooms have the best showers in the league. They are semi-powerful, warm and each team has its own set of showers. This is virtually unheard of in Sunday football; with most showers at the grounds the water barely trickles out and they are either too hot or too cold. The only people that tend to use them are the people who clean their boots in them.

The showers at some grounds can't really be described as showers – like the ones we encountered in Richmond the other week – and some don't even have showers. At these grounds I make sure as little skin as possible is showing; I wear gloves, make sure my socks are pulled up high and I always wear a long pair of shorts.

While the showers resemble the kind that wouldn't be out of place in a fancy health club, the pitches, although flat, are usually covered in too many stones. Half our warm-up, if we have one, is spent chucking the stones off our pitch into the bushes.

As usual I'm the first to arrive and am almost tempted to have a shower before the game, they are that good, but decide against it. Phil is the next to turn up and enters the changing room singing 'Flower of Scotland'.

"We stuffed your boys yesterday," he says, curtailing his flat rendition of the song.

"I wouldn't say you stuffed us, mate. It was a last-minute goal by one of the young lads you had up front – who I'm sure wasn't Scottish."

Every year on his birthday Phil organises a Scotland versus the Rest of the World fixture which is basically Scotland v England with the odd Irishman thrown in such as Damo, Hugh and Paddy. Yesterday Scotland actually won the annual game for the first time in about ten years although the bloke who scored Scotland's winner was about as Scottish as Paddy. When asked at the end of the game where he came from in Scotland, Phil shouted out "Fife" and the lad followed it up with saying he was down for the weekend in the worst attempt at a Scottish accent I have ever heard.

Jack comes in. "Phil, have you got that Geordie lad signed up for Calcio today?" he enquires.

"Geordie lad?"

"Yes, that Geordie who scored for Scotland yesterday."

"OK, I confess. He was actually from Carlisle but that's pretty much Scotland. Most of you English think England ends at the Watford Gap anyway."

Miles interrupts. "Sorry to change the subject but didn't our opponents today stuff us 4-0 earlier this season?"

"No, it was five," recalls Phil. "They had two really quick forwards who gave Gibbo and Jack the run-around most of the game."

"Shit, they did as well, Phil," says Jack. "Just what I need with my dodgy back and lack of sleep."

"Big night on the piss, then?"

"You could say that. The little one wasn't sleeping well last night."

"How times have changed."

"Tell me about it."

"Where's Hugh?" Danny asks me. "He's meant to be playing today."

"Think he's the only one not here. Let me try and call his mobile."

"He hasn't got one – the only bloke I know over twenty without a mobile phone and he must be mid-thirties."

"He has, mate. He got one this week although I think work forced him to get it and are paying for it. Let me try it."

"Bet it goes straight to answer machine?"

"Yes, you're right," I reply just as he enters the changing room. "The bloke might as well not have one."

"Gibbo just tried to call you," shouts Miles.

"Yes, lads, I finally have a mobile phone."

"Turn it on then. It does help."

"I've left it home."

"It's a mobile fucking phone. Does the word 'mobile' trigger anything, like the fact you can bring the phone with you so we can contact you?"

"Perhaps I should've done, but in all honesty I hate them."

"I bet it's switched off, lying next to your landline?"

"Could well be, Miles."

We get changed, pick the team and decide to start with Mark on the bench.

"Listen up lads," I say. "This team is pretty useful and we're having a slight change of formation. We're playing five in midfield, with Nick sitting in front of the back four, with Danny and Paul just in front and then Miles and Anton on the wings, but supporting Damo as much as possible in attack. When Miles has the ball on the left, I want you, Anton, moving more central and supporting Damo."

"Fuck me, Gibbo," scoffs Danny. "Been reading your UEFA books? We can barely master the basic 4-4-2, let alone this Christmas-tree formation. Also think you named twelve then."

"Whatever, Danny. Anyway, it's not the Christmas tree formation; that is when…"

"Whatever, mate. Let's just get out there get warmed up and score more than them."

The referee then pops his head round our dressing room door. "Excuse me, lads, but it's 10.30 and by this time the game should be starting. I should have also had your match-sheet, seen your first-aid kit and your linesman should have presented himself to me."

This referee is a complete stickler for everything. With the four points he mentioned that pretty much means a forty-quid fine. I'm sure this referee gets a cut of the fines he gets the league as he must bring the league thousands each year. I even got a bollocking last year for not having tucked in my shirt into my shorts, and I'm sure there's no law against that.

He is also guaranteed to book a few players. Any expletive results in a booking and if you direct it at him you will be sent off. Last year he managed to book seven players in our team and my brother mentioned to him at the end of the game that putting through seven bookings would be a lot of work for him and would cost us forty-odd pounds. He therefore suggested paying him twenty pounds in cash and he would forget about the bookings. To me this looks a win-win situation for both parties; we save ourselves twenty quid and the referee saves himself loads of paperwork and gets twenty pounds to go on top of his thirty five-pound match fee. Fifty five pounds – not bad for ninety minutes' work.

Unfortunately the referee didn't see it like that. When Jim mentioned this to him he got booked, and as he had already been cautioned it meant he was effectively sent off. So instead of the intended outcome of money being saved we got Jim sent off, which is another fine, and also received a letter from the league in the week fining us for trying to bribe the referee. That Sunday pretty much cost us a hundred pounds.

"Ref, we're leaving now," I explain. "I've got the team sheet and first-aid kit here. Please don't fine us."

"We will see about that. Now get out there," he replies as he exits the changing room.

"He sounds like my old English teacher and he was a right wanker as well," says Phil. "I mean, who does he think he is? He is refereeing Sunday football not the fucking Champions League Final."

Sure enough there are quite a few stones on the pitch which we do our best to clear, making sure the referee can see us being good citizens and carefully placing them into the bin by the side of the pitch.

I have a look at Real Sobad and the two quick, nimble strikers both seem to playing. They appear to be on good form as they are constantly hitting the ball past their keeper into the net. Of all the teams in our league they shouldn't be called Real Sobad; it is a name more suited to us. Perhaps we should swap names.

"The two forwards are looking good in the warm-up," says Danny ominously. "You could be in for a busy ninety minutes. They seem to have some kind of telepathy – they're like Shearer and Sheringham in Euro '96."

"Fuck me, Danny. It's just the warm-up. They're just passing to each other and then shooting past the keeper. I don't think any telepathy is needed for that, mate. Even you and Nick can pass to each other in the warm-up and hit the ball past Phil, but the only telepathy you two have is when you're trying to chat up two drunken birds at a nightclub."

We kick-off and the game is pretty much played in our half for the first twenty minutes, although our defence is holding firm and restricting them to shots outside the area which Phil is dealing with comfortably. They're playing the ball well amongst themselves with plenty of one-touch football but they're getting increasingly annoyed that they can't breach our defence.

Their frustration increases when a big kick from Phil sails over their full-back's head and Miles is left one on one with the keeper. Miles tries to get round him and stumbles and falls over, yet to our amazement the referee points to the spot and gives Damo a great chance to give us the lead.

"Never a penalty that, ref," protests their keeper. "He dived."

"Did you, mate?" I ask Miles.

"No, I didn't dive. I just lost my footing and fell over. I think the booze from last night is still playing havoc with me, to be honest. I'm not sure if the keeper touched me but I'm not complaining."

"He has to go for that ref, professional foul," I tell him as he approaches the centre-back who committed the foul that wasn't a foul.

"Come here, number six," he calls to me.

"I presume I'm number six, Damo."

"Funnily enough you are."

"Look, lad, I'm the referee. I make the decisions. You concentrate on playing football. Now what's your name?"

"Matt Gibson. Come on, ref, I was only having a joke," I reply as he books me as well as the player who allegedly brought down Miles.

Damo then steps up to the spot and sends the keeper the wrong way. We are somehow in the lead.

"As per usual you scuffed that, mate, didn't you?" I tell him as we head back to the halfway line.

"Sure did. They all count, though. It's all in the eyes, and the keeper thought I was going to put the ball to the left."

"Past the post."

The goal gives us some confidence and we begin to play some good football on the floor. With our new formation we are winning the midfield battle but Damo looks very isolated up front. Then again, you can't have the best of both worlds. Miles is clearly suffering from a heavy night on the piss and isn't running up and down the left flank like he usually does. However, we are restricting them to long-range shots and manage to hold on to our lead until half-time.

"We're doing well, lads," Phil tells us. "They may have a lot of the ball but they have had virtually no shots."

"Hate to say it but Gibbo's formation could be working," replies Danny.

"*Mais oui, mais oui*," I reply with a grin like a Cheshire cat. I'm sure Danny now regrets mentioning that.

"It may be working for the midfield but I'm completely on my own up front," says Damo. "I really need some support, or should I say quick support, when I have got the ball."

"Sorry, mate," says Miles. "I should be supporting more but my body is screwed. All I can feel it last night's ten pints and the chicken vindaloo I had down Brick Lane."

"The vindaloo certainly isn't given you the runs today, is it Miles?"

"Joking aside," I cut in, "another forty five minutes of this and we could earn an excellent away win and I fancy a few pints afterwards."

I'm not sure what our opponents had at half-time but they come out all guns blazing and within the space of five minutes they have had a few shots on goal and the ball seems to be spending the whole time in our half. The two lads in attack are both fast and are beginning to work well together with the big six-footer winning a lot of flick-ons for the younger, quicker forward to run on to. Luckily for us he seems to have left his shooting boots at home.

They are also beginning to boss the midfield and Danny is beginning to struggle. He is a good player when he has the ball and can spot a killer pass, but when it doesn't have it he might as well not be on the pitch. He never tracks back – doesn't think it's in his job description – and hasn't mastered the act of tackling.

"Come on, mate," I tell him. "They're making you look pedestrian at the moment."

"Yes, I know. I'll get into the game more now."

Danny is as good as his word, although he proves my point about not being able to master the act of tackling when he chops down one of their centre midfielders and goes into the referee's notebook.

With us tiring it is not long before the inevitable happens and they equalise from a goalmouth scramble after their third corner in succession.

"Can't say I didn't see it coming," Tom tells me as I punt the ball back towards the centre circle.

"I know you what you mean. Whenever we get rid of the ball it seems to come straight back to us. Their two lads up front don't seem to run out of energy either."

The equaliser should give us the kick up the backside. Sadly, it doesn't and they continue to pile on the pressure. Phil is making some good saves with little support from the defence. We are at least giving one hundred percent and we're still level.

What happens next is a first I have seen on a football pitch. A cross from their right-winger lands on the foot of the centre-forward, who volleys the ball powerfully towards goal from about eight yards. Phil somehow manages to dive to his right and push the ball over the bar which brings applause and congratulations from most of their team and ours.

"What a save, mate."

"How did you get your hand on that?"

"Their centre-forward had already turned round and begun celebrating."

"In all my time playing Sunday football I've never seen a save like that."

"I've never seen the opposition clap an opponent before."

"Well you know, lads, what they say about how great Scottish goalkeepers are," Phil tells us all while making a mental note of the compliments he has just received.

"Enough of congratulating Phil," says Damo. "Mark up, lads. We're facing a corner. Anyway, I think he should've held it," he adds, knowing we haven't heard the last of this save.

Their corner goes straight into Phil's arms and we manage to avert another dangerous situation. He launches the ball downfield and from this we have our first attack of the half when a cross from Anton ends up on the head of Damo, but he can only head it straight at the keeper. His clearance promptly sails over all our defence, their striker outpaces Jack and I and he manages to chip the ball over the advancing Phil to give them the lead.

"Fuck!" spits Danny. "Just when it seemed we could hold on to an undeserved draw we go and concede in the last few minutes."

"If I had a pound for every time in the last fourteen years we conceded in the last five minutes I would be a rich man," I say.

"You might as well go up front now, Gibbo. I can't believe I just said that."

Alas, my chances of being a hero and scoring the equaliser are quashed thirty seconds later when the referee blows the final whistle.

"Unlucky, lads. We battled well but they just had too much for us," Danny tells us as we take our stuff and head to the changing rooms.

On the way I get chatting to some of the opponents and they still can't believe how Phil got his hand to the ball. They also seem surprised when I tell them that the average age of our team was early- to mid-thirties especially as theirs is mid- to late-twenties.

"Lads, was speaking to the other team and they can't believe we are all in our thirties," I say on reaching the dressing room. "They all thought we were a lot younger."

"They can't think Paddy looks in his twenties," replies Miles, telling the truth.

"Didn't mention Paddy, but he thought I was in my mid-twenties," I reply dishonestly.

"Bullshit."

"Truth, mate, and from looking in the mirror now I think he's right."

"Do you want me to talk you all through my save, lads?" says Phil piping up.

"What save?" a few of us reply

"Well, as you asked, their striker shot from three yards and I somehow, still quite not sure how, managed to jump from one end of the goal to the other and somehow yes somehow pushed the ball over the bar. It was truly out of this world and probably… "

"Shut up," the whole team chorus, cutting him off mid-story.

We enjoy the five-star showers and get changed before Danny, Phil and I head off to the pub for a few pints.

"Well don't think it's me that should be buying the beers, eh boys."

"Why is that Phil?" I reply, knowing what is about to come.

"Don't encourage him, Gibbo."

"I just wish someone was at the game today that had a camcorder and recorded the save of the century."

"I'm so glad no one was," laughs Danny. "Anyway, it was probably the equivalent of one of my goals from inside my own half this season. In fact the second one I scored was probably better than your save."

"Not a chance. The reflexes I showed were out of this world."

"Exactly. I had to think about my goal – weigh up the distance, height of the keeper, positioning of the keeper and power to put on the shot."

"Think this will be my first and last pint this afternoon. I can't listen to you two going on about your save and goal all day. Anyway, Phil, who was in goal when we had our only clean sheet this season?"

"Knew you'd bring that up. I can't wait for my first clean sheet just to shut you up. If I didn't have you and Jack at centre-back with your distinct lack of pace I probably would have done."

"Come on, Gibbo, which was better, my goal – sorry, I mean goals from inside my own half – or Phil's half-decent save today?"

"I can't answer that, mate. I can't give either of you the satisfaction."

"It was mine, wasn't it, mate? It's OK, you can tell us."

"Thank God I've finished my pint. I'm off. I can't listen to you two anymore. Anyway Tworty's goal was better than your fluky goals, which were actually scored from inside the opponent's half, and your save was luck, Phil."

"Let's discuss how we can get some new players while drinking lots of beer"

I get woken at 9.00am by their captain phoning to ask whether the game is still on as it is pouring with rain outside and has been all weekend. I wish it wasn't as I only got to bed a few hours ago and the thought of running around in the pissing rain isn't a good one. However, when he tells me that they have only nine men the thought of playing isn't such a bad idea.

I turn on the television to watch *Match of the Day* but soon drift off back to sleep and get woken up again when Jim calls me.

"Mate, I'm going to be late today as trains are up the spout and I'm on the lovely bus-replacement service."

"What's the time now?"

"Why, are you still in bed?"

"No, mate, I'm virtually there."

"Funny, that. It's just that I can hear the TV in the background. Get a move on, its 10.00."

"OK, mate. To be honest, your call woke me up. See you at the ground. I need to get my arse in gear and you'll probably be there before me."

I call Nick. "Mate, running late will be there by twenty past. Traffic's murder this morning."

"But you cycle."

"OK, I got smashed last night, woke up at 9.00 thought I would have five more minutes in bed and Jim woke me up at 10.00 when he called to say he was running late."

"That's my boy. No worries, mate. I'll tell the lads some bullshit excuse why you're late."

"Cheers, mate."

I eventually arrive at the ground at 10.25. Most of the team are changed and about to go out on the pitch.

"How was your night?" says Danny. "Nick said you had a big one and overslept this morning."

"Cheers, Nick. So much for telling the lads a good excuse."

I quickly get changed and head out to the pitch which is heavily waterlogged with pools of water in both six-yard boxes and the centre circle.

"Looks like our fast one-touch passing game will suffer today," Danny tells me.

"It's been suffering all season, mate, waterlogged pitch or no waterlogged pitch."

"Anyway they only have nine, which is a result, so we should get a few goals today."

"I fancy a few today. Let's get the boys in for a team talk."

"Lads, I'm sorry for being late. I'd love to give you a bullshit excuse but Nick has told you the actual truth. The pitch is awful, especially in the middle, so let's try and get it out wide and make our extra players count. If we play simple passes and stay patient, the three points should be ours."

"Remember a couple of weeks ago when we played a team that only had nine?" says Danny. "For lads that had the pleasure of not playing that day, we really struggled. We can't just expect to turn up and get three points."

"But we only had ten that day," Jim points out.

"I know, but it still took a last-minute own goal for us to get the three points."

Today we're up against Chiswick Chancers, who we beat earlier this season. They are all around their early-to-mid-thirties and with them two men short we should really beat them again. The game should probably have been called off, but the referee won't cancel it as he will lose half his match fee and we don't want it cancelled as it would have meant we have got up early in the pissing rain, got drenched coming to the ground, and got changed only to be told that the match is off.

The pitches in Sunday-morning football are the second worst you can get. The only ones worse are Sunday-afternoon pitches and that is only because they have already been played on in the morning. I've played Saturday-morning and Saturday-afternoon football and the pitches tend to be flatter with more grass and clearer line markings, and you don't have to put the goal nets up each week. Saturday football is also a better standard and seems to be taken more seriously. The team I have played for a few times meets up an hour before kick-off, fines anyone who is late, has a coach who runs the warm-up and there's a club house where you can have a drink afterwards. The slow, pot-bellied player who turns up five minutes before kick-off with a fag in his mouth doesn't exist in Saturday football.

The referee we have today is chairman of the league and whenever he takes one of our games he always introduces himself as such, hoping it will mean we will give him an easy morning because we will want to be on our best behaviour. He must be one of the poorest chairmen as he always arrives in a clapped-out old Fiesta, but at least it means all the fines we have paid over the last few weeks aren't going towards a new car for him. If he suddenly turns up in a brand new BMW saying the league is struggling for money I will begin to get suspicious.

We kick-off and as they only have nine we all seem to think that we can play centre-forward or out on the wing. I have to admit being a culprit when, after about five minutes, I find myself on the left flank which is a long way from my position of centre-back.

"Gibbo, what the fuck are you doing over there?" shouts Tom, my fellow centre-back.

Danny joins in as I jog back to my correct position. "You are no left-winger and if you were you would be a right-back's dream. You have no pace, no skill and no left foot. Apart from that you would be fucking fantastic."

"Sorry, mate. Don't know what came over me."

The game is a truly awful spectacle. The pitch doesn't help matters but even if it was full of grass and it was a dry day I doubt we would be much better as we are playing poorly. We don't seem to know how to make the extra players count and still hoof the ball down the pitch aimlessly. We also seem to be unable to pick up any of their players in dangerous positions and our opponents have two good chances to score in the first half-hour. Luckily, Phil spares our blushes on both occasions.

The referee tells me he may have to call the game off if the rain persists, which to be honest I wouldn't mind as with the torrential rain blowing in our faces you can barely see five metres in front of you. Last year, during one away game, it was hailing so badly that the referee took us off for ten minutes until it died down. We were 4-0 down at the time and we were hoping he'd abandon the game. Sadly the hail eased and we ended up losing 6-0.

Phil is soon blushing himself when a cross-cum-shot from out wide drifts over his head into the net to give them the lead. They celebrate as a team with nine men would do while we all look at Phil with blank faces. It was a bit of a howler but I can't really criticise Phil; he rarely makes mistakes and he has saved me enough times this season when I've made mistakes at the back.

We begin to raise our game and Nick comes close with two chances. The first he manages to completely scuff from about six yards which makes me chuckle. Then from three yards he misses an open goal with a header and ends up cracking his head against the goalpost before going down in agony. I rush over and he looks in a bad way so I delay taking the piss for a few seconds.

"How did you miss that, mate? That was an absolute fucking shocker."

"Heading never has been a strong part of my game."

"No shit, although you managed to head the post pretty well."

"Fucking hurt that did, mate."

"I was dying to take the piss but thought I would wait until you were better."

"You're too kind, waiting all of five seconds."

Nick manages to make up for his earlier misses when, following a cross from Jim, he scuffs the ball past their keeper to give us the equaliser. Strangely, our goal seems to give our opponents some more energy and when half-time comes you would think that it was us with nine men, not them.

"Lads, this is fucking shit," says an agitated Nick. "We're making playing against nine men look the hardest thing in the world."

"He's right," responds Danny. "Our passing is all over the shop and you would have thought we've never played with each other before. Come on, we have forty five minutes left to sort this mess out, I don't want to be leaving this pitch with anything less than three points."

We head back out and we still struggle to break down our opponents' defence and begin to get frustrated with ourselves, them and the referee. Danny, Paul and Tom all pick up unnecessary bookings and I can safely say that I'm not enjoying the game one bit. I'm feeling hung-over, cold, wet, seem to have no energy and long for the end of the game.

Chiswick Chancers, in contrast, appear really up for the game. I'm not sure what they had for breakfast but they are all giving one hundred percent, they're getting stuck in, and if they lose the ball they are busting a gut to win it back. Their long-haired and bearded keeper, who looks like something out of ZZ Top, is very vocal and marshals their defence well. Their four defenders seem to be winning every fifty-fifty ball and aren't giving Paul and Anton any time on the ball. They also seem to be quicker than both of them, which shouldn't be the case as they must be carrying a couple of stone more and look a good few years older.

They're playing with three in midfield against our four, yet you would think it is the other way round. Our midfield seems to be chasing shadows while the three of them are happy to let the ball do the work and are easily finding their lone attacker, which shouldn't really be happening as there are four of us in defence.

The lad they have up front is a real bruiser who I must have played against around twenty times over the years. With his straggly red hair and long, pointed beard, he looks like a fatter version of the old USA player Alexi Lalas. Whenever their keeper boots the ball downfield he has his elbow digging in my ribs and his hand pulling down my shirt, and I don't know if it's his ugly, scary face but the referees over the years never book him. At the end of each game he always shakes my hand and remarks on what a good, clean game it had been, despite the fact that he has been fouling me all morning.

The contrast to us couldn't be starker. I look at all my teammates and everyone looks pissed off, as if they would prefer to be anywhere but here. God knows what they're all thinking, but I imagine it would be something like this:

Phil – what the fuck do I have to do to get a decent defence? We're playing against nine men but still seem to give them chance after chance. However, I can't have a go as I completely fucked up for their goal and let a tame cross end up in the top corner. I also wish I had got to Greggs this morning and got a sausage roll as I'm starving. Actually, make that two.

Pete – I'm completely soaked, the wife is drenched and my young son is screaming his head off. What the hell am I doing here? The wife has a face like thunder and the little one will probably come down with the 'flu.

Tom – give me a centre-back that actually plays centre-back and doesn't think he is a left-winger, right-winger, centre-forward or every position bar centre-back which is where he is actually supposed to be playing.

212

Hugh – I've barely played this season. First game I managed to lose my contact lens and don't even start the game, and today I start and we're getting made to look shit by a team of nine men who are virtually bottom of the league.

Paul – why the fuck did I get up at an ungodly to drive down from Peterborough to play in this? Thirty quid in petrol, five pound subs and I've just got booked, which is another seven pounds. Best part of fifty quid down the drain which I would have saved if I was still in bed like I should be.

Nick – my fucking head hurts. Why can't I play one game without getting injured? At least I scored but I know no one will mention this as we've been shit, and if anyone did mention it they would take the piss as I pretty much shinned the ball in the back of the net.

Danny – playing centre midfield with Nick is like trying to play the violin without a bow, but I have to admit I have been shit today and best keep quiet at the end of the game.

Jim – can't believe I still agree to help out my brother most Sundays when every week I say it's going to be my last. It's pissing with rain, I'm cold and it's such a contrast to Saturday football where I play on flat pitches with grass and we have substitutes, which is an alien concept to Real Calcio.

Anton – I've touched the fucking ball once all game. Every week the lads say get the ball out wide to Anton but do I ever get the fucking ball? No, I fucking don't!

Miles – when will Pete actually pass me the fucking ball instead of trying to take on their winger? He is a fucking full-back, not Pele; he is meant to tackle the winger and pass to me. The few tackles he has won he has then hoofed the ball up front, completely bypassing the midfield. Just pass me the ball! You would think I am having an affair with his wife.

Paul, though, soon cheers us up when he gets on the end of a cross from Jim and puts us in the lead with ten minutes to go. This must be the first time we have beaten the full-back all game and Paul has beaten his marker to the ball.

However, our opponents still don't give up and their heads don't drop. They continue to apply pressure and a shot from their centre-forward just clears our bar. Phil then looks to take a quick goal-kick out to Hugh, but succeeds only in passing it straight to their centre-forward. He runs in on goal and just as he is about to shoot Phil brings him down. The referee points to the spot.

"Shit! Sorry, lads."

No one says everything as most people can't believe what just happened. Alexi Lalas takes the penalty and sends Phil the wrong way to bring them level.

We kick-off, but almost immediately the chairman of the league blows for time and we trudge off back to the changing rooms.

"Lads, we were truly fucking awful," says Nick. "We just seemed to forget the basics of football today."

Phil lets out a heavy sigh. "Sorry, lads. Don't know what happened to me today."

"You're like a London bus, Phil – no mistakes all season and then two come along in one game."

"Lads we can't blame Phil. He's saved us enough times this season from our mistakes," I say, knowing that I'm probably the main culprit.

"It's a slight change from last week when the opposition were applauding him," says Nick.

"I think they were pleased with him today," says my brother. "After all, he did give them two lovely gifts."

The changing room is silent after the game. No one feels like a drink. I have a shower, change and get soaked to the skin on the way home.

We've had some bad performances over the years, especially in recent seasons. There was one game last year when Danny was running the team as Nick, Damo and I were away and we lost 4-1 against nine men. We were drawing 0-0 at half-time, so Danny's team talk must have been inspirational. Danny took himself off at 4-0 down and we soon scored which gave Nick, Damo and I even more ammunition on him. He actually texted Damo the score when he came off. Upon receiving the text Damo, who didn't know Danny had taken himself off, realised that the game wouldn't have finished. So he texted back, telling him that he knew Danny did pretty much nothing in centre midfield, but texting mid-game took the piss.

There was another game last season in January when we all arrived at the ground and there was no sign of Danny, who had the kit. We must have rung him twenty times and texted him repeatedly asking his whereabouts, to no avail. Turned out he had forgotten to set his alarm and had overslept. We eventually had to call the game off as we couldn't play without any kit, which annoyed Damo the most as he had travelled up from Brighton. Failing to fulfil the fixture means an automatic 3-0 loss, though the team we were scheduled to play beat us 6-0 earlier in the season, so perhaps Danny's sleep-in saved us a thrashing.

Nick must have got straight on the email when he got home as when I check my emails there is already an email from him.

To: Damo, Gibbo, Danny
From: Nick

> We were fu★★ing diabolical today
> Discuss

To: Danny, Gibbo, Nick
From: Damo

> I take it you lost then without your star striker

To: Damo, Gibbo, Nick
From: Danny

Today was as bad as Calcio have ever been. We have way too many players who basically have no idea how to play the game. I am virtually repeating other emails I have written earlier in the season.

We just ran around the pitch chasing the fucking ball. They had nine men for God's sake and we were dreadful. I know people were moaning that I was being negative but it was soooo shit it defied belief. We have no team shape. Today should have been a doddle but it wasn't.

Another note I deliberately watched today, as the kit was filthy and ringing wet, who couldn't be arsed turning their kit the right way round before chucking it in the kit bag. I have now just had to turn round about half a dozen ringing wet shirts.

To: Danny, Gibbo, Nick
From: Damo

They only had nine men as well, this gets worse and worse!!

To: Danny, Damo, Nick
From: Gibbo

Have to agree with Danny we were awful, we need some decent players for next season.

P.S. Danny – I made sure my kit was the right way round – I think it was the only right thing I did right all morning.

P.P.S. Damo – Nick missed two complete sitters today.

To: Danny, Gibbo, Nick
From: Damo

Just checked the table they are pretty close to the bottom. Christ lads you have had a shocker.

To: Damo, Gibbo, Danny
From: Nick

You're enjoying this aren't you Damo.

P.S. I also turned my kit the right way round

P.P.S. Gibbo did fail to add that I did score albeit a sliced shot that their keeper should have saved but they all count.

To: Danny, Damo, Nick
From: Gibbo

Let's discuss how we can get some new players whilst getting drinking lots of beer; we need to get a date in the diary soon. I think it would be better if any potential players didn't see us play this season as this would probably put them off.

To: Danny, Gibbo, Nick
From: Damo

And scar them for life.

How about a Saturday night next month? Anyway I'm off now, got better things to do than hear about our dire performance today.

"We could do with signing up their podgy left-winger and ginger centre-forward"

To: Real Calcio
From: Nick

Morning Lads

I won't mention our worst ever performance yesterday. We all have bad days in the office; it's just that we have seemed to have had more than our fair share this season.

Anyway with Easter being this weekend we have no game but are playing the following week against River Saucer who have beaten us twice this season including once with only nine men. They are probably going for the hat-trick this Sunday and I really want to win and shout their mouthy centre-back up.

On another note, if we are going to do another season we really need some new young, fit and fast players as we have really struggled for numbers this season. If anyone has someone in mind let me know.

Try not to eat your body fat in Easter eggs this weekend and try and go for a run or two before the next game.

Cheers
Nick

Great, I think to myself, that's all we need to get our confidence back – playing against a team of fast twenty-year-olds who've already beaten us twice this season.

During the week I meet a friend of mine for some food. She mentions she has started Bikram yoga and tells me it is good for your flexibility, hamstrings, core strength and balance. These are things I lack or in the case of hamstrings something I have been prone to pull, although remarkably this season I haven't. She suggests that perhaps I should give it a go as her boyfriend tried it six months ago and it seemed to have prevented him getting injured as much playing sport.

I don't tell the lads I'm going and head off to my first class on Thursday. The initial joy of being one of only three blokes in a class of thirty scantily clothed ladies is short-lived when the class starts. I straight away seem to struggle with the breathing exercises, which doesn't bode well for the rest of the class, I sense. I'm correct and the next ninety minutes are painful; I'm hurting in places I never thought existed. I also sweat like I've never done before and seem to have pools of sweat either side of my drenched towel.

The most embarrassing occasion is when my mobile phone goes off during one of the relaxation exercises and I have to amble over most of the class to go to the shelf where everyone's valuables are to turn it off. If I had any chance of having a friendly chit-chat with any of the lovely ladies after the class I think my phone going off with the *Test Match Special* theme music at full volume has put paid to that.

The best bit of the class is the last five minutes when we get to lie on the mats and are told to relax our minds and think of nothing. I fail with this as the only thing I can think of is whether Tottenham will win this weekend and whether the tasty girl lying next to me is single. Not that I would stand any chance if she was as I'm looking close to death and I ruined one of the exercises with my phone ringing (although if she's a cricket fan she might have loved it as it's a cracking ringtone).

The class eventually ends and I virtually collapse in the changing room, barely able to move. I eventually muster up the energy to have a shower and upon getting out I sweat even more, and when I get home I need to have another shower.

Nick, Damo, Danny and I decide to meet up later in the week but the only time we can all do is the night before our next game which isn't the most professional.

"Hands up if you've been for a run," Damo says as he walks into the pub and sees Nick, Danny and I sat at the bar.

"Can't say I did to be honest but I also didn't eat my own weight in Easter eggs, main reason being I didn't get any. Not that I want to come across as bitter," says a bitter Danny.

"I nearly went for a run," says Nick.

"Nearly? You were the one who sent the email telling everyone to go on one."

"I know, Damo, but I got as far as getting my running gear on and then the phone rang, it started raining and then *Soccer Saturday* started."

"I would've gone on one but I've been getting sharp shooting pains in my knee the last week or so and thought I better not risk it. Not sure what I've done."

"You OK to play tomorrow, though, Gibbo?"

"Prefer not to, but I doubt we have enough, do we Nick?"

"We have eleven with you, mate."

"I'm playing, then, by the sounds of it as again we have no subs. By the way, lads, you can call me Sting from now on."

"Why, have you suddenly become a multi award-winning music star or become a so-called master in tantric sex?" replies Danny, whose knowledge of Sting's sex practices worries me.

"No, mate. I've started Bikram yoga in Balham."

"What the hell is that?"

"Well, it's yoga in forty-degree heat."

"Fuck me, has there been some kind of heat wave in Balham or something? It's been bloody cold in Hounslow all week."

"Very funny. No, it's yoga done in this temperature-controlled room and it's bloody hard."

"But you've never done yoga before, have you?"

"Yes, thought I'd bypass yoga and just start with Bikram. In hindsight perhaps I should've started with normal yoga – walk before you can run, and all that."

"Isn't Bikram yoga for birds and tree-huggers, though?"

"Yes, around ninety percent of the people in there were girls, of which at least half were tasty. And I am prone to hug a tree or two on the way home now."

"Ninety percent girls? That's me sold then, Gibbo, and I imagine that's what sold you as well. When's the next class?"

"Thursday. It's not easy though, Danny. It's certainly harder than kicking a football round a pitch."

"And you've found that pretty hard this season."

"Enough of Gibbo and his new hobby, which like most of his other hobbies he is shit at," says Nick. "We need to sort out next season – do we knock it on the head and enjoy the Sunday lie-in again or do one more season?" He seems to be in favour of the latter.

"At the moment, especially with our last performance in mind, I'm tempted to jack it in," I say. "This season hasn't been the best. We all seem to be a lot worse than last season and the average age of our team is well over thirty now. We also really struggle for numbers and I just haven't enjoyed it as much."

"Agreed we have had our problems this season, Gibbo," says Danny. "But Sunday morning is an excuse to get out the house and escape the missus. I don't want to spend my Sunday mornings shopping nor being made to do jobs round the house."

"If we do jack it in, you don't have to tell her, Danny. You can just go and play golf instead."

"Can't see her believing that as I walk out the house with my golf clubs saying 'See you later, love. Just off to play footy'."

"I'm fifty-fifty; travelling from Brighton on a Sunday morning, and then playing when it seems as though half the team can't be arsed is beginning to piss me off," says Damo. "I might just find a team down in Brighton."

With a three-hour round trip, I can't say I blame him. Danny sees it differently.

"Judas! You can't do that, mate," he says, fearing we are about to lose our star striker – well, striker who scores the odd goal in home games against teams in the bottom half.

"Despite all the problems we've had I reckon let's have one more season. Think of all the good things, the banter we have, the odd goal we score, the end-of-season trips, getting pissed at the pub after some games, winning the cup."

"Yeah, winning the cup was great the other season, the highlight of my football career, although to be honest there haven't really been many apart from that and winning the cup when I was in the Cubs."

"That was the best day in the history of Calcio. Come on, boys, with a few new players we can win it again next season. It's just a question of us finding them."

"We need your website, Nick and Damo, to bring in some players," I say. "And preferably ones that are reliable, unlike Mark who keeps letting us down and is also shit. Two years ago it was great: we had subs each game, I scored eleven goals including a hat-trick in twenty minutes – remember that, lads, one with my left, one with my right and a bullet header."

"Here we go, Gibbo. You've perked up. How can I fail to remember your only ever hat-trick against the team that was bottom of the league and only had ten men?"

We end up staying at the pub until closing time which isn't the ideal preparation for the game tomorrow, but by the end of the drinking session we come to the conclusion that we need to get six more players within six weeks. If we do we'll have one more season; if not we'll fold the club.

"I feel like shit," Nick tells me over the phone early on Sunday morning, "and I feel even worse now because Anton has pulled out as his kids are ill, which is fair enough."

"Bloody marvellous. So we have ten. Well, nine with my dodgy knee."

"Make that eight – I've got a banging headache," counters Nick. "Why did we choose to go out last night? Can't remember much beyond about half nine."

"I'll give Jim a ring and see if he fancies playing, but he was playing yesterday and his bird isn't a great fan on him playing twice in a weekend."

I try to call Jim, whose phone rings and rings but he doesn't answer. He will know that the only reason I'm calling is to ask if he can play, and I imagine he can't be arsed so he doesn't answer. Ten it is then.

My sister is away this weekend so I have the joy of using her car to get to the ground, and unlike most weekends when I get soaked cycling to football, the weather is pleasantly sunny. I'm sure if I didn't have the car it would be pissing down.

I get to the ground just before 10.00 and some of their team are already out on the pitch warming up which is being run by their foghorn centre-back who looks more and more like Carlos Puyol every time I see him. It's not often you arrive to see a team already warming up and they look very well-run, but then again I imagine they would get a severe bollocking from Carlos if they mucked around.

We are lucky if we have two players in the changing room at 10.00. Sure enough, when I walk through the door there's just Miles in there.

"Have you seen the keen gits?" he says. "They're already out there – seems like they're doing some kind of structured warm-up with cones and stuff. It's not the Premiership."

"It beats our warm-up of shooting waywardly at the goal all at once."

"Isn't this the team that has an average age of about twenty with a loud annoying centre-back?"

"Sure thing, although he didn't play last time. Pete and Jack are old enough to be most of their players' fathers."

Tom makes it three. "I can't believe their warm-up," he says. "What's wrong with a banana, a can of Red Bull, a jog across the side of the pitch and a light stretch of the right hamstring."

"Lads, if we get here on time we could have a decent warm-up," I say as the rest of the team turn up. "Having said that, with a decent warm-up and our lack of fitness we'd be screwed after about ten minutes. Anyway, as we know, this team are young, fast and seem to have bundles of energy, so all ten of us have to be on our toes today."

"Bloody hell, Gibbo. Only ten again," says Jack, anticipating a long morning. "Great, we really need some new players next season. I'm forty-odd, and playing with only nine others against this lot doesn't fill me with confidence."

"Come on, lads. Heads up. We'll just play with Damo up front."

We don't even have time for us to fire shots at Jack, who is in goal today as Phil is away, before the game starts.

"Come on, Saucer!" comes their centre-back's rallying cry. "From the off, let's have a big ninety. Remember what we worked on during the week."

"They must train, Gibbo," Tom tells me in astonishment.

"Other teams do train, mate."

"Training is cheating, but they must fear us if they worked on certain things in the week."

"Mate, they've beaten us twice this season, once with nine men, so I doubt they fear us."

From pretty much the word go the ball is spending the whole time in our half, although we're defending well and Tom, in particular, is playing a blinder. He may moan at times but you can never doubt his commitment to the cause. After fifteen minutes

Nick goes up for a header and clashes heads with one of their midfield before falling to the ground in agony.

"Mate, you're great at heading goalposts and people's heads," I tell Nick as he lies dazed on the floor. "If only you had the same accuracy with that round leather thing you missed again."

We continue to defend well and Jack, who still insists on wearing no gloves in goal despite the fact that it is now raining, pulls off a great save. Well, I say a great save – from about six yards, their centre-forward volleys the ball straight at Jack, who saves it with his knees.

"Keep pressing, Saucer. Let's get the ball out wide and get round the back of them," their centre-back issues another commandment to his troops.

They continue to attack and whenever we get the ball out our half it seems to come back at us. I'm feeling shattered and am getting the run-around from their young, sharp and pacy forwards. They must be about ten years younger than most of us and there doesn't seem to be an ounce of fat or stubble on any of their players apart from the centre-back. It's scary to think that just as we were starting out in Sunday football all those years ago most of their team would have been playing for some under-twelve team.

They say in football that the older you get, the more savvy you become on the football pitch and that you can't buy experience, but I'm not sure I buy into that. I've been playing Sunday football for years and to be honest you wouldn't want to buy our experience. We haven't had much success in the last dozen years; we rarely get eleven fit players out on the pitch and they say that an experienced team doesn't let goals in the first or last five minutes, yet we usually do.

I also don't buy into the expression that the first five yards are in the head. I'm sure it's true if you're in your mid- to late-thirties and playing in the Premiership, like Giggs and Scholes, but I doubt it applies to us. If the first five yards are in my head, by the time I start running the bloke I am marking is already ten yards ahead of me.

However, half-time comes and it's still goalless and we feel pretty satisfied with ourselves, although if it was a boxing match the referee would have stopped the fight.

"You sure the ref played the full forty five minutes?" I ask an exhausted Damo as he comes over.

"If he did it must be the quickest forty five minutes ever."

"He must be planning to go to the pub. Either that or he is bored shitless refereeing this 0-0 classic."

We grab some much-needed water and head out for the second half still exhausted. Our luck changes, though, and with our first attack a through-ball from Nick puts Damo clean through. He manages to side foot the ball past the keeper to give us the lead, and we all pile on top of him, celebrating as if we've just won the cup, instead of taking the lead in a meaningless league match.

"Thank God for me," Damo tells Danny and I as we head back for the restart. "Up against four defenders today and still come up with the goods."

"I can't believe we are actually winning this game," I reply. "It's a fucking injustice but I'm not complaining. I just hope the referee only plays half an hour like he did first half."

"Keep pressing, Calcio. Let's get the ball out wide and get round the back of them," shouts Danny, using the same line as their centre-back did in the first half.

"I've got an awful feeling he might regret saying that," Tom tells me.

"I know. Him and his big gob."

The ball is soon back in our penalty area and Jack makes a great point-blank save from one of their forwards. Tom follows this up with a fantastic last-ditch tackle from the rebound. Just when I begin to think that we can hold on for a memorable win their winger outpaces Pete and cuts inside and scores in the far corner.

"Sorry Tom, got done for pace and age then," says Pete honestly.

"They're on the rack now," barks their centre back. "This game is ours for the taking, Saucer."

"I hope to God Danny doesn't fucking say anything," Tom tells me.

"Keep pressing, Calcio. Let's get the ball out wide and get round the back of them," Danny shouts out again, taking the piss as Tom and I try not to laugh.

We are really struggling now and seem to have run out of energy, while they appear to be gaining it. I'm sure that Danny's words were more of an encouragement to them than to us and the inevitable soon happens when another good move down their left side results in a tap-in for their centre-forward who has completely lost Tom and I.

"What have you got to say for yourself now, fat boy?" their centre-back shouts, drawing laughter from their team and a few of ours as well. "Think we got the ball out wide then and got round the back of you. Eat your words and judging by the size of you, you probably will."

Danny is surprisingly quiet and lost for words as we kick-off again, although it isn't long until we concede another goal from slack marking at a corner. They then score their fourth with a carbon copy of the second goal. By this time we're just begging the referee to blow for full-time as we're all completely shattered. I'm pretty sure he has played an hour in the second half to make up for the short first half. Eventually, just as they are looking for their fifth, the referee blows his whistle.

"Heads up, lads. That was a good performance considering we only had ten men against eleven fit youngsters," Danny tells us in the changing room. "We only let in the last three because we had no energy left."

"Old Carlos Puyol was on form today," says Tom. "Loved his response to you, Danny. Even you must admit that was a good one. I even congratulated him on it at the end."

"OK, I admit even I was speechless after that."

The changing room is pretty quiet as most people are too tired to talk and still out of breath. I have to shoot off to return the car before my sister gets back from her weekend away, so I leave the lads sitting motionless in the changing room.

Later in the afternoon I get a text from Rich, who runs Chiswick Chancers, saying that they are disbanding after this season. Some of his team might be looking for a club next season and he asks whether we would be interested in having them. I text back saying that we'll take them all especially their ginger centre-forward, blonde centre midfield player and left-winger.

"Mate, I've got some new players for next season," I tell Nick on the phone.

"Have you been out scouting and signing up players this afternoon, then?"

"No, I've been approached with the offer of some players."

"What for, money? We only have two hundred quid in the club account and that's for the piss-up in Sofia."

"Rich texted me from Chiswick Chancers and said some of their players might be looking for a new team."

"We don't want Rich, though. He's hopeless."

"Don't worry, I will tell him that."

"But we could do with signing up their podgy left-winger though and ginger centre-forward who caused our four defenders all sorts of problems last time, despite the fact that he was their lone striker and they only had nine men."

"Don't worry, I told him that. I'm surprised he approached us, though, seeing as we've had a poor season."

"Reason is, mate, he saw how shit we were a few weeks ago when they played us, and by joining Calcio their players would be guaranteed a start."

"Anyway, if it comes off we should have a decent squad next season and I fancy myself to have a blinding season. Can see the Gibson of old coming back, running the game."

"I take it you had a liquid lunch again with that rubbish you're talking. Anyway, got to go to buy some paint."

"You live the life. Speak in the week."

I come off the phone feeling happy. This season hasn't been the best, but with some new players I'm sure we can turn things round next season.

On a personal basis I could really do with a good season. Up until I hit thirty I like to think I was one of the better players in the team, and back then we were also in a higher division. Since I hit thirty I seem to pick up injuries more frequently, have become even slower and sometimes struggle to pass it to a team-mate less than five yards away.

I really don't want to end my career with a shit season next year, and it would be great if we could finish towards the top of the league and perhaps win the cup again. I've been playing football for best part of thirty years and I think the only things I have won are a cup whilst in the Cubs, the plate whilst playing for school (the plate was for the schools that got knocked out of the first round of the cup so I'm not sure it really counts), a league title and the cup with Real Calcio.

Three cups – well, two cups and a plate – and one league in thirty years isn't great. I'm also struggling to remember great performances I've had in the past ten years of Sunday football. Pretty sure the last really good game I had was when I was at university when I scored four goals in a twenty-minute spell. The rest of team couldn't believe it and to be honest neither could I. I should've retired then and gone out on a high.

"Blind me... comparing Man Utd to Real Calcio"

Our final game of the season is scheduled to be at home against the team who beat us in the first match and had their supporters on the touchline drinking cans of Stella Artois.

As the season has gone on longer than it should, getting a pitch for the last game of the season is difficult, to say the least, because the council have taken down our goalposts as well as all the other pitches in the borough. To be honest I'm not that bothered; we can't get relegated, can't get promoted and I'm away this weekend and can't play anyway. So I email the league secretary suggesting that we just call the game a draw.

He emails back saying that our opponents can still get promoted and will want to play the game as a victory over us will give them second place in the league and promotion. He gives me some details of some pitches that might be available, but luckily by the time I get round to phoning them up on the Thursday, knowing full well I've left it too late, they are full so the league has no choice but to cancel the game and call it a draw.

If Wandsworth Milan were a good set of lads who we should beat I would have tried to find a pitch. As they're bunch of arseholes, with a particularly annoying, dirty centre-forward, I'm quite proud that I have scuppered their bid to get promoted. It's probably the best performance I've put in all season. The league secretary asks me to drop the other captain an email so I do so.

Dear Terry
Matt here from Real Calcio. I'm sorry to be the bearer

of bad news but the game this weekend will have to be cancelled as we can't find any pitches available. I have tried all week to find a pitch and we were really looking forward to playing you again as the game last time was played in such a nice spirit. I was especially looking forward to marking your centre-forward, who stunk of booze and spent most of last match fouling me and calling me a fucking carthorse, fucking wanker and my personal favourite a fucking-son-of-a-bitch wanker.

To be honest with you I think you have would have won as we only have eight players this week and they are probably the worst eight players in our squad. *C'est le vie* I think the expression is and I hope you don't think your whole season has gone to waste now.

Have a fantastic summer.

Very best wishes

Matt

My mobile goes about ten minutes after I have sent the email, and as I don't recognise the number I presume it's Terry. Sure enough, I get an email ten minutes later.

Dear Matt

You have to play us, all our players have been looking forward to this week and we can't miss out on promotion. They will be well fucking upset when I tell them. I am pretty sure I can get a pitch, leave it with me.

Cheers

Terry

P.S. Jonty, the lad up front, has calmed down now. He wants to apologise to you about the last game. He is a good lad really, he is a teacher in real life and all the kids love him.

I call Nick. "Mate, I can't get a pitch on Sunday and the league have called it a draw."

"Bet that has pissed Milan off. Aren't they looking at promotion if they beat us?"

"Yes, mate, and that makes it even sweeter. I have also just had an email from their captain begging for us to play them this weekend. Apparently their thug of a centre-forward is a nice guy and wants to apologise to me before the game. He's a teacher in real life and the kids love him."

"Real life? Is Sunday-morning football make-believe, then?"

"Not sure, but this season has been a fucking nightmare for us."

I come off the phone to Nick and later in the afternoon switch my computer on and see an email from Rich, from Chiswick Chancers, who says he is talking to four other teams about whether they would be interested in their players next season. I call Nick back.

"Mate, I'm not sure that we definitely have the players from Rich next season."

"Why?"

"Well, Rich is talking to four other teams as well."

"Thought it was a done deal. Four teams, blind me. They came bottom of the league – surely his players can't be in that high demand?"

"Thing is our ground might be too far for them to travel to as most of them are based Ealing way. He asked if there was any way we could move grounds more towards Putney or Wandsworth."

"No way. Our ground is a five-minute walk from my house. It's a bit like Messi telling Alex Ferguson that he likes Man Utd and would sign for them but could he move Old Trafford a bit closer to London as his missus likes the shops of the King's Road and Manchester is a bit far away from it."

"Blind me… comparing Man United to Real Calcio."

"Anyway, we can't move grounds. We'll just have to find a Messi type of player in Earlsfield."

"Should be a piece of piss that, mate. Apparently, Earlsfield is full of them."

Damo sends an email later in the week asking for our various nominations for our end-of-season awards.

To: Real Calcio squad
From: Damo

Forget your Emmies, Oscars or Nobels... the Real Calcio Awards are upon us. It's the same as usual. Everyone gets to vote and nobody can vote for themselves (Danny, year after year...)

1) Lionel Messi Player of the Season
2) Trevor Sinclair Goal of the Season
3) Gordon Banks Save of the Season
4) Ronny Rosenthal Miss of the Season
5) The Zizou Moment of Rage Award
6) Joe Cole Gone Missing Award
7) Roy Keane 'Cut me open and I bleed green' Dedication Award
8) Vinnie Jones Shortest Performance of the Season
9) Jamie Redknapp Injury of the Season
10) Chris Kamara The All-Round Comedy Moment Award

Other categories welcome.

I will announce the winners in Sofia. For those not coming they will be emailed upon our return. Don't make me chase you up, vote now.
Cheers
Damo

Fair play to Damo. He organises the end-of-season awards every year. It's usually a good night and this year will be held in Bulgaria's capital on our end-of-season tour. I have won a few in my time; Miss of the Season seems to come my way most seasons as has the Comedy Moment award. Sadly I have yet to win, or been close to, winning the Player of the Season and I can't see myself doing it this year.

My vote for Player of the Season goes to Tom. Despite the fact that he loves a moan and occasionally loses his temper he has performed brilliantly this season and marshals our defence really well.

Goal of the Season has to be Tworty. He has only played for us just once this season but he scored a cracking goal. Danny, although I would never tell him, has scored a few good goals, but I could never bring myself to vote for him.

Save of the Season has to be Phil's incredible save when he made a point-blank stop from Real Sobad's centre-forward. Despite not being able to keep a clean sheet all season, which has pleased me immensely, he is probably the best keeper in the league. Having an old and slow back four in front of him doesn't make his job that easy.

Miss of the Season will be my shocker against Hounslow Hangovers. I will though vote for Nick.

Zizou Moment of Madness award has to be when one of our opponents ran on the pitch wielding a baseball bat after he was sent off against us. I have seen a lot of things playing Sunday football for ten years, but this has to be the most surprising and scary.

Gone Missing award has to be Paddy. Sometimes it takes me eighty eight minutes to realise he is playing. If not Paddy, then Tworty, who no one has seen since the first game of the season.

I'm not sure who deserves the Cut Me Open and I Bleed Calcio award. Danny did come straight from a long-haul flight to play, which is no mean achievement; I have to admit that I would head straight to bed after such a journey. Paul travels from Peterborough to play and Tom would play if he had one leg. Nick has bled a lot this season with his various injuries, but not sure if that counts.

Shortest performance of the season and injury of the season has to be Hugh, who managed to lose his contact lenses on the way to one of our games and therefore couldn't play as he is blind without them. Nick comes a close second after lasting less than ten minutes in at least one game.

All-Round Comedy Moment has to be Danny who, on seeing the chap run on the pitch with the baseball bat, shouted out the name of the only baseball player he'd heard of.

I send my email back to Damo and look forward to the awards evening this weekend in Sofia. There are fourteen of us going, including the infamous "Graham Jones" and Matty, who both love a good piss-up.

I've managed to organise a football game when we're out there, which should be fun. We are apparently playing a team of referees and journalists. I'm sure we'll give a good account of ourselves on the Monday morning after two big days on the piss.

"I need to get to the fetish club urgently – it's an emergency"

We agree to meet at Gatwick at 7.00am for our flight to Sofia. If we had to meet at that time to play football there would be no chance that any of the team would be here, but as I approach the check-in desk every one of the team has arrived.

"Jack, can't believe you're actually on time for a change."

"I'm actually early, Gibbo. No danger of me missing a weekend on the sauce. Besides if I miss the flight it means I have to spend it with the other half."

"If only everyone could get on time for footy we could have a decent warm-up and be much more switched on come kick-off."

"Whatever, Gibbo. I just find it easier to make sure I'm early for a holiday in the sun with the lads rather than a Sunday-morning game which is usually in the pissing rain, on a shit pitch, against a set of wankers who we usually lose against. Funny, that."

We all check in and head over to the nearest bar for a couple of pints. I can't drink at the best of times and I find it difficult trying to get two pints down me thirty minutes after having cornflakes. The rest of the lads don't seem to struggle and Danny is even having a vodka Red Bull. I'm sure if everyone had a choice between a large fry-up with a cup of tea and a few pints, most people would choose the former, but no one would dare suggest it.

The flight continues in the same vein. Everybody seems happy enjoying a cuppa with their breakfast before Danny orders a gin and tonic, as you do at 9.00 in the morning, and everyone follows suit with the same or a can of warm beer that costs four pounds.

We eventually arrive in Sofia, with a few of the team tipsy, and jump in taxis and get to the hotel. The receptionist's face immediately drops when she sees all of us enter, talking loudly, with some of the lads drinking beer. I'm sharing a room with Damo and we all agree to meet back in reception in fifteen minutes.

"The rooms seem alright, don't they?" I say to Danny when we come back down.

"Not bad for a three-star. Mine even has a balcony."

"No sign of a balcony in mine."

"What Danny failed to mention is that his room is the only one that has a balcony," says Miles. "Funny that, seeing as he booked the hotel."

"Pure coincidence," laughs Danny. "Anyway, get your drinking boots on and let's head out. The Man United game is on at the Irish pub down the road."

"Could've stayed in London and done that."

"But not at a pub that's a pound a pint."

We all head off to begin our sightseeing of Sofia at the Irish bar and settle down to watch the football just as Paddy, Chris and Hugh arrive after a brief look around town.

Paddy puts a guidebook on the table. "Lads," he says, "not that it's an issue, but you know that our hotel is a gay hotel in the gay district. Look at this."

"I wandered why Damo and I had a double bed with satin sheets," I say.

"Thank God he's joking," says Damo, "though our beds are pretty close together and we do have pink towels."

"I also found four condoms in our bathroom which I thought was strange. Damo isn't my type anyway, so they'll be wasted on us."

"Lads, it's not a gay hotel," Danny assures us. "I realised this when I was doing some research last week. It's a gay-friendly hotel, whatever that means."

"Hope its heterosexual-friendly as well," Damo replies as United take the lead.

We watch the game and then head out and wander around the town before heading to the park for a kick-about. The sight of fourteen tipsy blokes playing football rather badly draws Real Calcio's biggest crowd of the season and the game ends about 12-12. We head back to the hotel, get changed and go to a local restaurant. The food is lovely, or everyone thinks it is, apart from Phil who only eats the bread rolls and can't believe they don't sell chips. They have a local three-piece band to entertain us, and we in turn entertain them when Graham with his two left feet starts dancing badly in the restaurant.

We then head to a bar and Damo starts the annual awards ceremony. We add in a couple more categories including 'How the hell did you get an invite for the end-of-season tour,' which is won by Manny who has never played for us before but who Jack invited along. In second place comes Matty, who played badly in goal for us a few times, and in third place is Graham with his solitary appearance.

Danny, much to his annoyance and everyone else's pleasure, doesn't win the Goal of the Season which goes to Twenty instead. Hugh wins Injury of the Season due to the fact he managed to lose his contact lenses on the way to a game and couldn't play; Tom wins Player of the Season convincingly, although somehow Nick gets one vote which no one owns up to but I imagine this vote was bought by Nick. His one vote also means he comes in third place as the only other person who gets any votes is Phil in goal with two.

Save of the Season goes to Phil; I win Miss of the Season again but Nick is only one vote behind me. The Zizou Rage and Comedy Moment both go to the lad who ran on the pitch with a baseball bat. The Gone Missing award goes to Twenty, who seems to have disappeared for good after the opening game of the season. Shortest Performance of the Season goes to Nick as he barely lasts five minutes in some games, while the Cut Me Open and I Bleed Calcio award goes to Tom who never misses a game and never ducks out of a tackle.

"Look at that," Nick tells me and Danny at the bar. "Third place this year in Player of the Year, a previous winner. What an asset I am to Real Calcio."

"How much do you pay someone to vote for you year after year? I mean you were injured in most games after ten minutes, you headed goalposts and missed sitters."

"Ah, missed sitters. We really should rename the Miss of the Season award the Gibbo of the Season award."

"How come I didn't win Goal of the Season?" Danny moans to Nick and I. "I bet you guys rigged it."

"Reason you didn't, Danny, is because Tworty did," I reply. "Anyway, I could never vote for you on principle."

We carry on drinking at a local pub where we see a very pissed bloke sitting at the bar. Next to him is a statue of an old woman with her elbow on the bar and the bloke has no idea that it's a statue and is talking away to 'her', much to our amusement. We think he has cottoned on to the fact that it's a statue when he eventually turns away from it to face the bar. However, a minute or so later he turns back to face the statue and he has only gone and bought it a drink. At this point all of us start crying with laughter, leaving him to carry on chatting up the statue and hoping that he asks it for its phone number.

The pub closes around 3.00am and most of us head to a club, which I can't remember much about, and then to the twenty four-hour McDonald's, which isn't open. Apparently it isn't open between 4.00 and 6.00am. Maybe they should rename it the twenty two-hour McDonald's.

When we arrive back at the hotel Danny bursts into the reception.

"It's Graham. He has been kept in a fetish club in some cellar and I need to get him out."

"Doesn't sound too bad to me being kept in there," chuckles Paddy.

"It's a fucking nightmare. We didn't have any dances or drinks and we got given the equivalent of a six hundred pound bill and we don't have any credit cards on us."

"Christ," says Damo, checking how much money he has in his wallet. "I dread to think how much they get charge you if you actually have a drink and some fetish."

Danny dashes up to his room and grabs his credit card and comes back downstairs.

"Shit I haven't got a clue how to get back there. I need the address," he says just us the hotel manager comes into the reception.

"I need to get to the fetish club urgently. It's an emergency," Danny tells the manager who looks as him as if he needs his strange fetish-fixation fix. The rest of us would probably be in stitches if the situation wasn't so bad.

Danny gets the address of the club and heads back there with Matty, who is over 6ft tall and I imagine would be quite handy if anyone kicked off. The rest of us wait in reception. We're all actually rather worried as Graham would have been by himself for some time.

About half an hour later, Graham, Danny and Matty come back to the hotel. Graham looks quite shaken up.

"Thank God I've got out of there. I had two big fucking lads watching over me, threatening to beat me shitless if Danny didn't turn up."

"Did Danny end up bailing you out then?" asks Hugh.

"Danny did and what makes it even worse was that they didn't take American Express so I couldn't even get any air miles. Had to pay with me and the wife's other credit card which must be over the limit by now. I felt like asking for some champagne and at least some dances for my six hundred pounds but thought against it at the end."

"How come they gave you a six hundred pound bill, then?"

"Well, Graham did shout out champagne and dances as he entered the club, the pissed old fart."

"What did you say, Danny?"

"I said 'No, no, no, no' to everything."

"Yes, of course you did, mate."

"God knows what they'll put on the credit card statement. Might have some explaining to do to the missus."

"Hope they put Fetish Club," says Chris with a smile on his face.

"Yes, good luck explaining to her that although you spent six hundred pounds in a fetish club you had no drinks and no dances," Matty tells Danny with a smug grin. "Can't see her believing that one."

"Nor me," adds Graham.

"Don't you start," says Danny. "You and your mouth have cost me six hundred quid."

We have a few more drinks, taking the piss out of Danny and Graham before finally heading to bed and passing out at around 6.00am.

The phone wakes me the following day and I reach out for it, half asleep.

"Good morning, welcome to our nude massage parlour, how can I help?"

"Urm, is that Mr Gibson?" a female voice answers as it sinks in that unless one of the lads has mastered a female Bulgarian accent overnight it's unlikely to be one of them.

"No, it's Mr Sheridan."

"It's reception. Do you want us to make your room today?" she replies sounding slightly embarrassed.

"Yes, please."

I wake Damo up and we head down to reception and he gets a few strange looks from the receptionist as we head out the hotel.

"Swear the receptionist and her mate were laughing at me when

I handed in the room key," he says en route to meet the rest of the lads at the cafe down the road, which makes me chuckle.

Most of the team are there. Everyone looks pretty hung-over and conversation isn't exactly flowing. We have some food and I go with a few others to do some sight-seeing and take a few photos while the rest of the team head back to the Irish pub.

After an hour the heavens open and we go back to the pub to catch up with the rest of the lads and spend the afternoon drinking and exchanging stories. We learn that Matty streaked at Lord's during the Ashes for two hundred pounds, and that Danny took his first ever date to the fairground and was sick all over her when they were on the waltzer. This can't have been a pretty sight as I imagine he would have had a fair few toffee apples and candy floss beforehand.

We then return to the hotel to get freshened up and on the way there my mobile rings.

"Hi Matt. It's Stefan here from the team you are meant to be playing tomorrow."

"Oh hi, Stefan. Was going to give you a ring and see what time you want to meet."

"Slight problem, Matt. The pitch I've booked is double-booked and I can't seem to find another pitch. It's a bank holiday and most of the pitches are being used."

"Shit. Can we just play at some park, then?"

"Not really. Besides, most of my team have now booked other things tomorrow but next time you come over we can arrange a game."

"Sounds good."

"Have a good rest of your weekend."

"There's a slight problem about tomorrow's game, lads," I announce as we head back to the hotel.

"I fear a Gibbo fuck-up," says Chris. "What's up?"

"Well, let's just say we're going to be unbeaten on our end-of-season tour. They have no pitch and they can't get a team."

"Fucking hell, Gibbo. We give you one job to do on our tour and you can't even do that. I was looking forward to a game to try and burn off all the booze I drank last night."

"Mate, you barely run during a game and drank for twelve hours yesterday. You would need a twenty four-hour sauna to burn off the booze."

"At least it means I remain Real Calcio's all-time European leading goalscorer," says Phil, who has a total of one goal.

"I was looking forward to playing against some Bulgarians," complains Danny.

"Apparently they were looking forward to playing against a gobby Scouser as well, mate," says Damo.

We're a bit disappointed that we have no game to play tomorrow, but I doubt we would be in any fit state to play anyway. We go to a few local bars and manage to befriend some locals and finally head to a nightclub at around 2.00am.

"Not you three," the huge bouncer tells Jack, Damo and Manny, the three black members of our team. "You're not welcome here."

"What?" replies Damo.

"Not welcome."

"You are having a joke, aren't you?" says Danny, hoping he is.

"No," comes the stern reply.

"Fucking unbelievable," adds Jack. "This is the twenty-first century, not the stone age."

"Fuck this," says Danny, looking crestfallen. "I don't want to go in now even if I was paid to. Let's go before I say or do something I could regret."

"I have never experienced that before, not in forty-odd years," Jack tells me as we walk away.

"We did the right thing walking away. The bloke was fucking huge and however wrong he was, it wouldn't have been in our interests to get involved in anything."

We all walk off in disbelief and head back to the Irish bar to continue drinking, although the night has been soured with what happened at the nightclub.

The following day is one of the longest I have encountered. We have to check out of our rooms by midday and have the whole day to kill before our flight back at 10.30 that night. God only knows why Damo booked us all on that flight. We are all hungover, it's pouring with rain and we all just want to get home. We end up spending most of the day in the cafe drinking coffee and playing cards, though a few of the lads go to the monastery just out of Sofia.

Paddy and Chris are heading on to Greece for a few days and we say our goodbyes before heading to the airport.

"How many holiday days do you get, Paddy? Every time I email you I get an out of office."

"I lose track, mate. Fucking loads, though, Gibbo."

"Don't you also get extra days off at Easter and for the Queen's birthday?"

"Sure do, mate."

"It'll only be a matter of time before you get a day off for Prince William's best mate's next-door neighbour's birthday."

"Sounds good. Might suggest that."

We eventually get to the airport and check in. Nick, Danny, Damo and I are all sat together at the back of the plane.

"So lads, what shall we do about next season then?" Nick wonders. "We have to let the league know next week if we're going to continue."

"Not sure," I reply. "We keep talking about it but never seem to reach a decision."

"I'm up for one more season," says Danny. "I'd get bored on a Sunday morning without footy and it would be harder for me to get a pass to go to the pub all afternoon if I hadn't played footy in the morning."

"Surely it would work the other way," says Damo, "i.e. you can take your wife for a nice walk in the morning, thus get some brownie points and then go on the piss in the afternoon."

This seems more logical to me.

"Got to tell you about my mate and how he gets brownie points from his missus. He has a calendar in the kitchen and puts fictional nights out on there, such as Dave's birthday drinks or watching the footy with Andy. Anyway, his wife expects him to be out those nights but of course he comes home, as he has nothing on, with flowers for his wife and mentions that she has looked rushed off her feet with the kid so he thought he'd stay in with her and help her with the cooking. So when he has a stag weekend to go to in Eastern Europe, she doesn't bat an eyelid as he has built up a huge array of brownie points."

"That's fantastic, Gibbo," says Damo, already planning one or two fictional nights in his head. "I might try that as well. Has she ever been suspicious of anything?"

"Occasionally, mate, but when she asks who Bruce or another fictional character is he just says you know it's the lad Bruce from accounts, or words to that effect, and it seems to work."

"Fantastic work by your mate. I'm going to buy a calendar from WH Smith at the airport and see if it works on my missus," says Nick before returning to the business in hand. "Seriously, though, what shall we do about next season?"

"Travelling from Brighton is becoming more of an arse with unreliable local buses, cancelled trains etc," replies Damo. "Going back on the bus-replacement service to Brighton after another thumping makes me think 'Why the hell I do this?'"

"The reason it's an arse is because people let us down time after time," I say. "I've mentioned this before but I don't understand how people can't reply to emails when we send them out on Monday asking if they can play on Sunday. How hard is it to say 'Yes I can play' or 'No I can't'? It's not as if I'm asking them to give me their thoughts on Newton's law."

"And if they did you wouldn't know what they talking about anyway, Gibbo," says Nick.

"Very funny. But you see what I mean – surely on a Monday you know if you are around the following Sunday morning."

"You're right, mate. It's the same with people getting to the ground on time. Surely if people can get to work on time they can get to footy on time."

"Although I reckon half our team are probably late for work as well."

"We really do need a squad for next season. If we can get a decent-sized squad and have fourteen regularly turning up on Sundays, any latecomers can start on the bench," says Danny optimistically.

"If we also had a decent squad we could also say that if you don't reply to the email by Tuesday we presume you aren't playing," I remark.

"Any ideas on how we can recruit more players, then?" asks Nick.

"We need to advertise. I reckon we need to get an advert on gumtree, on your play4ateam website and perhaps put some A4 bits of paper up at leisure centres, at GJ's or any other local pub in the blokes' toilet."

"If we do make sure it's your mobile number on there. I don't want pissed blokes phoning me mid-slash from the toilet at midnight thinking they are Pele."

"I won't mate. I'll put Danny's number."

"No you won't. We also need to remember, lads, that it's not just the football we need to base this decision on but the pub in the afternoon as well with all the banter we have. Having said that, the pub is a lot more enjoyable if we have had more than eleven players and won, which doesn't happen as much these days."

"Also the end-of-season tours are fantastic," says Nick. "I agree this weekend hasn't been the best, especially with the racism we encountered, but the trips to Amsterdam and Krakow were fantastic, as were the weeks in Crete and Ibiza. It will also be harder for me to convince my bird that I can go off with the lads for a long weekend or a week if we don't still have a football team."

"Good point that," concurs Danny. "My bird thinks that our end-of-season trips are actual football tours although she had her suspicions in Ibiza as she texted me mid-trip to say that I'd left all my football gear at home and how was I meant to play football with no kit."

"What did you tell her?" asks Damo, no doubt thinking he might try the same trick one day.

"I told her it was a beach-football competition and everyone played in their board shorts."

"Bet you also told her we won."

"I did as well, with me scoring the winner. My bird thinks I'm even better than I actually am. I know it's hard for you boys to gauge that. She thinks we're top of the league."

"So lads, are we in conclusion that getting a week away from the other half is much easier if we carry on playing for another season, as we can continue to lie to them and tell them that our week away in May is an end-of-season football tour and not what it really is, which is a big week on the piss?"

"Sounds good to me, Gibbo," adds Nick. "Can't believe the main reason we are carrying on next season is so that we can have a week on the piss in May."

"I know, mate, but we do also need to make sure we get a big squad. May will seem along way away if we're playing with nine men in December in the freezing cold getting spanked 5-0."

"Great. Glad we've got that sorted, though not convinced it's the most practical reason to carry on," says Danny, who seems happy that Real Calcio are playing another season as it means another year of Sunday afternoons in the pub. "But sod it, we're all in agreement."

"Now where's that air hostess?" says Damo, looking around and beaming broadly. "I think four large vodkas are in order right now."

Links
www.twitter.com/realcalciofc
www.facebook.com/realcalciofc
www.bleedinggreenrealcalcio.com